TAROT ACADEMY

SPELLS OF FLAME & FURY

ISBN-13: 978-1-948455-16-9

ALSO BY SARAH PIPER

TAROT ACADEMY

Spells of Iron and Bone

Spells of Breath and Blade

Spells of Flame and Fury

THE WITCH'S REBELS

Shadow Kissed

Darkness Bound

Demon Sworn

Blood Cursed

Death Untold

Rebel Reborn

ONE

STEVIE

Their touch is my anchor.

I focus on the cadence of Doc's voice, allowing his words to flow over me like a warm bath, its gentle current urging me into the dream. *My* dream, and the otherworldly realm we believe holds the sacred Arcana object—the key to our survival.

Or possibly to our doom.

Don't let go…

Baz's voice is in my head, as clear as if he'd whispered in my ear, and I answer in turn, tightening my grip on his and Kirin's hands. Letting go is *not* an option here. We're connected by flesh and blood now, our magick and life force and sheer will keeping us tethered to one another. If there *is* a way back from this nightmare, this connection is it. We can't lose it.

Doc continues reciting the dream meditation, his voice drifting away as Professor Broome's potion works its mysterious magick. Everything inside me feels heavy and slow. Baz and Kirin squeeze my hands, the heat of their skin a stark reminder that even as the darkness of the dream realm takes hold, all of this is very, very real.

As are the consequences of our failure.

"No tricks, Devane," a hard-edged voice temporarily breaks through the haze. "Or the ginger dies first."

Rage ignites inside me, and it takes everything I have not to snap out of Doc's meditation and charge at the bitch holding my friends hostage.

Hurt so much as one of those ginger strands, and I will destroy you...

Casey Appleton and Janelle Kirkpatrick may be possessed, but they're still dangerous. Until Doc and the other professors can figure out a spell to break the possession or immobilize our captors, their guns speak louder than magick, and they won't shut up until we return from the realm with their prize.

The promise of finding the Sword of Breath and Blade is all that's keeping us alive, and bringing it back intact is our best shot at fighting our way out of this mess with Casey and Janelle. If it's not in the dream realm where I believe it to be, if we can't infiltrate the magick likely protecting it, if I'm wrong and I didn't inherit Mom's talent for dream retrieval...

Fear scrapes the edges of my heart like some kind of wild beast, but I tamp it down, bury it with the rage. Breathe. Take comfort in Doc's warm voice and Baz and Kirin's protective touch, again and again and again.

With or without that blade, whatever awaits us in the dream realm or upon our return, I've got my Arcana brothers by my side. More than the threat of guns and whatever else awaits, their fierce loyalty keeps me going. Fighting.

Don't let go, Baz's voice comes again. But it's watery and distant now, swallowed by some deep and endless magick, and when I finally open my eyes and find myself standing in the misty dream version of Arcana Academy, I'm utterly alone.

"Baz?" I call out. "Kirin?" I can still feel their touch in my hands, still sense our connection, but they're nowhere in sight.

Goosebumps prickle the skin on my arms, and I glance down to see I'm dressed in a wedding gown again. Unlike the last time, however, this one is finished—an elegant, elaborate affair in cream and silver, with flowing gossamer skirts and a fitted satin bodice dusted with crystals. My hair is styled too—braids of all different thicknesses woven into a complex fall that drapes over my left shoulder, studded with delicate purple hyacinth flowers.

But like the bouquet of black dahlias in my hand, the beautiful gown and accessories are no more than warnings.

"Kirin?" I try again.

I'm met with empty echoes. No sign of my Tarot princesses either, which means I'm going to have to make my way to the cathedral of standing stones alone.

Disappointment settles around my shoulders, but I have to trust they'll find their way to our destination. This realm is even more dangerous than the one we just left behind—I know better than to call for the guys again.

Our best shot at success is avoiding detection by the realm's other visitors—namely, Dark Judgment.

My gut clenches as I recall the cruel determination in that monster's eyes on my last visit, watching him devour a baby to fuel his own magick, then lift his staff and incinerate my men. Turn them to wasted ash with a gleam in his eye and a wicked smile on his face.

Called to confess, called to atone. Beg for your flesh, your blood, and your bones...

Unworthy! Unworthy! Unworthy!

I take a deep breath, shoving the memory aside.

Time to move.

Ditching the creepy bouquet, I hike up my skirts and cut a path through the mist in what I hope is the direction of the standing stones my Princess of Swords led us to the other day. If my intuition is right, the Sword of Breath and Blade will be buried directly beneath those stones. And if I truly share my mother's gift for prophecy and dream retrieval, we'll be able to yank it out of its secret hiding spot and bring it back to the material realm.

Casey and Janelle? As far as I'm concerned, they're another problem for another time.

The deeper I move into Breath and Blade's lands, the thicker the mist. When I glance down, my feet seem to have vanished; I can no longer tell the difference between the roiling white fog and the swish and swirl of my gown.

"This is pointless." With zero visibility, my vision is little more than a hindrance. Closing my eyes, I reach out for the energy of the elements instead—the earth beneath my feet, the soft and cool breeze in my hair, the tiny droplets of water in the mist, the very fires of creation that made this place.

Everything inside me stills, and I recite the first words that come to mind.

> *Magick of earth, of air, and of fire*
> *Of water and spirit, please hear my desire*
> *I call on your guidance through this shadowed*
>   *place*
> *For wisdom and courage, for strength and for*
>   *grace*

A golden light washes over me, immediately followed by a warm, loving energy that pulses before me and makes my heart soar. I know at once that I'm safe. That the magick of this place has brought me exactly what I most need.

My brothers.

I open my eyes, and the mist before me parts, revealing a gateway made of two stone slabs, a figure standing between them, back turned.

"Kirin?" I whisper. "Baz?"

But when the last of the mist fades away and reveals my company, it's not one of my brothers that await. It's a woman, short and slender, with lustrous black hair streaked with white. A dark blue cape flutters in the breeze, lifting to reveal the rest of her ensemble—a tattered gold tunic paired with a long navy skirt. The stars dotting the fabric shine as bright as any I've ever seen in the night sky.

"Hello?" I call out, but she doesn't startle. Just turns slightly and nods, as if she's been expecting me all along.

When she's finally facing me full-on, gazing at me with penetrating chocolate-brown eyes, I have to stifle a gasp.

I've seen those eyes before—in a much younger-looking face.

Eulala Dominga Juarez, the woman with the tiny house in the desert. The little oasis where Doc brought me after he broke me out of jail, where he fed me tacos and promises and a side of hope.

"Lala?" I ask softly, still a bit uncertain. The smooth, golden-brown skin I remember from my jailbreak visit is now wrinkled with age.

I shouldn't be surprised; Doc told me she'd just turned eighty-four.

"In the dream realm, I am in my truest form," she says suddenly, as though she can read my thoughts. "And my most intuitive."

I nod, some primal part of me already understanding her cryptic words, even if I don't know why she sought me out here. According to Doc, Lala only speaks when she's got something super important to say.

"Should I be terrified?" I ask.

She's literally never said a word to me before. Why else would she come all this way—track me down in an entirely different realm—if not to deliver bad news?

But Lala only smiles, then reaches inside the folds of her

tunic and pulls out a worn leather grimoire. The cover is engraved with a simple pentacle, the cover secured with a frayed leather cord.

A stone altar rises from the earth before her, much like the one inside the Fool's Grave, minus the carvings. She sets the book on the slab, opens to a page in the middle, and raises her arms, muttering an ancient incantation in a language I don't understand.

Glancing down at the book, I try to make sense of the symbols, but I don't recognize any of those, either. It reminds me of the dream book Professor Maddox gave me —the one my mother supposedly pulled from this very realm.

As Lala wraps up her incantation, the mist swirling above us parts, revealing a blanket of glittering stars and a bright crescent moon. Beyond the stone gateway, an ocean comes into view, softly lapping the shore like a cat at the milk bowl.

"What is this place?" I whisper, momentarily entranced by its otherworldly beauty.

"The dream realm, of course," she says. "Within you and without, ever shifting, as you yourself are always in motion."

"How are you here?"

"The dream realm is my most sacred domain. I am here more than I am there, though not always so out in the open like this. Some journeys must be undertaken in the lonely darkness of one's own soul. However, you have asked for guidance on your quest for the sacred objects, and I am here with an important message."

"But what about Kirin and Baz?" My voice is shaky with panic. As much as I'd love to pull up a stone slab and wax mystical with one of the most powerful witches in existence, who also sounds like exactly the kind of emo badass queen I need in my life right now, I *really* need to find the guys. "We're dream-sharing," I explain. "We're supposed to go to the stone circle beyond the spires."

"To find the Sword of Breath and Blade," she says.

"Yes! Have you seen or spoken with them?"

"They are walking their own paths, as all are meant to in this realm."

I stretch out my fingers, automatically seeking the warm touch of my brothers.

"I really need to find them," I say, but Lala is already shaking her head.

"In time, you will. Though time is something we cannot take for granted here. The longer you remain, Starla, the more difficult it will be for you to return home."

"But this isn't my first trip."

"Precisely. Each time you visit, you leave a piece of yourself behind—sacred knowledge your enemies can and will exploit. The Dark Arcana will press every advantage."

"What sort of sacred knowledge?"

"Secrets. Fears. Shame and guilt. Regrets. The usual mental baggage all humans carry." She tries for a smile, but her eyes are dark and serious.

A chill settles into the marrow of my bones.

"But how could the Dark Arcana exploit that stuff?"

"Oh, quite simply and quite thoroughly. Consider: if the Tarot in its purest form is a guide to your innermost self, then what would the darkest, most twisted version of that guide do?"

She doesn't elaborate, and I don't ask her to. The answers are already rushing through my mind unbidden: sabotage, torment, manipulation.

I swallow hard, picking at one of the crystals on my wedding dress. I really hope that was the worst of it. I don't think I can handle any more bad news at the moment.

Offering what I hope is a welcoming smile, I look at her and say, "So, what's this about a message? Please tell me you have a map, and maybe some snacks. Actually, at this point I'd prefer the snacks."

Lala smiles mysteriously. Definitely a thing with her. Behind her, the crescent moon winks over the sea, the salty night air drifting toward us on a warm breeze. It reminds me of Doc—his ferocity, his wildness, the almost-kiss we shared in his classroom—and I smile. I swear I can feel his protective presence, even here.

Come back to us...

His earlier words float through my mind, settling in my heart and giving me a much-needed shot of strength and determination.

I blow out a breath, squaring my shoulders. I think of Doc and Ani back in the material realm. I think of Isla and Nat, of Professor Broome and Professor Maddox, of everyone coming together to help us tonight, no questions asked. And I think of my best friend Jessa, never losing faith in me, even when I sometimes lose faith in myself.

Of course I'll come back to you, Doc. And when I do? Fair warning... I'm probably most definitely going to kiss you...

My smile stretches wider, a warmth spreading inside my chest as I make that silent promise to myself. I picture the look of shock on his handsome face, the moment's hesitation before he finally gives in to his desires and claims me in a ferocious kiss of his own.

Something to hope for. And sometimes, hope is all you need to pull you through the worst of it.

For a minute, it almost feels like things are looking up. Like we might actually stand a chance against this unfathomable terror.

Then Lala grabs my hands in a crushing grip and says, "Starla. I need to tell you how you're going to die."

TWO

ANSEL

My mother once told me I'd never know love.

She said I was too naive, too foolish to recognize it. That being alone would forever be my curse, just as I'd cursed her to the same fate.

This, from the woman who'd just gotten caught in the midst of a decades-long affair by the man she claimed to love.

The man who—until that moment—I'd called Dad.

It was the manifestation of my magick—magick that shouldn't have existed in the child of two mundane parents —that gave away her ugly secret and broke apart the only family I'd ever known.

To this day, I still don't know who my real father is. Backed into an impossible corner, my mother admitted her indiscretions, but she refused to implicate her partner in crime. For all I know, he's not even aware of my existence.

It was easier for her and everyone else to blame me, as if

I somehow divinely conceived myself, all for the sole purpose of decimating their happily ever after.

"You're cursed, Ansel," she said matter-of-factly one day, turning her back on me and ashing her cigarette into the kitchen sink. She took one last drag, then dropped the butt down the drain, flicking on the garbage disposal as if it could destroy the evidence of every terrible thing she'd ever done. "Cursed as the red hair on your bastard head."

I was ten years old.

I should be able to laugh about it now, right? All that ancient history. Water under the bridge, as the saying goes.

But here's the thing: I've *never* been able to laugh about it. Not then, and certainly not now. Some wounds just cut too deep, even for the guy who lives to make everyone else laugh. The guy who finds the silver lining in just about *every* disaster I've had the pleasure of navigating.

For all her faults, my mother was nothing if not convincing; I spent my entire adolescence believing I was the ungodly, unloved *thing* that broke my family apart. Once that seed took root? Well. Just add a little water and a healthy dose of resentment from the man who spent a decade loving another man's son, a mother who turned day drinking into an Olympic sport, and a baby sister caught in the crossfire, and *voila*! A life and all its infinite potential —*my* infinite potential—derailed.

There was a long time—dark, shadowy nights curled up with a bottle of pills and a razor blade—when I wondered if my mother was right. If maybe I *was* cursed to be alone, to skirt the edges of real love like some desperate spectator who could look but never touch. Never know. Never feel.

Then I came to Arcana Academy—a last-ditch effort to get myself back on track after barely passing high school. Here, I learned to embrace my magick rather than be ashamed of it. I met the guys, connected with my fire energy, discovered my Sun Arcana. I made an oath to the Keepers of the Grave and learned what it meant to have real brothers. To stand for something so much bigger than your own petty crap.

And just when I thought things couldn't get better, Stevie rolled onto campus—a mass of wild curls and crazy energy and pure, uncut happiness. A woman who turned my world inside out, shone a light in all the dark places, and rescued my heart.

Even now, despite our dire circumstances, just the thought of her name brings a smile to my lips. After all the time we spent together—the hikes, the laughs, the hugs... That kiss tonight was everything. A promise, a gift, a future.

So no, maybe I can't laugh about all the messed up shit my parents put me through. But I've got the next best thing.

Vindication.

My mother? That woman was dead wrong.

I *do* know love. And it's not the twisted, conditional bullshit so many families try to pedal in the wake of their own colossal failures at it. This love is real. Vast. Perfect, even when we ourselves are anything but.

And that kind of love? Friendship? Brotherhood? There's *nothing* I won't do to protect it.

To protect them.

"Don't get any smart ideas," Casey Appleton warns, as if she has *any* fucking clue how bad things are about to get for her.

"Oh, I've got *plenty* of ideas. But don't worry, Case." I grin, sweet and disarming. "None of them are particularly smart."

She presses the gun into my forehead and gives it a hard shove, but her lazy smirk is a dead giveaway: she doesn't see me as a threat.

No one ever does.

I hold back a smile, thinking of that game where someone asks, "If you could have just one superpower, what would it be?"

Flight, invisibility, mind reading, healing—sure, those are the obvious answers.

You know what no one ever says?

I want to be perpetually underestimated.

But that's *my* answer, and it's where the real superpower lies. Because being perpetually underestimated? That makes you the most dangerous person in the room, every fucking time.

Casey finally turns her back on me and wanders off to issue a few lukewarm threats to Isla and Nat, but when I catch Isla's defiant glare across our makeshift circle, I know she won't be cowed either.

I lift a brow in question, and she nods, magick rippling before her like a heatwave. I can feel it simmering in the air like the moments before a lightning strike—the pungent smell of ozone, the sharpening of the senses, an invisible current strong enough to raise the hairs on my arms.

Casey and Janelle should be able to sense it, but they're either too amped up to notice, or too confident in their weapons to worry about it.

They *should* be worried, though. Isla and Nat, the professors, me—we're all gearing up for a fight. And though we may not be able to hear one another's thoughts, one thing is certain: when it comes to taking these bitches down, we're all working from the same playbook.

Isla holds my gaze a moment longer, and I give her a quick nod before glancing down at Cass.

In the center of our circle, he and the other professors are huddled closely on the ground. At first glance, it appears they're just watching over Stevie and the guys. But I know how Cass's mind works; he's gearing up to make a move too. I can tell the moment the magickally charged air hits him; he glances up at Isla, then at me, his eyes narrowing as he tries to pinpoint the source.

He gives me an almost imperceptible shake of the head, but I've got a plan, and I won't be deterred. Seeing Casey and Janelle threaten my brothers flipped a switch inside me, then broke it clean off. There's no going back.

I glare at Cass, imploring him to focus on our friends and leave the rest to me.

He holds my gaze another moment, then sighs, finally returning his attention to Stevie and the guys.

Janelle and Casey are bickering now, impatient and bored as they pace around our circle. I don't know which one of them is the ringleader here, but their plan is obviously rushed and half-assed, and it's clear they don't trust each other. Despite the guns, both women are distracted, antsy, and quickly losing their edge. They're so fixated on the promise of the Sword, on their swift victory, it doesn't even occur to them that any of us might be plotting against them.

That they themselves are likely plotting against each other.

It's time to end this.

I shake out my arms and blow out a swift breath. Beneath my feet, red dust rises in tiny eddies, drawn to the magick simmering inside me.

"What did I tell you, Red?" Casey's got me in her sights again, and now she crosses back to me, waving the gun in my face. "You seem twitchy. I don't like twitchy."

"Twitchy? Maybe I'm just allergic to death threats."

"Don't push it," she snaps.

"Sorry, sorry." I flash her a grin and a wink, raising my hands in mock surrender. The Ace of Wands card flickers into my mind's eye, an image of a powerful wooden staff thrusting upward from a massive stone crevice, the sun blazing overhead. It's the ultimate Big Dick Energy card, and I can't help but feel that energy coursing through my veins now, throbbing in my gut, everything in me winding tighter and tighter…

Fire magick prickles across my skin, itching to be unleashed.

Casey narrows her eyes, a shadow crossing her face. "Red?"

"Yes, Miss Appleton?" I'm all smiles, all teeth.

"We've got guns," she says, raising hers to eye level as if I've somehow forgotten this crucial piece of information. "And I can be *very* dangerous when provoked."

"Fair point." I consider the warning, then shrug. "But here's the thing, Miss Appleton. *I've* got fire. And you can go fuck yourself."

Faster than lightning, I call upon the magick of the Ace and recite a spell, my hands trembling with potential magick, my cock hard with so much unspent energy, my voice so fevered even Cass's eyes go wide with shock.

> *Flames of fury, flames of rage*
> *From spark to fire, forge this cage*
> *Burn the skies and scorch the ground*
> *Their blackened hearts shall now be bound*

Blue and silver flames crawl along my palms, quickly engulfing my hands, my arms. Casey steps closer, her mouth twisting with anger and fear, but she can't touch me now.

No one can.

Closing my eyes, I dig deep in my subconscious, mining the oldest hurts, the rage, the betrayal, the loss, the steady diet of neglect and blame my mother fed me. I call up memories of razor blades and pills, the sharp sting of the blade slicing against my wrist, the bright red of the blood that welled up, the fear and shame that always forced me to stay my hand. I remember her cruel words, my father's coldness, the bitterness that hardened my baby sister's heart until even that sweet little girl could no longer stand the sight of me.

Every memory, every echo—I channel it all into fuel.

Deeper I plunge. Darker. In my mind's eye, the sun in the Ace of Wands card dims, then dies, the sky turning black, all the light sucked away until nothing remains but pure anguish.

In that agony, where those old wounds still fester, still burn, I find the *real* fuel.

I open my eyes and let out a roar torn from the darkest, most terrifying recesses of my soul.

Casey gasps and drops her gun.

And with no further warning than another wry smile, I thrust my hands forward and set the night ablaze.

THREE

STEVIE

"Is that, like, a metaphor?"

I stare at Lala, waiting for the explanation that will make all of her craziness coalesce into some logical thing, some definite answer I can grab onto—and maybe beat the shit out of.

Because I did *not* come all this way—under extreme duress, mind you—just to be told by some mysterious age-defying oracle that I'm about to bite it.

I fold my arms across my chest and continue the glowering, but instead of a response, I get a Tarot card. It slips out from between the pages of her grimoire and lands at my feet.

"One of Mom's, or one of yours?" I ask.

"The messenger matters not." Lala lowers her eyes, silence engulfing us as I crouch down to examine the card.

On its face, an old woman draped in a green cloak holds

a skull before a steaming cauldron. Just beyond her window, a black raven circles.

Death. Trump Thirteen. The same card that filled up my bathtub after I dreamed of my mother, right along with Judgment, thousands and thousands of tiny images whispering the same ominous warning in my mind.

The darkness is already rising. Judgment will come for us all.

I stand up straight again, leaving the card on the ground. It promptly vanishes.

"It's a spiritual awakening, right?" I say, fighting to keep my voice steady. "That's what this all means. I will quote-unquote *die* so I can be reborn. Close one door, another opens, the seeds fall in death so that new life may bloom, etcetera, etcetera. Yes?"

"*All* death is an awakening," Lala says, calm as ever. "But no, Starla. I'm afraid this is about your literal death— one rising on the very near horizon. Your mother foresaw it long ago, before you even chose her to bring you into this world."

"*Chose* her?" I squeeze my eyes shut, desperately trying to maintain my questionable grasp on reality.

"The rebirth of an ancient Arcana soul is a complicated—"

I hold up my hand to stop her, certain my brain can't handle a deep dive down the rabbit hole of Arcana reincarnation right now.

"Let's get back to the part where I croak. How does it happen?" I open my eyes and tap my lips, pondering the exciting possibilities of such a ridiculous outcome. "A mix-up in potions class that melts off my entire face? No, too gruesome. Professor Maddox assigns another essay on Tarot cups as a symbol for the womb, and I write myself into an irreversible coma? Wait, maybe it's a more epic end for Starla Milan. Death by toppling cheese fountain?"

Lala's frown deepens.

"Oh, come on, Lala. I can think of worse ways to die than drowning in smoked gouda."

"Your sense of humor is admirable," Lala says, glaring with a look that's anything *but* admiring, "but this is no laughing matter. Your mother—a great seer with abilities far beyond even my comprehension—witnessed your death as clearly as she witnessed your birth. She passed that message on to me, where it remained in safekeeping until the proper time for its emergence."

"And you decided that proper time is *tonight*? In the middle of a hostage situation, two Arcana mages gone MIA in the dream realm, an explosion at a popular campus bar, sanctioned witch hunts, the militarization of half our non-magickal cities, and a near-impossible search for the magickal objects that could very well destroy us all?" I gape at her, incredulous. "For a bunch of so-called prophets, you witches have *shit* timing."

Without breaking her calm demeanor, Lala says, "It is only now that the images in your mother's vision make sense to me—only now that all other forces have aligned to make that particular outcome possible." She picks up her grimoire and heads through the stone gateway. "Follow me."

I do as she asks. Down at the shoreline, the tide eats up my footprints, water nipping at my bare toes and soaking the hem of my wedding gown. Far out across the sea, the turquoise water slowly bleeds into a deep navy blue, its tranquil darkness rippling with a phosphorescent glow.

Under almost any other circumstance, the moment might be beautiful. Magickal. Instead, tears of frustration well up, my cheeks quickly turning as wet and salty as the ocean.

Baz and Kirin... Where are you? What's happening? Am I really so close to death? How could Mom not have told me about this?

"Can I stop it?" I whisper. Despite their confusing presentation, my mother's visions have never been wrong. But I have to believe that Lala wouldn't be sharing this if there wasn't a chance, however dim, that I could alter my fate.

Her gaze turns soft, her black hair shimmering in the moonlight. "That is a question I cannot answer."

"Then why are you telling me this at all? For the rest of my life, however long or short it is, I'll have this shadow hanging over me. What's the point? Why not just let me live my life in relative peace?"

She takes a deep breath, gazing out at the shifting phosphorescent waters. "Sometimes there *is* peace in knowing what lies ahead. Acceptance. When that moment is finally upon you, my hope is that you will not fear death, but embrace it."

The image from the Death card flickers in my mind, and

I picture the old woman knocking on my door, offering up that skull as if it were a tuna casserole.

"Oh, yes," I say. "Let me just invite her in for a mug of calming lavender vanilla tea and a chocolate scone."

"Actually, I've heard she quite enjoys a nice smoked gouda." Lala winks. It takes me a few beats to realize she just made a joke.

We both laugh, but the tide is coming in quickly, the water now soaking the dress up to my knees. I try unsuccessfully to fight off a shiver.

"I'm telling you this," she continues, "so you can prepare those who will continue in your stead. This war does not end with your death, nor does your legacy."

"My legacy?" I look down at my hands, empty and plain. The soaked wedding gown hangs limp, a cruel hint of something that was never meant to be.

"Starla, you have to understand. Your mother—"

"It's Dark Judgment, right?" I ask. "He's going to incinerate me, just like in the visions."

Lala shakes her head.

"How does it happen, then?" I ask. "In battle? An act of magick? A sneak attack?" I glance out across the ocean. "Here in the dream realm, another Dark Arcana enemy hiding in the shadows?"

"In this war," she says, "you will suffer great losses—a terrible fate for which nothing can prepare you. The unbearable pain will drive the prophecy to its completion. By your mother's own accounting, it is said, 'Thus her ache shall find no ease, so shall the daughter of The World surrender to the emptiness, to the void within and without. By her own hand, of her own volition, The Star shall fall. Henceforth she shall take her eternal breath in utter darkness.'"

Deep inside me, a spark of anger ignites, an ember that quickly becomes a flame, a flame that becomes a fire, burning through the last of my fear and confusion.

By my own hand? My final breath in darkness?

Is she fucking *serious* right now?

I turn toward her, eyes blazing, heart pounding so hard it's like I've just run a five-minute mile. "So after all this spirit-blessed, Star Arcana, super-special snowflake-ness, *that's* my destiny? To kill myself?"

"It is foretold."

"I don't think so, Lala."

"I know it's hard to imagine now, but your mother divined—"

"No. I don't accept it. I would never do that."

"You wouldn't do that right now," she says. "In *this* moment. But you can't know what you'll do in the next moment, or the one after that."

"But my mother knew? *You* knew?"

"That's how prophecy works."

"This one is wrong, Lala. I'm telling you. There has to be a loophole."

Lala shoots me a dubious look, but I press on.

"Every spell has one. Prophecies are no different, right? Aren't they basically like spells in reverse? A prediction of the events rather than a direction of them?"

She considers my logic. "I suppose that's one way of

looking at divination magick. However, even if there *is* a loophole—"

"There *totally* is. You said it yourself—my mother foresaw this death sentence before she was even pregnant with me. Before I'd supposedly chosen her to bring me into this world. I didn't *exist* as a person yet. You, my mother, even fate itself... None of you had any idea who I'd become, what power and strength I'd ultimately possess. And maybe I'm still figuring that out too, but one thing I know beyond all doubt? Your girl here is *not* going out like that."

Another surge of fire rises inside me, my whole body buzzing with energy, with magick, with possibility, with determination.

No one gets to decide this for me.

"My friends and I—we're going to *fight*, Lala," I continue. "All of us. Fight for our magick. Fight for the right to practice our craft or totally ignore it, however we see fit. Fight for our freedom. And most of all, we're going to fight for one another. If anyone in this fucked-up mess is headed for great losses, unbearable pain, and an ending of utter darkness, it'll be the assholes who try to stop us."

Across the sea, dark clouds gather, their silver-blue bellies flickering with lightning. It reminds me of that first night at my academy suite and Jessa's epic pep talk.

You're gonna walk straight out onto that campus—every single day for the next four years—and learn your magick like a fucking boss bitch. And you're gonna own your power, be ruth-

25

lessly unapologetic about it, and rock that shit like the Goddess-damned, sparkly-ass, witch queen of the desert you are...

My face splits into a grin, her words echoing, bolstering me all over again. I *am* a boss bitch. Even my best friend knows me better than fate does.

Lala tries to remain stoic, which I understand. I mean, you can't exactly do jazz hands while you're telling someone they're fated to die a gruesome death. Still, the twinkle in her eye is unmistakable, her lips twitching as she holds back a smile of her own.

"You are very much your mother's daughter, Starla Milan."

I flip my braid over my shoulder and fold my arms across my be-glittered bodice. "I'll take *that* as a compliment."

"As it was meant, I assure you."

In the distance, a bolt of lightning arcs across the sky, the clouds finally blotting out the stars. The waters at our feet begin to churn and froth, the waves growing restless. We take a step backward to avoid a direct hit.

Lala's demeanor turns serious once again. "You must listen now, Starla, and listen well. We don't have much time."

"No," I say as the wind kicks up, stealing some of the hyacinth from my hair and casting it out to sea. "I need to find my friends. We're looking for the Arcana artifacts—I'm almost positive they're here in the dream realm."

"Indeed they are," she says.

"Wait. You're sure?" My heart leaps, my smile stretching wide once again.

But Lala isn't smiling.

The air between us changes, and suddenly it's like I can't get enough of it into my lungs.

"Absolutely sure." A wicked grin twists her lips, and in this moment, I know I've made a terrible mistake in trusting her. "I hid them here myself, though unfortunately for you, I am unable to recall their precise location."

Reaching into her tunic, she retrieves a silver athame, its blade blackened with old blood. The sight of it sends a cold prickle down my spine.

"Lala, what are you talking about?" I pant, still struggling to catch my breath. "You—"

In a blur of madness, she grabs my hand and yanks me close, slicing the blade across my palm. I yelp at the sudden pain, desperately trying to wrench free, but her grasp is fierce and unyielding, squeezing my flesh until blood spills onto the pages of her spellbook.

"Stop!" I cry. "Stop!" But my pleas fall on deaf ears. Hot, uncomfortable magick burns through my insides as Lala casts her spell.

Dark of water, depth of dreams
Nothing here is what it seems
On sacred seas we now set sail
Grant me sight beyond the veil

All around us, the water churns and swirls, imprisoning

us inside a whirlpool that rises higher and higher each time she repeats the verse, a massive column of water that leaves us just enough room to breathe, but cuts us off from all else.

"What are you doing?" I shout, my blood on fire, lungs burning, voice nearly swallowed by the rushing water.

Lala's eyes roll into the back of her head, showing me only the whites. Her lips don't move, but her voice reverberates in my mind—the voice of a haunted, ancient goddess whose power threatens to bring me to my knees.

"You asked for guidance in this realm," she says. "Illumination. Painful as it may be, that is what I offer."

"By mutilating me and stealing my blood? Like the Dark fucking Hierophant?" Fear sours my gut, but I will *not* back down. I don't care who she's working for or how many dark minions the Magician has. This is *my* dream—*my* nightmare—and she will *not* overtake me here. "Who *are* you?"

"The messenger matters not," she repeats, and in the wall of water before my eyes, another Tarot card swirls into view, larger than life.

It's the High Priestess card, featuring an elder witch standing between two stone pillars before a sacred ocean. She's dressed in a skirt full of stars and a golden tunic, arms raised toward the moon, an old grimoire placed on a stone altar…

"It's you," I breathe, the pieces clicking into place. "You're the High Priestess."

Lala says nothing, her eyes still milky white, the water swirling faster and faster. The Tarot card vanishes, and suddenly the frothy turquoise water turns pitch back, shot through with tiny white bolts of lightning.

All around us, the alchemical symbols I saw in her grimoire appear, each one glowing like a fiery ember in a bed of black coals. Swirling through the whirlpool, they rearrange themselves into new symbols and pictures, a sacred language only Lala seems to understand.

The magick of her spell burns a fresh path through my veins, the pain making me dizzy.

"Do not resist this," her voice echoes.

Before I can utter another word, the column of water collapses, stealing the last of my breath and sucking us under, way down to the darkest depths of the sea where no light can ever shine.

FOUR

BAZ

I wake up—if you can even call it waking up on this fucked-up acid trip through the dream realm—on my hands and knees. Can't even get a damn breath out before I'm puking up saltwater, gasping for air.

Not good.

My lungs convulse as the sea burns its way out. I dig my fingers into the muddy earth, squeeze my eyes shut, and wait for the water and the excruciating pain to pass. But Death's got me in a tight grip, and that bitch does *not* want to let go.

This is worse than any of my own nightmares by far. I can only hope that Stevie and Kirin are faring better.

How long have I even been here? A minute? An hour? No idea. Feels like forever before I finally get a good clean breath, before the burn starts to cool. I manage to get to my feet... just in time for the next wave of total suckage.

Pain and pressure duke it out behind my eyes, the agony enough to knock me on my ass. Red-hot runes swim in my vision, lighting up the darkness and slicing through my skull like tiny branding irons.

I unleash a scream of agony that echoes across the landscape of Breath and Blade, and I'm pretty sure that scream's about to be my last word before I bite it.

Then, as swiftly as it took me down, the pain vanishes. The runes evaporate.

I'm on my feet again, holding my breath for the next attack.

Nothing comes.

I take a beat to get my bearings. Definitely somewhere in the middle of Breath and Blade, but there's so much mist I can't see more than ten feet in front of me. Despite the fact that I arrived here like a half-drowned rat, I'm completely dry. And dressed, inexplicably, in a too-small pair of fuzzy black pajama pants covered with glow-in-the-dark zombies.

No shirt, no shoes, no service.

If this is Stevie's dream, I can only imagine what her subconscious is trying to tell her about me.

"Stevie?" I call out. "Kirin?"

Nothing.

They're not here—that much is obvious. More than the deathly silence, I can feel their absence. My hand is cold now, Stevie's touch no more than a memory.

Fuck.

Not that I want anyone to see me in these juvenile pants,

but losing the crew before we've even started this journey is a bad fucking omen.

Doing my best to orient myself, I reach out for a connection with earth, hoping my magick works the same way here as it does in the material realm. It's tenuous, but it's there—the slight buzz in my veins as I make the connection.

It's quiet—a gut feeling more than anything else—but it's the first real sign I've gotten since my painful awakening. I cling to it, heading off in the direction I hope will bring me to the standing stones. To Kirin and Stevie.

Lightning arcs overhead, making the misty landscape flicker like a disco. The moment it passes, a dark shadow takes shape on my path. Human. Hulking.

Terrifyingly familiar, and in that moment, I realize my fatal mistake.

Hope.

Shoulda known better than to have any in a place like this.

"You look like day-old dog shit, kid." His voice slithers out like a serpent from the basement of my memory, coiling around my chest and squeezing the salt-stained air from my lungs.

"Ford?" I croak out, which is bullshit, because here in the realm of nightmares, who the fuck else would it be?

"I don't know," the shadow calls back. "Is it?"

"Show your face, you dickless wonder."

Lightning flickers again. The shadow vanishes.

"Ford?"

No response but the echo of wind through the spires.

Maybe it's all in my head.

I close my eyes, try to shake off the ghosts. Remember why I'm even here.

Stevie. I need to find Stevie and Kirin, get that cursed sword, and wake the hell up out of this forsaken realm...

Forcing myself to keep walking, I peer through the flashing mist, hoping for a glimpse of my girl. Willing her to step out from behind the stone spires, grab my hand, and plant one right on my lips.

One step in front of the other. Don't look up. Don't stop. Just keep walking. I just have to get to that stone cathedral. They'll be waiting for me there. They have to be—I can feel it in my gut.

"Forget about me already?" comes the voice. The shadow darkens my path, then vanishes behind a thick spire.

"Trying to." I bark out a laugh, but I can't pretend this shit doesn't affect me. I feel it all the way to my bones. That cold, icy dread, fresh and familiar, as if my big brother never left my side.

Fucking Ford.

I was so sure I was finished with him. So sure I'd never have to see his terrifying face again, and that even if I *did* see it, it wouldn't faze me. It's been what—a decade and a half since they locked him up? And I managed to survive more than a few shitstorms since then. Hell, before I met Stevie, Shitstorm Survival Mode was my default setting.

This sonofabitch? He shouldn't even be a blip on the emotional fucking radar.

But then, like a damn apparition, my big brother steps out from behind the rock, and my house of cards blows away in the wind, leaving me holding my dick in one hand and a pocketful of lies in the other.

"Ah, so you *do* remember me," he says, and the moment I see that torturous grin, I realize how much power he still has over me. How much I wish things could be different. How much I wish we could go back to a better time—a time when he was still my brother.

"Been a few, Baz," he says. "Been a few." He walks with a limp, no doubt courtesy of the daily prison beatings— abuse Janelle's money can't seem to prevent.

Guilt churns inside me.

I'm the one who put him there. I may as well be beating him with my own bare hands.

"Go ahead and ask how I got it." As if he can read my mind, Ford smacks his hand against his bad leg and hobbles a few more steps toward me. "No need to stand on ceremony with me, kid."

My gaze jerks back up to meet his. There's a challenge in his eyes, a dark rage that's been brewing for years.

He *wants* me to start this with him—if for no other reason so he can be the one to end it.

I was a fool to hope there could be anything left of the brother I once knew—the boy who snuck into my room when our parents were having one of their epic battles and helped me build a blanket fort. The one who taught me how to play Bullshit and Blackjack and gave me my first cigarette when I was six so I'd puke and never, ever pick up the habit.

Unfortunately, *that* boy—the one I loved and idolized—became a man, and that man died a decade ago, set on fire with the mage he burned alive.

My own guilt aside, Ford *earned* his ticket to hell. And I'm guessing he's not here looking for redemption.

He's not here at all, I remind myself. Just some projection served up by my guilty conscience. My own nightmares come to life.

"Thanks for the family reunion," I say, "but I've got somewhere to be. Take care of yourself, Ford."

In a swift move that belies his injuries, nightmare-Ford lunges forward and grabs me by the throat, his eyes wild. "Oh, you can't walk away from me. It doesn't work that way—not even here."

I let him hold me. Let him think I'm still scared of him. "So this is what—a test?"

"Of a sort."

"I get it. This place fucks with your head, makes you relive the darkest parts of your past. Am I close?"

He releases my throat, grabs hold of my hair instead. Gives me a few good tugs before finally shoving me away. "You always were the smart one in the Redgrave gene pool, you little fuck."

"Yeah? Well, here I am. Do your worst. I guarantee it won't be as bad as the life you left me with."

"Ooh, and there it is." He grins again, smug as all get

out. Real or not, it takes every ounce of focus I have not to pummel his ass into the dirt. "In all this little blame-and-shame," he continues, "you're forgetting the part where *you* turned *me* in. Ratted me out like some little street punk looking to make a name for himself."

"Ford, you..."

You set a man on fire. Burned him alive. Took pleasure in it. You fucking died that day—died before my eyes and left me alone in a world of monsters and ghosts I had no idea how to fight...

But all the words die on my tongue, leaving only this: "Fuck off, Ford. You're not even real. None of this is real."

"Aww, now that hurts." He presses a hand to his heart, but malice still shines bright in his eyes. "Real or not, I can still fuck you up. Get inside your head."

Lightning arcs overhead again, a bright flash followed by a deafening crack of thunder. Without warning, a sharp pain slices through my head, dropping me to my knees, filling my mind with images of Stevie. She's running toward us. Toward *me*. I try to shout, to stop her, but I can't find the words, can't get off the ground, can't stop the blood pouring from my nose and into the dirt, the pain in my skull blinding me—

"Baz! Baz, get up!" She's shouting as she gets closer, her scent preceding her, wrapping me in its warmth.

"Stevie," I breathe. Suddenly she's here, dropping to her knees before me. Her hair is soaked, fat water droplets falling onto my skin as my fingertips brush against her hand. I fight against the pain, will myself to open my eyes as I reach for her face...

"Not so fast, kid," Ford says. "This one looks like a handful. Think I'll keep her for myself."

Stevie's snatched out of my grasp. Her scream cuts through the blinding pain, and I force open my eyes just in time to watch my brother pin her to the ground, one hand fisting her hair, the other pressing a knife to her throat.

Stevie doesn't make another sound. Doesn't struggle. Just looks at me with those impossibly blue eyes, tears staining her cheeks. Her clothing is soaked, stuck to her skin as she shivers in my brother's grasp.

A trickle of blood beads on the blade.

Pure, white-hot rage incinerates the pain in my head, and I launch myself at Ford, slamming straight into him. We both hit the ground with a thud, his cruel laugh making my skin crawl.

Stevie vanishes, along with the knife.

She was never there at all.

Even flat on his back, with my knee pressed against his chest, my brother laughs and laughs.

"Get out of my fucking head," I grind out, shoving off of him and getting to my feet. All around me, the mist eddies and swirls, flickering white with the intermittent lightning.

"Are you sure it was me?" he teases, climbing to his feet. The knife appears in his hand again, and he presses the tip to his thumb, drawing blood. "Maybe you're just your own worst enemy."

Stevie flickers through my mind again, but now she feels far away, lost on some distant ocean. Her wild curls whip around her head, her gaze reflecting fear and determination in equal measure. I squeeze my eyes shut to block out the image, but it has the opposite effect, bringing her into vivid color. Her screams echo inside my skull as a column of water swirls around her, lit with magick.

"Stevie!" I shout, frantic, helpless, but it's too late. My mouth fills again with the briny taste of the sea, and I cough up water.

"There, there, kid." Ford's serpent voice is in my ear, hot and close, his hand clamped around my shoulder. "It's over now."

Stevie's image shatters, the water in my mouth evaporating, leaving me alone once again with the guilty conscience and a brother whose ghost will probably haunt me for the rest of my damn life. Maybe longer.

"Did you enjoy my little show?" he asks.

"That was your doing?"

"What do you think?"

I shrug off his hand, turn my back on him. I refuse to let him see how much he's getting to me.

"That all you got, you sick son of a bitch?" I grumble.

Ford hobbles over to stand in front of me. Folds his arms over his chest and leans back against the rock, taking the weight off his bad leg. Making sure I notice it. That I feel bad about it.

Lightning splits the sky, chased by thunder so loud I feel like I should duck.

I don't move. Just glare at him, wishing him out of existence. Wondering if maybe, when this is all over, I'll tell

Janelle to take her dirty money and shove it up her ass, let the bastard die in that prison for all I care.

Ford turns his head, spits into the dirt. "You know what the best part of all this is?"

"That you're just a figment of my imagination, easily obliterated by a bottle of whiskey and half a joint?" The idea buoys me. Something to look forward to later, after we find this damn sword and put this night behind us. I can almost taste the whiskey, feel the warmth of the booze hitting my gut, see the haze of smoke as it works its particular brand of memory magick on everything that happened here…

"Sorry, kid. Wrong answer." His eyes turn cold, then coal-black. Suddenly his smile is too wide for his mouth, his limbs too long, his teeth too sharp.

I watch in awe as he transforms before my eyes, my heart lodged in my damn throat.

Nightmare is too tame a word for the vile beast standing before me.

Ford opens his mouth, and dozens of oily black scorpions scurry out, their bodies sliced to ribbons by his razor-sharp teeth. They fall dead to the ground, only to be reformed again, bigger and stronger, faster and deadlier. Like some horrible insect army, they converge on me, devouring my bare feet, stabbing, biting, their poison burning through my flesh like acid.

I'm on my knees again, gasping in pain, begging for help. For a hand. For an end.

But Ford only laughs.

My body convulses as the poison takes hold. I can feel my heartbeat slowing, my lungs giving out, my cells dying.

When my brother finally speaks again, his voice is that of a ghoul, haunted and ancient, half-dead, terrifying.

"The best part," he hisses, "is that you actually believe I'm the worst thing you'll have to endure here."

FIVE

KIRIN

Nothing looks familiar to me here; even the spires themselves have taken on a sinister new cast, like the pale, knobby fingers of corpses clawing at the mist.

Baz and Stevie are nowhere in sight.

I'm not quite sure who decided on the wardrobe for this adventure, but I'm dressed in a black tuxedo, complete with silver bowtie and the tightest dress shoes imaginable. Not ideal for trekking to the stone cathedral and digging up the magickal sword to end all swords, but I suppose they'll have to do.

Since the monkey suit didn't come equipped with a compass or map, I spin around, pick a random direction, and make my way into the mist. With any luck, I'll find a familiar landmark or—better yet—run into Stevie soon. I have no idea how long we'll have in this realm—whether something back home will yank us out of the dream before we've even tracked down the sword—but it can't be long. I can feel the clock ticking down already; my skin itches as though I'm being watched, tracked by some nameless shadow waiting to pounce.

And home? What awaits us there?

I shudder to recall the scene we left behind—to think of my sister. Of some horrible monster possessing her and forcing her to do its bidding.

Ten years without a word exchanged, pretending I was better off without her. Now she's finally back in my life, and I'm *this* close to losing her for good.

And it's all my fault. If I hadn't pushed her away again, maybe she wouldn't have gotten involved with Janelle. Whether it was her choice or just a case of being in the wrong place at the wrong time, it doesn't matter. I could've prevented this.

Emotion wells inside me. Why are we both so damn stubborn? Why couldn't I have picked up the phone or sent an email just once in the past decade?

I think about what Stevie said to me the day we found the stone cathedral, how my Tower energy is so much more than just chaos and destruction.

It's about clarity—those shocking moments of insight that make you question everything you've ever held true. It's about knocking down all the old shit so we can heal and rebuild…

I wanted so badly to believe her that day. To believe her even now. But how can I? When Casey unexpectedly came back into my life, I didn't try to heal and rebuild. Didn't even give things a chance. I fucked it up all over again, locking her out of my life. Refusing to budge even the slightest bit.

And look where she ended up.

My sister could die tonight, and I can't even remember the last thing I said to her.

Only that it was probably something shitty.

Emotion surges inside. Picking up on my distress, the spires around me begin to vibrate. Tiny stones skitter down the sides, pinging off my head and shoulders like hail—a warning of what's to come if I don't pull it together right now.

I take a deep breath, bury it all deep inside. I can't risk losing it out here—I could set off a chain reaction that destabilizes the entire realm.

Swallowing down the bitter tang of regret, I march onward, putting all of my faith in Cass, Ani, and the others to figure things out back home.

And in Baz, Stevie, and me to figure it out here.

It's five minutes, maybe ten before the ground starts rumbling again, but this time, it's not my doing. Barely perceptible at first, the vibration picks up quickly, rattling up through my bones and making my teeth chatter. Overhead, larger stones and loose rock tumble from the looming spires.

And then, in an instant, the world is tilting sideways.

An earthquake. In the dream realm.

The sound is indescribable, a deafening roar like nothing I've ever heard before.

The researcher in me is practically hard over it, my fingers itching to pull out a field notebook and a camera.

But the scientific method won't save my skull from getting crushed by a rock.

Calling on my air magick, I temporarily clear the mist around me, desperate to locate a safe place to ride out the quake. But nowhere is safe here—the whole area is an obstacle course of towering rocks and rutted earth, just like it is back home.

A boulder the size of a suitcase smashes down in front of me, barely missing my feet.

Any closer and I would've been a human pancake.

With no choice but to run, I release my spell and bolt into the mist, hoping that a moving target has a better chance at dodging the worst of the falling debris. I'm so focused on keeping my head covered that I almost don't notice the earth splitting open before me, cracked down the middle like an over-baked loaf of bread. The force of it knocks me backward on my ass.

And then, as quickly as it arose, the rumbling stops.

An eerie, absolute silence engulfs me, and from the three-foot-wide rift in front of me, a shiny mass of blackness oozes upward, seeping across the earth.

Oil?

I scramble to my feet and take a careful step toward the edge of the rift, unable to avoid the black ooze.

But the sudden crunch beneath my shiny shoes tells me it's not ooze at all.

It's scorpions. Thousands upon thousands of them, each

one mangled and mutilated, half-dead, yet still surging forth en masse.

"What the *fuck*?" I breathe, taking an unsteady step backward.

As if in response, a vision of Baz flickers through my mind. He's on his knees beneath a stone tower, scorpions devouring his flesh. Behind him, a dark mage in a blood-stained robe stands tall, his wand raised to the heavens, fire licking his palms.

Despite the flames at his command, his eyes hold no spark of life, no sign of humanity.

I know in an instant it's Dark Judgment, just as I know it's not some imagined vision. It's happening. Somewhere in this forsaken realm, my brother is under attack.

And from the looks of it, he's not going to survive it.

Fear sours my gut, tightening my muscles in preparation to fight.

"Baz!" The fevered pitch of my own voice breaks through the haze, bringing me back to my own doomsday scenario. In mere seconds, the mangled scorpions have surrounded me, spilling over my shoes and skittering up my pant legs.

I stomp hard to dislodge them and launch myself across the rift, charging onward through the mist, hoping like hell I don't fall into another rift or come upon more dangerous foes. Despite the fact that I'm running blind in too-tight dress shoes, I don't dare stop. Not until I find my friends. Not until we find what we came here for and get the fuck out.

My heart pounds a frantic beat in my chest, my lungs burning for more air, sweat stinging my eyes. I need to rest, to find water, but before I can talk myself into slowing down, another bone-rattling rumble shakes the earth, knocking me to my knees.

I get back to my feet just in time to see the fire.

Just a few dozen yards ahead, it chews through the mist, a swath of white flame scorching the earth. My gaze tracks it to the source—a golden chariot led by two wild horses, their driver lit by some terrible rage.

My mouth goes dry. It's the Dark Chariot, exactly as Stevie described her from her nightmares.

She makes a wide arc, then returns, heading in my direction. I spin around in search of a new escape route, only to realize I'm not alone out here.

And, my instincts warn, I'm not her primary target.

Just behind me, two children cower beneath a rocky outcropping, their arms wrapped tightly around each other, their eyes wide with fear.

"Help us," the little girl says. She's wearing a white dress embroidered with tiny bumblebees, her hair tied into two shiny blonde pigtails.

"Casey?" My jaw falls open, my heart sinking into my gut as the recognition hits. That's my sister. I remember the dress, the pigtails.

My gaze shifts to the boy in her arms.

Derrick, our younger brother. It's definitely him—the freckles and big brown eyes are a dead ringer—but for whatever reason, he's the same age as Casey right now. They could almost be twins.

They're not real. This is all a trick of the realm, a trick of my own guilty conscience...

An ear-piercing howl breaks through my momentary confusion, and I whirl around to see the Chariot closing in fast.

"She came right out of the ground," Casey says, her young voice bringing me right back to our childhood. "After it was shaking and stuff was falling on us."

I curse under my breath, but Derrick picks up on it instantly.

"Did I do something bad?" he asks, lip quivering.

The whole thing is so fucking insane, but whatever it is, something in me believes it's real. It's happening. And it's breaking my heart.

"No, buddy." I crouch down before him. "It's my fault. All of it."

The Chariot is barreling down on us, the fire so close I can hear the hiss and pop as the flames devour everything in their path. The earth trembles before her, and in that moment I know it's over. There's nowhere for us to run. Nothing to do but say goodbye.

I pull the kids close to me, do my best to shield them from the view of our impending doom.

"Mom and Dad were looking for you," Casey whispers into my ear, her body trembling. "They wanted to tell you it's okay."

"I know. Shh." I press a kiss to the top of her head. "Close your eyes."

"But you didn't even say goodbye," she says. Tears leak from her eyes, dampening my shoulder. "Now they're dead, and you never even said goodbye."

Before I can even ask her what happened to my parents, two bodies appear before her in the dirt, their eyes open and glassy, their skin sallow.

My parents.

Grief seizes my chest, and I fall forward and reach for my mother's hand.

"It's too late, Kirin," Casey says. "You should've come sooner."

Casey's right. The moment I touch my mother's cold fingers, the skin melts away, along with her hair and clothing. My father's body follows suit. Bit by bit, I watch everything recognizable about my parents seep into the earth until there's nothing left but bones.

"You *were* right, you know," a dark voice calls from behind me, his shadow falling over the bones. "All of this *is* your fault."

I jump to my feet and spin around to confront this new enemy. The Chariot has vanished, but in her place a darker presence lurks, looming over us. He looks like some kind of ancient druid priest, dressed in white robes stained red with blood. Evil and powerful magick emanate from his very core.

Judgment. Just as dark and terrifying as Stevie described him.

From inside the folds of his filthy robe, he retrieves a wand, already glowing with power. I try to reach for my siblings, but I'm suddenly seized by darkness, completely paralyzed. In a blur, Judgment touches his wands to the bones, incinerating them.

Casey and Derrick scream, the sound of it so horrifying it crushes my lungs.

Unable to move, to blink, to breathe, I watch my family turn to ash.

"You have brought great shame upon your home, Kirin Weber," the robed man says. "Upon your family."

I want to deny it, to stand up for myself, but his magick is already working its way deep into my mind. I can't fight him, can't lash out. I can only stand mute, enthralled by the raw power in his voice.

"This is your doing." He gestures across the ruined landscape, all of it crumbling and smoldering around us. "And it is but a glimpse of the pain you will eventually unleash. Yet despite this destruction, this chaos, you live. Always, you live."

He releases me from his hold, and I fall to my knees, nodding up at him. I hate myself for succumbing to his influence, but I'm powerless in the face of it.

Even without his magick, the words themselves are a spell, seeping beneath my skin and poisoning me from the inside out.

"You don't deserve to be here," he says.

"I don't deserve to be here," I parrot back. Inside, my

mind is shouting at me to fight, to run, to do something other than give up, but my will is bent to his command.

"You don't deserve to live," he says. "You've known this for many years now."

"I don't deserve to live."

"You are an abomination and you must be eradicated."

"I am an abomination. I must be eradicated." I look up and meet his eyes, cold and dead, even as his mouth twists in pleasure. He wants this to be the last thing I see before he incinerates me.

With the last shred of self-respect I possess, I close my eyes, calling up a new image. It's a tiny act of rebellion, but it's all mine.

Instead of the dark mage before me, I picture Casey and Derrick. Not as children, but as I last saw them together in London with my parents, before all hell broke loose and I fled. Derrick, still just a kid then, wriggled uncomfortably in his tuxedo. Casey was dressed in a blue satin gown the color of the sky, her cheeks pink with pride and excitement. It was the night of her official acceptance into the Association for the Preservation of the Occult Arts, the night that would kick off her brilliant career. I'd never seen her or my parents so happy.

A faint smile touches my lips, and then the image changes, my family fading away to reveal a stunning woman in a wedding gown, her curly hair studded with purple flowers. She walks toward me, carefully picking her way through the rubble.

Stevie...

I smile as she approaches, but she doesn't smile back. Her eyes are wide with fear, her mouth stretched into a scream.

"Kirin!" she shouts, reaching for me. "Don't you dare!"

I reach for her in return, but no matter how hard I try, I can't touch her. Can't feel her silky-smooth skin or smell the intoxicating scent of her hair.

"I'm sorry," I whisper. "I have to go."

Unable to bear the weight of this loss, I open my eyes.

Stevie vanishes from my mind.

Before me, Dark Judgment raises his wand and grins. His teeth are like barbed wire. When he speaks, I feel my heart turn to stone.

"By decree of the Dark One, the first son, the sole and rightful heir of magick... *All who are deemed unworthy shall burn.*"

SIX

STEVIE

The sea coughs me up on the shoreline in an unfamiliar landscape, then hastily retreats, calm and serene once again. All around me, the broken remnants of majestic sandstone towers smolder, black smoke curling to the sky. It looks as if the whole place was set on fire.

I take a deep breath, my lungs still burning. At least I can breathe again.

I get to my feet, unsteady and a little queasy. I haven't even begun to process what just happened when Lala washes up next to me, offering a wet but apologetic grin as she quickly rights herself.

"You are alive and unharmed," she announces, holding her hands up in surrender as if I might just murder her. Despite her friendly demeanor, the idea is not off the table. "Bear that in mind as you allow me to explain. Now, take a few cleansing, calming breaths, and we'll—"

"What. The hell. Was that?" Digging my fingernails into

my palms to keep from throttling her, I stare the woman down, hard, my blood running so hot I don't even feel the icy wet dress clinging to my skin.

"It was only a water spell," she says. "To reveal what lies on your path in this realm. It was for your own good, child. To help you see."

"And you couldn't have mentioned that part before you knifed me and sucked me out to sea?"

"There was no time. The water was becoming unstable, unreadable."

"So you sent me through a cosmic spin cycle? Lala, I nearly drowned!"

"But you didn't," she says. "Besides, the vortex itself wasn't my doing. That was simply the dream realm's response to my water magick. As you may have gathered, things are not quite as predictable here as they are back home."

"Oh, I've gathered all right. Gathered enough tricks and manipulations to last a lifetime. So please forgive me if I'm not interested in hearing any more of your whimsical visions right now." I heft up the heavy, wet fabric of my gown and clomp toward a rise of dry land, trying to get my bearings. "I just need to find Kirin and Baz, so unless you can help me with that, please leave."

"You will find them, Starla."

"I don't even know if they made it to the dream realm." I glance out across the landscape. The mist has dissipated, revealing deep rifts that scar the scorched earth. Jagged, smoking rocks jut out against the horizon.

"Your friends are here with you," Lala says. "I assure you."

This gets my attention, and I turn back to face her. "You know that for certain? Where are they?"

"The precise location I cannot see. I can only sense their nearness. They're not far now."

It's the first bit of good news I've gotten all night—almost good enough to make up for the fact that she nearly killed me.

Keeping my smile to myself, I turn to scope out the landscape again, picking out a clear path through the maze of decimated boulders. "If they're close, I'm pretty sure I can find them. Maybe I can do a revealing spell or something."

"You *will* find them." She reaches for my arm, her touch warm but unyielding. "But you must know what the magick has revealed to me. You must know what lies ahead."

"Ah. And there it is," I say, my momentary hope fading away. "The other shoe." I feel it drop to the bottom of my gut, cold and painful. I should've known it wouldn't be a simple matter of finding my guys and getting the job done. Not here. Not now.

I turn back to face her, trying to keep the disappointment and frustration at bay. A calm, clear head—that's what I need right now. Not to mention an ally, even if she is prone to dramatics.

"What did you see?" I ask.

"In addition to the myriad external enemies you'll likely

encounter, all of you will face great personal adversities on this quest. It is only through your bond—your shared strength, love, and loyalty—that you will endure. Ironically, it is that same bond that brings such traumas to light."

"What sort of traumas? What do you mean?"

Lala's eyes darken, taking on a sorrowful cast. "The pain and guilt that haunt your waking hours shall come to life here, in whatever ways your subconscious chooses to manifest them."

"But how does that work if it's a shared dream? Will we all see the same things?" I cringe inwardly, hoping I don't have to bare my entire soul to the guys tonight. Not here. Not like this.

"The dream realm is deeply embedded within you, but it is also a place—a place through which you and many others pass. Yet every experience of it differs, as every dreamer creates her own world from the fathomless depths of her subconscious mind."

I glance down at my wedding dress, wondering what kind of craziness my fathomless depths are up to. "So I've got a wedding fetish? No offense, Lala, but I'm not looking for a ring just yet. A sword, yes. Not a ring."

"That's not a wedding dress." She brushes her knuckles along the beaded bodice, her gaze full of concern. "It's a sacrificial gown."

"A what now?"

"In times of old, when humans first came to understand the magick the First Fool brought forth, women deemed unworthy of possessing such magick were adorned in fine white gowns and sacrificed in elaborate rites. They believed it would prove to the elemental deities and the First Fool himself that they revered magick more than even life itself." Lala shakes her head. "The fact that you're wearing such a dress in your dreams suggests that deep in your soul, you don't see yourself as worthy of magick."

The words of Dark Judgment echo, the memory of his viciousness permanently seared in my brain.

You are unworthy of the magick you carry...

"Why can't my subconscious be lounging on a secluded tropical island, piña colada in hand, hot naked guys rubbing coconut oil on my thighs?"

"That sounds divine, doesn't it?" Lala's eyes glint with humor, but once again, it doesn't last. She reaches toward me as her smile fades, lightly touching my braid. "You don't believe you deserve such pleasures, Starla. The purple hyacinth flowers speak to a deep regret and sorrow from your past—a forgiveness that has not been granted, but must be, if you are to become whole."

"You sound like my Tarot cards. Always telling me what I already know, but don't want to deal with."

"I am the High Priestess, child. What is my purpose if not to guide you through the murky depths of your subconscious?"

"I know. I just wish my depths were a little less murky."

Lala's eyes twinkle. "Much like the cards, I cannot tell you what to do. But I will offer something for consideration, if you'll allow me?"

Beyond our little rise of land, the rocky towers still

smolder, tingeing the air with a dark, sulfuric scent that makes my skin prickle. Whatever happened here, it can't have been good.

I can only hope Baz and Kirin weren't in the vicinity when the place got leveled.

Fresh fear surges inside, but I tamp it down. Lala just sensed them close by. She assured me I'd find them.

"Please," I say. "Offer away."

"Often the person we most need to forgive is ourself."

A soft laugh escapes my lips. "Well, that sounds super easy, right?"

So many people have been hurt because of me. Have died. And still, at this very moment, I'm leading two of the men I love straight into the mouth of hell.

Forgive myself? I wouldn't even know where to begin.

Tears sting the backs of my eyes, but I keep them at bay. Right now, my murky inner demons need to take a number —we've got much more dangerous monsters to wrangle here.

"Where do the Dark Arcana fit into this?" I ask, getting us back on track with the highlights reel of my previous dream realm encounters: The Chariot running roughshod across campus, hunting my friends in cold blood; Judgment's baby-eating, pyromaniacal freakshow; the Magician's cruel army. "If that's all just a subconscious projection of my personal baggage, then I'm even more messed up than I thought."

"The Dark Arcana do not exist in your subconscious," she says, gesturing for me to follow her back down toward the water, toward cleaner air. "All Arcana energy—light and dark—exists on another plane until it manifests in its physical form. That manifestation typically happens quickly, when one human emanation of an Arcana passes on and another is chosen as the vessel."

"So there are always twenty-one," I say, recalling what Doc and the others had told me when I first learned I was the Star. Every witch and mage possesses elemental gifts— air, earth, water, fire, or some combination—and a few rare witches like myself possess spirit magick. But twenty-one of us are also emanations of the Tarot's major Arcana. As one dies, another is born, cue the Circle of Life song.

"Precisely," Lala says. "But through much reflection and study, I'm coming to understand that the Dark Arcana do not always follow the natural order, manifesting the same way the rest of us do. I now believe they seek out weaknesses and vulnerabilities in their Light Arcana counterparts, exploiting those weaknesses in order to turn others to the darkness."

The sea turns frothy once again, the smoke surrounding us rising to blot out the stars.

An ominous chill creeps across my skin.

"So Professor Phaines... he wasn't always dark?" I ask.

"No. It's likely he began his magickal journey as the emanation of the Light Hierophant, but was corrupted by the dark energy in his later years."

"The other Dark Arcana energies—they're still here in the dream realm? Just... just floating around until the time is right to invade someone else's body? That means any one of us is at risk of attack or invasion."

"Yes, it does." Lala pulls her cape over her shoulders, drawing it close against the oncoming chill. "Remember, Starla. All of this is ever-changing, the legends and lore shifting with each generation like sands in the wind. We don't know precisely how any of this works. But I can tell you that the dream realm is highly permeable. Any spirit or energy form can travel here, and as you've experienced, their actions here have very real consequences."

At this, a full shiver breaks through, shaking me to the core. Until now, I've traveled here alone. No matter how real it felt to witness Dark Judgment incinerate my men in my dream vision, it was all just that—my dream.

But tonight, two of my brothers are here with me.

If Judgment finds them...

"Make no mistake," Lala continues. "The dark energies you encounter here can and *will* harm you. That they haven't seriously hurt you already is a sign of your inner strength and the spirits that protect you. But even the most powerful guardians and magick can't prevent every attack, particularly when you're still burdened with your own deeply private demons. That pain, that guilt I mentioned... It's all going to be magnified here."

"I'm still not following you. I've never experienced anything but the Dark Arcana here. Why would my subconscious dredge up all that stuff now, of all nights?"

"Oh, Starla." Lala slips an arm around my shoulder and pulls me close, a kind, grandmotherly gesture that takes me completely off guard. Swallowing the sudden tightness in my throat, I rest my head on her shoulder, allowing myself a momentary comfort.

"It's an effect of the dream sharing," Lala says softly. "Your bond, your love for one another... Love like that makes you stronger, but it also makes you vulnerable." She pulls out of our embrace and turns to take my hands, her eyes shining with new emotion. "True love is a formidable force on its own. When it sees itself reflected in the heart of another, it will lay bare and burn down *anything* that stands in the way of that union. The process can be terrifying and painful, but it's wholly necessary. Only love has the power to dismantle our fears and set free the pure, limitless heart within."

My heart swells, as if it recognizes itself in her words— once pure and limitless, now imprisoned by a lifetime of pain and guilt and fear. I'll admit, it's hard not to get caught up in Lala's breathless proclamations and the idea that maybe love really *can* save us all. Thinking of Kirin and Baz, my deepening feelings for them, the simmering tension between me and Doc, the butterflies that swirl through my stomach anytime I'm with Ani... I know she's right. Love *is* a formidable force.

Unfortunately, now is not the time to get swept away by romantic notions, no matter how badly I want them to be true.

And time, as Lala said, is not something we can take for granted here.

"Lala, I appreciate your many insights, particularly the

ones that pertain to my complicated love life. But we need to back-burner the couple's therapy, okay? Right now, our prime objective is to get that sword and scoot back to the material realm before the Dark Arcana figure out what we're up to. And then—assuming we survive the night and whatever craziness is waiting for us back home—we'll need to do it all over again for the rest of the sacred objects. Beyond that, I have no idea what happens next. I'm just really banking on that whole 'survive the night' part. So anything you can do to help me in that arena would be completely amazing."

"So you're seeking the sword, the wand, the chalice, *and* the pentacle, then?" Her eyebrows lift in question, but I have a feeling she already knows the answer.

Which means she's just stalling before dropping another bomb in my lap.

"Well, normally I'm all about an eclectic vibe," I say, forcing some levity into the darkness. "But in this case, we really need the matched set. Trademarked, one-of-a-kind, ancient Arcana artifacts—no imitations, duplications, or substitutions accepted."

Lala doesn't even crack a smile. Just releases my hands and shakes her head, her mouth pressed into a grim line.

Whatever news she's holding onto now, hearing it is going to hurt like hell.

I squeeze my eyes shut, as if the act alone could bring me back home, back to my bed. Back to the safe, protective arms of my men. Back to a world where witches and mages are never persecuted, magick is never wielded as a weapon, and love really can conquer all those old ghosts.

"Just tell me," I whisper, letting the fantasy blow away on the sulfur-scented breeze. "Whatever it is, I'll deal with it."

"It's the spell protecting the artifacts. The very act of retrieving them will bring its own terrible dangers." Lala touches my hand again, and behind my closed eyes, four new Tarot cards flare to life—the Aces of each suit, vivid and beautiful, a promise held in each one.

But before I can fully appreciate their messages, the edges of the cards begin to smoke. In one simultaneous *whoosh*, the cards burst into flames.

I gasp and open my eyes.

"It's complex, ancient cloaking magick," Lala says. "Bound to the objects and to this realm, just as the objects are bound to each other. The moment one of them leaves here, the spell protecting them will shatter."

"Shatter?" Panic rises inside me as I picture the Aces catching fire. "What does that mean, exactly?"

"Any objects remaining here after one is removed will be vulnerable, protected only by the physical barriers that hide them, making them much easier to track down. Any object brought back to the material plane will become material again too, reclaiming its full power. Not only will its cloaking magick vanish, but the sudden infusion of ancient Arcana power on the material plane will leave a massive magickal signature. The Dark One will eventually sense it— he's been working toward this end for millennia."

"So by bringing back the Sword tonight, we're basically creating a homing beacon. Awesome." I rub my temples, trying to see a way around this fuckery. "Okay, so we'll need to find all the objects tonight. And then we'll have to cast a new cloaking spell once we get to the material realm. There might be a small window of time when things go unprotected, but the Dark Magician can't just find us and break through the Academy wards that quickly, right? I'm sure Doc and the other professors can figure something out before that happens, and… and…" I narrow my eyes, scrutinizing her face. "There's more, isn't there? You've got that bad-news wrinkle between your eyebrows again."

"Made manifest," she says, "the objects will not only act as homing beacons, but as anchors, allowing the Dark Arcana to manifest their energy through the objects without having to manifest in a physical body. Academy magick will be no match for the Magician's connection to those objects. They were forged from his father's body, blood, breath, and bones—they call to him ceaselessly. He *will* find you there, Starla. He will use the tools to manifest his darkness back home. And from there, he will unleash all hell to get what he wants."

"Complete control of magick. His birthright." I fall to my knees on the shoreline, soaking my dress once again. It's almost too much to bear. At every turn, another new obstacle befalls us, each one more impossible than the last. "But my mother's prophecies… The clues… All of my research with Kirin… Even the dreams I had as a child…" I look up at her with wide eyes, desperate for someone to tell me everything will work out okay. That there's even a *shred* of hope here. "I feel like everything in my life set me on this very path. Led me right here. Like my *mother* led me here."

"Indeed, she has."

"But why would she do that if I wasn't meant to retrieve the objects?"

"Oh, you *must* retrieve them. The risk of leaving them here poses a much greater threat. In hiding and cloaking them, I've only prolonged the inevitable—paused the falling dominoes long enough for you to come into your power, just as your mother knew you would."

"But I *haven't* come into my power," I protest. "My parents forbade me to use magick at home, and I've only been at the Academy for a semester. Kirin just started teaching me air magick... I'm not even sure I'm passing all my intro classes. This doesn't make any sense, Lala." Stating it out loud like that, I hear the ridiculousness of it all, magnified by a hundred.

But I also hear something that shakes me right out of my funk: defeat.

Dark prophecies, doom and gloom, impossible odds? Since when do I ever back down from that stuff? I practically get off on it these days.

The waves lap at my knees, inviting me back in. Back to the bottom of the sea, where I can close my eyes and all of this can be swiftly forgotten.

But screw that.

I get to my feet, take a deep breath. Right now, in this very moment, everything is fine. I'm alive. In the dream realm. Ready to complete our mission. Until those circumstances change, I will do what I came here to do.

As for the rest? We'll figure it out like we always do—when it drops on our heads, and not a moment sooner.

When I look at Lala again, she's beaming at me, her eyes shiny with tears.

"Are you a mind reader?" I ask. "Just wondering."

"No. More like a mirror." She winks, then pulls me in for a tight hug. "Find your friends, sweet girl. You need one another, now more than ever."

"Wait, you're not coming with me?" I pull back, imploring her. "But I need you, Lala. You're one of us—a Keeper of the Grave. What if I run into Judgment or the Chariot? Or worse, the Magician himself?"

She shakes her head and covers my hands with hers, holding tight. "For long years, I have protected the objects in the dream realm—long enough for you to find your way to them. That was my task, and now I must leave you to yours."

"Can't you just, like, add a new task to your list? They even have these notes apps for your phone now, with reminders, and you can just..." I trail off with a resigned sigh. My charms are obviously lost on her.

"Not all Arcana are meant to fight," she says. "I have shone a light upon your path. A small sliver, perhaps, but a light nevertheless. It is up to you to see what lies beyond."

Lala leaves me with one last mysterious smile, then turns and walks straight into the sea, vanishing before my eyes.

Okay, girl. She's right—it's up to you now. You've got this.

More determined than ever, I tear off some of the excess fabric from my so-called sacrificial gown, shortening it to a much more respectable miniskirt length, perfect for kicking ass. Jogging back up to the rise, I mentally psyche myself up for the night ahead by visualizing the victory celebration that will most definitely happen later. In my bed.

That's the spirit!

I've just crested the incline when I catch sight of a lone figure at the edge of the chasm, his shoulders slumped. Even from this distance, I know he's one of mine.

"Kirin!" I cry, but he doesn't hear me. I skid down the other side of the incline and break into a run, pushing hard to reach him.

Something is definitely wrong.

He sways on his feet, then falls to his knees, revealing another figure behind him—a man in a dirty white robe, fire sparking between his palms.

I would recognize him anywhere—the monster who's been burning his way through my nightmares for weeks.

Judgment.

And he's about to incinerate the man I love.

"Kirin!" I shout again, but he's deaf to everything but the dark mage standing before him. I pour all of my fear, all of my hatred, all of my rage into that vile beast. "Don't you dare!"

But Judgment only grins as he lifts his wand, his lips muttering a spell certain to bring pain and death.

The wand shines in the moonlight. On the very tip, the first ember sparks to life.

I've got maybe ten seconds before my worst fears materialize and I lose Kirin forever.

I don't speak. I don't think.

I run. I charge.

I fucking *fly*.

SEVEN

CASS

A wall of silver-blue fire explodes before my eyes, the shockwave knocking us flat on our asses.

I spring to my feet, desperate to get a read on what's happening. Aside from a lost blanket, Stevie, Baz, and Kirin look unruffled, the professors scrambling to cover them up again. Nat and Isla are at my side in an instant.

"Is everyone okay?" I ask, looking them over. The girls nod, already rushing toward the fire, shouting Ani's name.

Ani...

It's in that heart-paralyzing moment I realize he's not here with us. He's trapped on the wrong side of hell with a raging inferno and two possessed, gun-waving psychopaths.

Worse? I'm fairly certain he's the one who lit the blaze. I could see it in his eyes—that eagerness to pounce. To save Stevie and the others by any means necessary, even if that means putting himself in harm's way.

"Ani!" I shout, but the fire blazes higher and hotter, damn near singeing the eyebrows off my face.

"I can't even see him!" Nat shouts, reaching out toward the flames with her own fire magick, as if she's testing Ani's spell for weaknesses. "It's so intense—I've never felt anything like this."

Isla lifts her hands, her lips muttering a chant that seems to wring every drop of available water from the landscape, but it's not enough. The water sizzles into steam the moment it hits the fire, the flames surging brighter.

"He can't control it," I say, fighting to keep the alarm from my voice. The flames are creeping closer, growing, consuming the air around us. Stifling a cough, I spin around to check on the others. The professors are still on the ground, their worried faces flickering in the firelight.

"How long until they wake up?" I ask.

"We can't know that." Professor Broome sweeps a lock of Stevie's hair from her forehead, a gesture that makes my chest ache. "They're still in the dream realm. They'll come back to us in their own time."

"They don't have their own time." Abandoning the fire, I crouch down to scoop Stevie into my arms. "We need to move them. Those flames get any closer, and the fire will incinerate us all."

"Leave her be, Dr. Devane." Professor Broome stops me with a surprisingly firm grip on my forearm. "The realm is highly unstable, and we're essentially hacking into it with our magick. The fact that all three of them went under at the same time is a miracle in itself, but we can't assume the rest of their journey will be smooth."

"What are you saying?"

"If we move or wake them now, we risk cutting off their tenuous link to our realm, trapping them there."

Fear and frustration war inside me.

"Trapped there or dead here," I snap. "Who wants to make the call?"

"I'll make the call!" Professor Maddox shouts. "Put out the damned fire, for Goddess's sake!" She grabs my arm, hauls us both up. Hoping like hell she's got a plan, I follow her back to the most intense section of the firewall.

"Isla," she calls, waving the girl to my side. "All three of us are water blessed. Isla's magick wasn't enough on its own, but if we can combine our power, we might stand a chance."

Nodding, Isla and I offer our palms, allowing Professor Maddox to make a clean slice on each. She does the same to herself, then orders us to join hands.

"The River," I say. "It's our best shot. We need to induce it to help us."

"But it's so far away," Isla says. "I'm not sure I'm strong enough for something like this."

Magick tingles between us, already gearing up for the fight.

"For our friends, Isla." I smile and send a calm, steady pulse of energy her way. On my other side, Professor Maddox squeezes my hand.

"I know we can do this," I say. "Together on three, okay?"

Isla finally nods, and with nothing left to lose, I close my eyes, count down, and call on my water magick, pushing myself to the absolute limits.

River of Sorrow, River of Blood
Come to us now, by rain or by flood
Quench the flames that burn up the night
Lend us your power to snuff out this light

Isla and Professor Maddox join in, all of us chanting the verse three times. By the end, both women are trembling, and it takes all my mental focus to remain upright. Stars flicker behind my eyelids, and my knees threaten to buckle.

I'm nearly drained, nearly ready to give up when I finally hear Professor Maddox gasp.

"It's working!"

I open my eyes, peer into the heat and flame. Blood-red water seeps up from the ground, sizzling into clouds of steam.

But she's right; it's working. Inch by inch, the river is tamping down the fire.

With renewed hope, we resume our chant, four times, five, six, not daring to stop until the silvery flames shrink from a raging inferno to something more akin to a careless campfire.

"Ani!" Nat calls, and I peer through the heat at the ginger-haired Arcana mage on the other side. Smoke roils around him in massive gray clouds, blocking our view of Janelle and Casey. For all I know, they're passed out on the ground, or they're no more than fuel for the fire.

But it doesn't matter. Right now, there's only Ani. Relief hits me so hard, I nearly lose all composure.

But within seconds, it's abundantly clear that even with the fire under control and the guns no longer pointed at his head, Ani is far from safe.

"What's wrong with him?" Isla whispers at my side. "It's like he's in a trance or something."

She's right. His hands are raised, his lips murmuring a spell, his eyes wild with power. Even as the water beats it back, the remaining silver-blue flames continue to sway and dance at Ani's command. It would be beautiful to watch if it wasn't so horrifying.

I've never seen him so intensely focused. So captivated.

He's not just controlling the fire's movements. He's *casting* it, conjuring it from somewhere deep inside himself, giving it life and bending it to his will.

Ansel McCauley, what have you gotten yourself into?

I blink away the sting of sweat and smoke and take another look, still doubting my own eyes.

But there's no other explanation. This is ancient, power-ful, *highly* advanced pyromancy, totally forbidden, and I have no idea where he could've learned it.

We don't teach it at the Academy—not even at the highest levels of study. Because this level of spontaneous conjuration requires a mage to delve so deeply, so completely into his inner darkness that most who attempt it never return.

Not whole, anyway.

Fear chews through my insides, but I can't let Ani or anyone else see how absolutely terrified I am.

Ani, if I can't bring you back from this...

"Ani," I call gently, releasing Isla and Professor Maddox's hands and easing myself toward him. "Everything is going to be okay. You can release this magick now. Stevie, Kirin, and Baz are safe."

I can't know that for sure, but the immediate danger of our brothers being consumed by Ani's fire magick seems to have passed, so I'm pressing that advantage. Hell, at this point I'd say just about anything to bring him back, to save him from his own best intentions.

But my words make no impact. The look in Ani's eyes is so cold and lifeless, so utterly lost, I barely recognize the man I've come to think of as my kid brother.

"Ansel," I try again, softer this time, stepping over the last of the smoldering fire to get close to him. "Please. You need to rein it in now. I know you meant well, but you're putting yourself and everyone else here at risk."

No response. Even as I come to stand right beside him, Ani still doesn't acknowledge my presence.

"I need you to do this for me, Ansel." I place a hand on his shoulder, fighting the tremble in my voice. "Come back to us now. We can't do this without you."

It's a long moment before anyone speaks, the echo of my

own ragged heartbeat all that I hear as I wait for his impossible return.

But then, his shoulder twitches beneath my touch, and Ani looks up and meets my eyes, his gaze slowly coming back into focus, brows knitting together in abject confusion.

"Cass?"

"You little shit." Blowing out a sigh of relief, I haul him in for a hug. When I pull back, he's still confused, looking out at the scorched earth, the soot-stained faces of our friends, the devastation that he caused.

"Did I...?" He glances down at his hands, then back out across the smoldering embers. It's as if he's just returned to his body after a long trip away, completely lost and disoriented.

"It's okay, Ani. You're safe now. We're all safe." At my words, the last of the fire sizzles out completely. The river retreats into the earth, back to the lands of Blood and Sorrow. And the thick, churning smoke blows away in the breeze, revealing a cage of glowing silver-blue light.

Behind the ominously pulsating bars, two women lie slumped on the ground, breathing but clearly unconscious.

"So this was your crazy plan?" I say. "Imprisonment by fire?"

"Hey, work with what you've got, right? Stevie taught me that."

"You nearly worked yourself into an early grave. The rest of us too."

"But I didn't. And now we're no longer hostages, so... yay me?"

"Yay you." I shake my head, but I can't help but grin. Ani has always had that effect on me. On all of us.

Ani's return smile is as sweet and charming as a mischievous child's, and in that moment, I know he's truly back. That he's one of the rare, lucky few to survive a trip through his own private hell unscathed.

Perhaps I should have had more faith in our Sun Arcana.

Ani, the eternal optimist.

"Next time, give a man some notice before you light the place up," I say.

"I couldn't exactly communicate with you, and from where I was standing, it didn't look like anyone else had a better idea."

"Hell of a risk, Ani. Hell of a risk."

"Paid off, though." He shoots me another grin, but it does nothing to quiet the lingering voice in my head. Things may look good on the outside, but something tells me this is far from over.

"We'll be discussing this later," I warn, pulling him in for another hug.

"Live in the moment, Cass." He pulls back and winks at me, once again diffusing my anger. "But do you think you could make the moment a little shorter? I'm not sure how long that cage will actually hold. I should probably check on it."

"Be my guest." I stand aside to let him pass, not entirely sure I want to approach it myself. Instead, I busy myself retrieving their guns from where they dropped them.

After checking that the cage is still intact, Ani joins me with the others to check on Stevie, Kirin, and Baz.

"How much longer?" Ani asks, looking at Stevie with so much concern and longing in his eyes it nearly breaks me. More than anything, I want this to be over.

More than anything, I want her to come back to us.

I can only hope she'll keep that promise.

"We don't know, Ani," Isla says. "The professors say we just have to let this run its course."

"I can't promise that cage will hold Casey and Janelle all night," Ani says. "Physically, yes. But there's a spell within the fire keeping their magick on lockdown. That's the part I'm worried about."

"Good thinking," Professor Maddox says. "We have reason to believe both women are being possessed by someone—or someones—using them to steal the Arcana objects. Stevie sensed Fairy's Breath at play." She fills in Ani, Isla, and Nat on the whispered conversation we had with Stevie before she slipped under the dream spell.

"Dark Arcana?" Ani asks.

"A strong possibility," I say, "but it could just as easily be mages or witches eager to make a name for themselves. We can't rule anything out."

"Ah, well." Ani shrugs, his mood light despite the situation. "I guess we'll just have to torture it out of them."

Professor Maddox shoots him a stern glare. "We will do no such thing, Mr. McCauley. But we *do* need to bind them —prevent whatever's possessing them from hightailing it out of here before we've had a chance to question them."

"How do we bind them?" I ask.

"I've got a spell for that. I just need—"

"Licorice root, witch hazel, and Dragon's blood." Professor Broome retrieves a small glass vial from her bag. "That should do the trick."

Professor Maddox reaches for the bottle, all smiles. "We make a pretty good team, don't we?"

"I've been telling you that for a decade. Now stop fangirling and let's go put those motherfuckers in chains. Metaphorically speaking, of course."

Professor Maddox beams. "Of course."

I raise an eyebrow, but say nothing as I lead the women back to the cage, knowing deep in my soul that Stevie was right to trust them.

That I'm right to trust them too.

"There's just one more thing I'll need, Dr. Devane." Professor Maddox smiles, her eyes glinting with dark delight. "Your blood."

EIGHT

KIRIN

A shadow falls over me as the dark druid stands tall, one hand reaching toward the heavens, the other grasping his staff. At his words, flames lick along the wood, hungry for more.

> *Called to confess, called to atone*
> *Beg for your flesh, your blood, and your bones*
> *Unwashed and unworthy, you shall be cleansed*
> *For evil Arcana shall meet evil ends*

With a final wicked grin, Judgment thrusts the fiery staff into my chest.

The pain is like nothing I've ever endured, fire gnawing through my flesh, burning it clear to the bone. My vision swims, my ears ring, blood pools at the back of my throat.

Death can't come quickly enough.

I take a final gasping breath, choking on the acrid stench of my burning body.

"Unworthy," the druid hisses.

I'm fading. Falling. Disappearing…

But then, just before the last light dims, I see it in the distance, hovering just beyond his left shoulder.

A faint smile touches my lips.

Stevie….

In the span of a single heartbeat, the snowy owl dives at us like a literal bat out of hell, smashing its talons into the druid's neck.

With a bone-rattling howl, Judgment spins on his heel and swings the flaming staff. But the owl is too cunning, too quick. It launches away, then swoops back down for another direct hit. This time, Judgment manages to clip a wing, the white feathers singing at the tips.

The sight of those perfect feathers coming to harm fills me with rage so pure, so endless, all of my pain is forgotten.

With renewed purpose, I clamber to my feet and raise my arms, calling on the very last of my magickal and mental reserves. An image sharpens in my mind's eye—a Celtic knight on a white steed, blue cape flapping behind him, sword raised high, horse and rider charging headlong into battle.

It's the Prince of Swords, one of the knights of the Tarot, ready to answer my plea.

The spell comes to me easily.

Prince of Swords, majestic knight

I beg of your magick to aid in this fight
Call forth the wind, the lightning, the power
And I shall unleash the wrath of the Tower

At my fevered chanting, the wind whips into a wild frenzy around us, so fierce it nearly tears the tattered clothes from my back. Lightning strikes again and again, splitting the ground, toppling sandstone towers, setting the night sky on fire. It takes all of my strength and fortitude to stand my ground against the blustering storm, but the owl is unfazed, attacking the druid at will, navigating the swirling winds with grace, just as I knew the creature would.

Just as I knew *Stevie* would. She and her familiar are one, fused together by magick and a bond I can't even begin to understand.

Judgment attempts to fight back, but he's no match for the combined power of my spell and Stevie's owl magick. His neck is bleeding profusely, his filthy robe in tatters. Holding tight to the staff, he attempts to call in more fire magick, but it's no use. The wind steals his breath, battering his body until he has no choice but to retreat.

As the wind begins to fade, the owl makes one more slow, graceful arc overhead, and Judgment vanishes in the distance.

The storm is over, and I'm left once again among the smoking ruins of Breath and Blade.

Spent and close to death, I finally give in to the tremble

in my muscles. I drop to my knees with no more than a soft thud.

The owl lands soundlessly before me, preening its white wings.

I reach out and touch its downy head. Closing my eyes, I manage one more smile for the woman I love.

"You're magnificent," I whisper.

It's the last thing I do before I faceplant into the dirt.

NINE

CASS

Kneeling before the prisoners, Professor Maddox sets four Tarot cards on the ground in front of the cage—all swords.

Casey and Janelle are conscious now, alternately hurling obscenities and begging for their lives, but nothing will deter the professor from her spellwork.

Touching each card in turn, she recites her spell, our prisoners screaming in agony as the binding magick works its way into their systems.

> *Seven swords reclaim your power*
> *Eight shall forge your cage*
> *Before the Nine, weak minds shall cower*
> *Ten defeat the conquered mage*
>
> *Bound to bodies by the swords*
> *Silver blades of thirty-four*
> *Each an hour keeps the wards*

Until your souls return to shore

She repeats the verses three times, then unstoppers the vial, pouring its contents across the Tarot cards. Following her instructions, I quickly slice my palm, spilling my blood onto each card.

It instantly binds with Professor Broome's potion, the mixture turning the viscous silver of mercury. Sliding over the cards, it follows the path of the swords, fully coating each blade. When it reaches the tenth sword in the final card, the entire set bursts into flames, burning to a fine white ash that's swiftly carried off by the breeze.

The screams of agony cease. Casey and Janelle pass out cold once again.

Silence descends, and the professors and I let out a collective sigh of relief.

"Did it work?" I peer inside the cage. The bars still glow the eerie silver-blue of Ani's fire magick, but the women trapped inside appear unharmed and, more importantly, harmless.

"They're completely neutralized," Professor Maddox confirms. "No magick, no soul-swapping. Once they awaken again, they'll follow your command and yours alone."

"So they can walk out of here tonight?"

"Only if you order them to do so. Your blood ensures that."

"What about the cage?"

"It's no longer necessary—Ani can break his spell whenever he's ready. The women simply cannot leave without your express permission. Not until the binding spell wears off."

"When does that happen?"

"Thirty-four hours, times three," she replies. "'Silver blades of thirty-four. Each an hour keeps the wards.' I recited the spell three times, so that means you've got..." She taps her fingers on her lips, doing the calculations in her head. "A hundred and two hours—just over four days. I know that's not much time, but that was all I could manage. After our spell to call the river, my reserves were pretty tapped."

"You did great," I assure her, thoroughly impressed with her quick thinking and excellent spellcraft. "Once Stevie and the others return from the dream realm, Ani can disable the fire magick, and we'll relocate the prisoners to a more... secure location for questioning."

"Questioning?" Professor Broome eyes me warily.

"I'll need truth serum, if you've got it," I say. "As well as Devil's Fire."

Her eyes widen, then narrow. "You're going to torture them."

"Not if they cooperate."

"And if they don't?" Professor Broome asks.

I shrug, but don't elaborate. Despite my earlier reservations, I'm now fully on board with bringing the professors into our circle of trust, along with Isla and Nat. But that doesn't mean I'm signing up volunteers for the dirty work that comes next.

I won't subject them to that.

"Keep in mind, Dr. Devane," Professor Maddox continues. "That spell is a hard limit. When the clock strikes a hundred and two, they'll be able to yank their souls back at will, no longer obligated to you. You need to do everything you can to extract the information we need before that happens—"

"You have my word—"

"—*without* resorting to barbarism," Professor Broome adds sternly, and Maddox nods her agreement.

I lower my eyes, unable to hold their penetrating gaze. "I don't appreciate the preemptive accusation, Professors." *However true it may be...*

"Dr. Devane, please." With a gentle touch on my arm, Professor Maddox reclaims my attention. In her eyes, I find the humanity I was hoping to avoid.

"This isn't your concern," I say, but she's not going to give up so easily.

"Casey and Janelle are alive, essentially trapped inside their own bodies. They're aware of everything that's happening to them. They will experience—*feel*—everything. And they will remember it the rest of their lives."

I gesture to our prisoners, still passed out in the cage. "They are both on Fairy's Breath. They came here tonight with the intent to steal the Sword of Breath and Blade, and probably kill us in the process. Believe me, Professors. This is not the time for second chances."

Maddox shakes her head. "Stevie confirmed Janelle has been taking Fairy's Breath from the start, but not Casey.

And we have no evidence that either woman consented to the possession. It could've happened against their will. In fact, that seems likely—Casey was working for the APOA until this very evening."

I stand before them, quietly seething. Deep down, I know they're right. But we're essentially at war. The risk of compassion, of hope, is almost too great.

"If they *were* forced into this," Professor Maddox presses, "we're condemning innocent women to pain and suffering."

"I can't speak for Casey," I counter, "but Janelle? That woman is hardly innocent."

"Of this particular crime, she may be." She folds her arms across her chest and glares. "Capture her, yes. Interrogate her, by all means. But I won't stand by and let you torture anyone, even if they *are* guilty. The moment we give in to those baser instincts… That's when we lose the core of who we really are. Who we want to be. That's when we become the very enemy we want so badly to defeat."

As if that little pep talk weren't enough, Broome comes in for the big finish.

"Stevie would never stand for this," she says.

Rage simmers inside, my muscles clenching with the effort of holding back. "Stevie is risking her life to save us tonight. Do *not* use my respect and admiration for her to manipulate me."

I'm towering over her, practically shaking with fury, but Maddox doesn't back down.

"A respect and admiration she obviously returns," she

says. "But if you do this, Dr. Devane, she'll never look at you the same way."

The truth stings, but I can't let emotion cloud my judgment on this. We need answers, and I'd bet my life our prisoners aren't going to offer them up willingly.

"It doesn't matter," I say. "You know why? Because if we don't figure out who's behind this, who's seeking out those artifacts, Stevie—and the rest of the students and faculty here—won't survive the semester. So if keeping her safe and alive means risking her opinion of me, you can *damn* well bet I'll—"

"Cass!" Ani calls across the scorched earth. "Come quick!"

The professors and I exchange a quick glance—this conversation is far from over—then run over to check on Ani and the others.

"Something's wrong with Baz," Ani says. "His hand is turning black. That can't be good, can it?"

Professor Broome kneels down for a closer look, her deep sigh all the answer we need.

"What's happening?" I drop down next to her, pressing the back of my hand to Baz's cheek. "He's burning up."

"The blood connection between them is broken," Professor Broome says. "It means they've been apart too long in the realm. They should've found one another by now."

"What about Stevie and Kirin?" I ask.

She looks over the others in turn, their hands clasped

tightly over their blanket. "They have reunited. They're safe —for now."

The news offers little comfort. They won't return without Baz. None of us would leave one of our own behind.

"What happens if they don't find Baz?" Isla asks.

Professor Broome sweeps the hair from Baz's forehead, a gesture so sweet and protective it damn near breaks my heart.

When she looks up to answer, tears track down her cheeks.

"If they don't find Baz before they wake up, he'll be lost to the dream realm forever."

TEN

KIRIN

"Kirin! *Kirin!*"

Stevie's voice is so clear and rich, I'm almost afraid to hope it's really her. Because if it's some new trick of this terrible realm, I might just shatter.

"Kirin," she tries again, softer this time. Her touch on my face is like pure sunshine.

I take a chance. Open my eyes.

My heart stutters, and I gasp and blink and finally find my breath again.

"Stevie?" I whisper, reaching for her face. She's kneeling before me, blue eyes shining bright beneath a layer of dirt, frizzy curls and flowers slipping loose from her braid.

I've never seen anything so beautiful in my life.

"Oh, thank the *Goddess*." She helps me to my knees and pulls me close, wrapping her arms around me and burying her face against my neck. Her tears soak my collar. All I want to do is collapse again, but somehow, I find the strength to return her embrace.

"You're trembling," I whisper. "Are you all right?"

"No, I'm not all right!" Stevie says, finding her fire. She pushes me away to look me over, only to yank me close again. "I thought you were dead, Kirin. I thought I'd have to bury you in this awful place. I thought I'd have to go back home and tell Doc and Ani I'd lost you. Don't you *ever*—"

"You *didn't* lose me. I'm not going anywhere."

"I saw him though. Saw that wand ignite, and I just... I really believed it was over. That the monster had finally won."

"But he didn't. You fought him off." I touch her face again, staring at her in abject wonder. Each day, each hour, she becomes more of a mystery to me. A complicated, beautiful mystery I'd love to spend the rest of my life contemplating.

After several long moments, Stevie finally cracks another smile, letting out a shaky breath. "*We* fought him off. So don't get all hero-worshipy on me." She presses an all-too-brief kiss to my mouth, then stands, pulling me up with her. "We need to move. And this time, I'm not letting you out of my sight."

"I'm good with that plan."

"You sure?" she teases. "As I recall, you have a thing about running away whenever things get too intense."

I slide my hands into her hair, tilting her face up toward mine. "I'm not going anywhere. Not this time."

Casting aside all my previous reservations and fears, I claim her in a possessive kiss, stopping only when we've both run out of air.

"Believe me now?" I nip her lower lip, enjoying the dark flush I put in her cheeks.

"Okay, so that was... pretty convincing." Stevie grins, and I swear in that moment I'll never feel pain again. But all too quickly, her smile falls away. "I don't understand how you're not a pile of ash."

"Does it matter?"

"To me? Yes." Gingerly, she runs her hands along my arms and chest, checking every square inch for injuries. My tuxedo jacket is in shreds, the once-crisp white shirt scorched beyond recognition, but my skin is unmarred.

"This fucking *place*," she whispers, and a chilly, ominous breeze lifts the curls framing her face. "He was literally about to incinerate you."

I nod, barely suppressing a shudder. I don't tell her that despite appearances, my chest still aches with the ghost of that cruel burn, almost as if my flesh is still smoldering.

"Confession," I say, trying for a bit of levity. "Sacrilege or not, I'm totally going to burn the Judgment cards from all my Tarot decks when we get back."

"I'm on board with that plan." Stevie runs her hand along my chest again, her light touch temporarily soothing my burning flesh. "I don't know how this is possible, Kirin, but we should probably just count our blessings and move on. We still have a sword to find, and Baz..."

Sadness and worry fill her eyes.

I hook a finger under her chin and tilt her face up once more. "We'll find him, Stevie. I promise."

Nodding, she takes my hand, and together we make our way along one of the only pathways that wasn't decimated by my storm. All around us, rocks and boulders lay smashed and scorched, the entire landscape like some post-apocalyptic wasteland.

"I need to tell you something," she says, and I feel her hand tighten around mine, as if she fears she'll scare me off again.

I squeeze back, a silent promise.

"I met someone here," she continues. "Well, re-met, is more like it. Lala."

"Lala Juarez?" I can't quite wrap my head around it. Lala is a friend, but we don't see or speak of her much. Cass knows her better than the rest of us, but even he barely mentions her. From what I understand, she's extremely private and mysterious, and hardly ever leaves her home in the desert. "How the hell did she end up here, tonight of all nights?"

Stevie takes a deep breath, then says, "She's one of us, Kirin. The High Priestess."

She tells me the whole story—how Lala hid the sacred objects in the dream realm years ago, what we're risking by taking them out. Lala's theories about how the Dark Arcana manifest, and how they'll exploit our every weakness to get what they want. It's all so simultaneously terrifying and fascinating, my brain doesn't know how to respond. Fear?

Hopelessness? The nerdy excitement of a lifelong academic on the verge of a major discovery?

"None of this is in the lore books we've researched," I say, defaulting to the world where I'm most comfortable. Research is a puzzle, and puzzles can be solved. We just need to find all the pieces.

And tonight, we're closer than we've ever been.

"I'm pretty sure we'll have to rewrite *all* the lore after this," she says. "Along with half my mother's prophecies."

Her eyes go far away, but before I can ask her what's wrong, she's right back with me, filling me in on the rest of Lala's intense lessons.

"You're basically blowing my mind right now," I say. "You know that, right?"

"Yes, and if we were back in the library, I'd be happy to encourage your patented Genius Boy Arcana Lore hard-on."

"Noted." I crack up at the imagery. "But…?"

"Seriously? Look around!" She runs off the path, spinning in a circle and sweeping a hand across the ruined lands. "We're in hell, and all you can think about is how to work this into a thesis!"

I catch up to her, capturing her hand and pulling her back onto the path. "First of all, we're not in hell. And secondly… I don't know how else to explain it. It's just that it all makes sense now."

"It all… *what*?" A maniacal laugh bubbles out from between her lips. "Kirin, let's consider the facts here. We are currently stuck in a nightmare realm. You're wearing an extra crispy tuxedo and I look like a 1980s hair-band video reject. We're traipsing through this sulfur-scented wasteland looking for our missing brother and a magickal sword that will either save us or usher in the demise of the entire world. There are at least three psychotic dark Arcana mages on the loose, one of which has a wand in his possession that turns people into toast crumbs. And let's not even *talk* about my hair. Have you seen this monstrosity?" She grabs a fist full of her wild, flower-studded curls. "In what world does *any* of this make sense?"

"No, I mean... I thought I was going crazy. I just saw my whole family die here, right before my eyes, and I thought I'd finally lost it."

"Wait." Stevie's eyes go wide. "You saw your family die?"

"Yes. I mean, not exactly. It was more like a dream—like, my parents and siblings were here, but they were all the wrong ages. My siblings were little kids. My parents turned into skeletons. And this tuxedo?" I yank on what's left of the lapels, offering a cheesy grin. "Yeah, it's basically a funhouse version of the worst night of my life."

"Kirin, that sounds terrifying."

"It was. But now I understand it was just a projection. A manifestation of all the shit I haven't dealt with. Get it?"

She cocks a dubious eyebrow. "From the worst night of your life?"

"Exactly!"

"Kirin, I don't understand. What is happening?"

I blow out a breath, and she looks up at me expectantly, the mood taking a dark turn.

All the nonsensical humor of the last five minutes vanishes in a puff.

Damn it, I would've given anything to let the past stay neatly tucked under the rug. But that's the thing about trying to sweep things under the rug—no matter how hard you try, there's always more dirt.

"Ten years ago," I finally say, "I nearly killed my family —and a lot of other people, too. And there was nothing I could do to stop it."

Stevie must sense the sudden weariness in my voice, because despite the bomb I just dropped, she doesn't push for more.

Part of me—hell, *most* of me—wants to leave it at that. But I've been wrestling with this shadow for ten years. It's the whole reason I've been running from my feelings for her; it all goes right back to that night in London ten years ago.

I close my eyes, take a deep breath.

If anyone deserves to hear the story, it's her.

"My entire family—for generations—has worked for the APOA," I begin. "My grandparents still work in human-magickal relations. My parents are both research librarians —my father's specialty is ancient occult languages, and my mother works on cross-cultural magickal studies. I've got cousins there, uncles and aunts, everyone. Casey is the first field agent of the family, though—something she used to love lording over the rest of us."

I try to smile, remembering how excited and proud she was about that fact. But when I think of my sister now, there are three versions competing for attention in my memory: the Casey I remember from those days, before everything went bad between us. The Casey who waltzed into my office a few weeks ago, grilling me like a murder suspect. And now, the latest version: the Casey who took us all hostage and held my friends at gunpoint, all for her shot at the sword.

"There was an event in London for Casey's acceptance into the field," I press on, trying desperately to convince myself tonight's version won't be the last one we see. "A big formal affair at this fancy hotel with all the families and significant others, all the APOA bigwigs. We all went— Casey and I, our parents and grandparents, my little brother Derrick.

"Anyway, this all happened before I really knew about my Tower energy. By that point, I'd had a few outbursts, but nothing I couldn't keep under wraps. I just kept telling myself it was hormones, or new magick still manifesting, something I'd eventually learn to control. But that night, it all came crashing down." I swallow hard, fighting against a wave of terrifying memories. "Literally."

We crest another rise, more spires coming into view in the distance. The smoke has finally cleared, the worst of the wreckage behind us. With any luck, the stone cathedral still stands, the sword beneath it intact.

Instinctively, we pick up the pace.

"What happened?" Stevie asks softly, doing me the

courtesy of keeping her eyes on the path ahead rather than on my face. It's a small gesture—one I appreciate more than she realizes.

"There was a whole show," I say, "an act all the recent inductees put on for the guests. Basically, they staged a kidnapping in order to give the new recruits a chance to show off some of their moves."

"That sounds like… a terrible idea."

"Completely," I say. "But apparently it's tradition. At least, it was tradition. Not anymore." I take another deep breath, shake my head to clear the ghosts. "Looking back, I can see how obviously fake and over-the-top the whole thing was. There was no way any sane, rational person would see it unfold and think the recruits were in any danger. But for me… I don't know. I process things differently. The lights went out, the cheesy action-movie music kicked in, and when the lights came back on again, all I saw were three strange men grabbing my sister."

Even now, thinking back on that moment, the terror hits me all over again. Try as I might to hold it in, it's no use. Even here, Stevie can pick up on my energy.

And even here, she knows exactly how to help me. Looping her arm through mine, she rests her head on my shoulder, telling me without words that I'm safe. That she's here. That I'm not going to scare her off, no matter how crazy this story gets.

It's a long moment before I'm able to speak again.

"In my crossed-wires brain," I finally continue, "Casey was being attacked. Everything that happened next happened in a blur, faster than a gunshot. It's only in reliving it in my nightmares that I've been able to slow it down, piece it all together.

"My vision swam with red, adrenaline flooded my system, and a tremendous rage boiled up from inside. I launched myself at her attackers. They were trained agents, but I had the element of complete surprise on my side; by the time anyone figured out what was happening, I'd beaten one of them unconscious."

A faint gasp escapes Stevie's mouth, but there's no judgment there. She tightens her hold on my arm, silently urging me to continue.

"That wasn't the worst of it, though. All of a sudden, I heard screams. Not just the overdramatized stage screams they'd piped into the soundtrack, but real panic. The ground felt like it was crumbling beneath me, and when I finally stopped pummeling the guy long enough to look up, I was damn near trampled in a stampede. The hotel was collapsing, half of the ballroom engulfed in flames, the rest of it like a bomb just detonated. My parents were screaming my name, but I couldn't even see them in all the chaos. For three hours, I thought the worst—that they'd died in the accident. By the time we reunited outside, the hotel was nothing but rubble. And I learned, in that horrific moment, that it wasn't an accident or even a bomb. It was me. *I* was the bomb."

Stevie gasps, and I sense the questions on her lips, the words she wants to say to make this right. But I can't stop now, or I'll never get this out. I'll never be free from its terrible grasp.

"By some miracle," I say, "no one died. But my grandfather was paralyzed from the waist down, bound to a wheelchair for the rest of his life. At least a dozen people suffered broken bones, severe burns, internal bleeding. Three mages quit the APOA that very night, and one witch was injured so badly she lost her magick. She made a full physical recovery, but the emotional trauma of it... She just couldn't connect with it after that. And those are the cases we were told about.

"No one could prove the destruction was my fault. But everyone had seen me attack those agents, and without evidence of an outside attack, it wasn't long before the rumors began to swirl. Behind closed doors, Agent Eastman convinced my grandparents and parents that it'd be best for everyone if I chose a different career. He tried to boot Casey out too, but thanks in part to my family's stellar reputation and Casey's refusal to back down, she was eventually allowed to continue her work. But it wasn't easy for her. She got all the crap assignments, no one wanted to partner with her, and she had to work five times as hard as anyone else to get to where she is today. That night still follows her like a black cloud, and there's nothing I can do to make it go away. Not for her or any of the others I hurt."

Stevie stops along the pathway, and I finally turn to face her. Her eyes are filled with tears, and I wait for her to break the news—that it's all too much to bear. That she can't be with someone like me. Can't even be my friend.

She'd be right to go. To run as fast and far from me as she can.

Stevie doesn't say anything at first, which is just as well. I've spent the last ten years burying my head in books; if there were words of comfort for this, surely I would've found them by now.

But then she says simply, "*Goddess*, Kirin. I'm so, so sorry you had to go through that. It's horrifying, heart-breaking, and there is absolutely nothing I can do or say to take away that pain—not for you or anyone else in your family." She shakes her head, dashing the tears from her eyes. "So that's it, then. The moment in your past that hurt you so badly, you convinced yourself that you don't deserve love. That you're destined to destroy everything you touch. And you ran away from everyone you ever *did* love, just to protect them."

"As far as life-ruining moments go, I'd say it's a pretty epic one."

Stevie nods, but doesn't say anything else, the wheels of her mind turning silently behind her eyes.

"That day at the spires," I say, "you mentioned some-thing about the stories we tell ourselves. How we do it to protect ourselves from pain. But don't you see now? For me, this isn't just a story. It's an actual thing that happened, with real, far-reaching consequences. People got seriously hurt. A witch lost her magick. I lost my career and nearly derailed my sister's. And worst of all, my family... They never looked at me the same after that. I had to leave, Stevie. There was nothing else to be done."

"Maybe they just didn't know what to say."

"No, Stevie. They knew what to say. They were just too afraid to say it. Too afraid I'd lose my shit again and bring down the house on top of them."

"You were practically a kid, Kirin. You didn't even know about your Tower energy. That night was a horrible tragedy, and I'm not trying to minimize this in any way... But it was totally beyond your control."

"You're right. It was beyond my control back then because I didn't know what was happening to me. But now I *do* know, so I have a responsibility to—"

"To cut yourself off?" She looked up at me again, her eyes blazing with fresh anger. "To hide behind your desk and books so you don't have to take any chances with actual relationships? To push your family away and hope they just, what? Forget about you?"

"You don't know what it was like. Living with that disappointment, that fear in their eyes. My family suffered because of me. They're *still* suffering. Staying away is the best thing for all of them—believe me."

I turn away from her, stalk down the path, but she's hot on my heels.

"Actually, I *don't* believe you, Kirin. Because it's not true." She grabs my hand again, forcing me to turn around and meet her fiery gaze. "Do you remember what else I told you that day? About how the Tower isn't just about what falls, but what's left standing after disaster hits?"

Her touch disarms me, as always.

"What's worth saving and fighting for," I echo, recalling

her words. "The thing you hold onto when everything else is utterly lost."

Stevie smiles. "So you *do* remember."

I nod, because I can't find the words to tell her that what she said, what she made me feel that day… It's what *I've* been holding onto. Most of the time, it's the only thing getting me through the day.

But still. Compassion may be a balm for a broken heart, but it's not a time machine. I can't go back and fix it. I can't jump into the future and make sure it never happens again.

"You need to reconnect with your family," she says resolutely. "At least with Casey."

"Like I said, it's just easier for them if I—"

"Easier for *you*. That's what you mean."

"Stevie, I appreciate that you're trying to help me, but you don't understand."

"Maybe not the nuances of your family, but it can't be that simple, Kirin. You *matter* to people. You matter to me, and I'm only just getting to know you. How could you not matter to them? I can see it in Casey's eyes every time she looks at you. Whatever happened between you guys—ten years ago or ten days ago—she misses her brother. She's trying to reconnect, and you keep shutting her down."

Her words hit the mark, but my walls are going back up again, brick by brick.

"None of that matters now. Casey's… Casey's gone." My voice breaks, and I have to turn away to catch my breath. Because if I look into her blue eyes and find even one more shred of sympathy, I'm going to lose it for good.

"Look at me, Kirin."

I ignore her, but that infuriating woman stomps around to stand in front of me, grabbing my face between her hands, holding it until I finally meet her gaze.

I brace myself for the worst, but it's not sympathy I find there.

It's fury.

"We *will* get Casey back after this," she snaps. "None of us is giving up on her, and I'm not about to let you do it either. She needs you, now more than ever."

"You're making a lot of assumptions, Stevie. Casey and I are about as far apart as two people can be. You say you won't let me give up on her, but that's the thing—I gave up on her a decade ago. I can't just walk into her life and take all of that back. Whatever we had as kids, it's gone. I destroyed it, because that's what I do. I'm the fucking Tower."

Stevie doesn't back down. She stands tall, jabbing a finger into my chest. "Yeah, you're the fucking Tower, Kirin. So stop sifting through all that old rubble and build something new."

"Because it's that easy, right? Just forget about all the —Stevie?"

She's staring at me now, but she's not angry. She's gone totally still.

She gasps once, then coughs, pointing frantically at her throat.

I grab her shoulders, panic shooting down my spine. "Stevie? What's wrong?"

Her body begins to convulse, and she claws at her throat, eyes wide with fear. Suddenly, water gushes from her open mouth.

"Stevie!" I grab her shoulders and try to steady her, but the water keeps coming. Her face pales, her lips turning as blue as the night sky.

"This isn't happening!" I shout. "This isn't fucking happening!"

I lay her on the ground and try everything in my power to save her—CPR, magick, bargaining with any gods or goddesses within earshot, screaming at her to finally wake us up from this twisted, horrible nightmare.

But nothing works.

Nothing fucking works.

Her body finally stops convulsing. Her eyes go glassy and wide. And in the cold and bitter silence, all I can do for the woman I love is hold her hand and watch her drown.

ELEVEN

STEVIE

The force of the water hits me like a car crash.

Kirin vanishes, and suddenly I'm being sucked down a deep canyon, battered by rocks and debris as the water tries to swallow me whole.

Desperately I try to suck in air, but it's no use; the water surrounds me, tossing me around as if I'm no more substantial than plankton.

Panic sets in. Colder than the water itself, it reaches deep into my chest, freezing everything it touches.

It doesn't matter that Lala believes I'm fated to die by my own hand. That's no comfort when I can't fucking breathe.

Frantically I paddle, kick, claw my way to the surface. I buy myself about two seconds and take a big gulp of air, only to be sucked back down again.

Memories flicker behind my eyes—a lifetime of happiness with my parents, here and gone in a flash. All of our time together at Kettle Black, our tea café. All the laughs we shared, the Scrabble nights, the tea-themed birthday parties, even the stupid arguments.

Right up until the last one. The one where I stormed off during our hike, pissed off that they wouldn't let me attend the Academy. They gave me space to cool off, but then I wandered off the trail. By the time we reunited, exhausted and more than ready to go home, the weather had turned.

The flash flood came out of nowhere.

And my parents—the people I loved most in the entire world—died saving me from it.

"We wouldn't be here if you'd only listened," my father says. "It's your fault."

My heart seizes at his words. He's no longer speaking them in my memory, but right in front of me.

My father is here with me.

Not the boisterous, tea-loving man I remember, but the man who died because of me. Angry. Bitter. Betrayed.

His skin is bloated and blue, his head smashed in on one side, his lips black. He's wearing one of our best-selling shirts from Kettle Black—*Make Like a Tea and Leaf!*—but that's damn near the only thing recognizable about the man I adored more than life itself.

Oh, Dad... I'm so sorry…

He grabs my arms, cruel fingers biting into my flesh. Blood leaks from his massive head wound. Through the red haze between us, he looks at me and frowns.

"You're not worth it, Starla Milan," he says, his voice dark and hollow in my mind. "I should've let you drown."

"I'm sorry. I didn't mean for this to happen! I wish I could go back and—"

"You can't. And neither can we." A grimace splits his pale face. "Not anymore."

He stiffens, then finally releases me, his body sinking down to the black depths below. I try to grab hold of him, to cry out, to follow him, but at that moment, an icy hand closes hard around my wrist.

Not my father's grip this time. Someone else's. Someone from above.

I'm yanked hard and fast from the deep, my body bursting out into the cool night air. I suck in big gulps of it, so certain it's a trick, that at any moment I'll be pulled back under for good.

But my savior doesn't release me. He hauls me up into a boat that bobs calmly on a tar-black river.

I lean over the edge and retch, water and grime burning up my throat, making my eyes sting. When I finally turn to see the face of the man who pulled me from Death's jaws, I gasp.

"*Luke?*"

"Now who else would row all the way out here just to save you from yourself? Come here, girl. Let me see you."

My heart nearly bursts with joy at the sight of my childhood friend from Tres Búhos. I throw myself into his arms and laugh right along with him, and in this moment he feels so whole and alive, I almost forget that he isn't.

But... the man who just saved my life *isn't* my friend Luke. He can't be. Luke was possessed and turned into dark-mage barbecue before I even set foot on Academy grounds.

More tricks of the realm. More deadly traps.

I wrench free and back up to the edge of the little rowboat, my hand curling around an invisible pommel as if the Sword of Breath and Blade was already in my possession.

Don't I fucking wish...

Immediately the imposter's eyes turn black, his smile melting into a menacing scowl. "Is that any way to treat an old friend, witch girl?"

"You mean a monster *posing* as an old friend? Yeah, I'd say it's *exactly* the way to treat you."

I raise my hands and call on my newfound air magick, throwing a little water magick into the mix too. If all elemental magick operates on the same basic principles, it's worth a shot, right?

Wind whips the water into foamy white peaks. The boat lurches, knocking the imposter on his ass. But me? I'm *more* than ready for this wild ride.

I'm creating it. Channeling it. Manifesting it with all my magickal might.

> *Air and water, sword and cup*
> *Turn this river bottom up*
> *By the winds the waters churn*
> *Break this vessel bow to stern*

I shout to be heard over the wind as it buffets us on all sides, threatening to toss us both overboard. The imposter scrambles to his feet, desperate to find purchase, but the magick is at my command, and I stand my ground inside the little boat.

Closing my eyes, I repeat my chant, envisioning my Princesses—Swords, with her black raven and tattered blue gowns, raising her silver sword high. Wands, that fiery badass, standing her ground with her staff at the ready. Pentacles, the young girl always eager to learn, to share. And Cups, holding her golden chalice to the heavens.

They appear in my mind and clasp hands, their power rising and swirling, merging into a tempest worthy of legend.

It's mine for the taking, and I take it *gladly*, unleashing it with a ferocity that makes my Princesses beam with pride.

"By the winds the waters churn," I repeat. "Break this vessel bow to stern!"

Magick flows from my hands, my lips, my hair, spinning us faster and faster and faster, a toy boat set atop a whirlpool.

"Stop it, you crazy bitch!" the imposter shouts. "You're going to kill us!"

"That's the idea, maggot."

The water churns, the little boat no match for the storm, for the magick. I spin us until I lose all sense of gravity, until my own stomach is threatening to revolt, until the imposter looks up at me with terror in his eyes and begs me to spare his life.

When I've finally had enough, I close my fists, cutting myself off from the magick. At once, the Princesses vanish, taking the tempest with them.

We crash back down to the surface, the wood splintering beneath us, back on rocky terrain once again.

The water is gone. Our boat no more than a pile of kindling.

And there on the edge, the body of the monster impersonating my friend lies broken, his blood seeping into the earth.

But he's not dead.

I watch in horror as the vicious monster fades away, replaced again by my old friend.

"Luke?" I whisper.

His eyes flutter open, the skin around them turning black with bruises, as if he's being beaten by an invisible assailant. By that same hand, an invisible blade carves a pentacle into his forehead, then slices off his hands and feet.

It's the same torture he endured back in Tres Búhos. The same violence I saw in the police photos Cass shared with me while I was still in prison.

When he meets my gaze again, his eyes are glassy with emotion, so real it punches me right in the chest.

"Why did you let this happen?" he pleads. Tears stream down his face.

And then his eyes melt away, leaving two black pits.

Gone is the terrifying mage who possessed him, the monster who tried to kill me up on El Búho Grande this summer. Now there's only Luke, confused and scared, mutilated, the pain of betrayal lacing his every word.

"We were supposed to look out for each other, Stevie," he whispers. "I thought you were my friend."

His anguish washes over me in heavy, icy waves, the guilt I've been trying to outrun for months finally catching up to me, barreling straight into my chest. For the second time in minutes, it hurts to breathe.

"I'm so sorry. I couldn't help you. I tried, but..." I reach for him, but it's already too late. White flames crawl up from the ground, consuming his flesh one torturous inch at a time.

"Luke!" I shout, useless. Hopeless. Worthless.

His screams hollow me out inside, but there's nothing I can do but watch, bearing witness to this cruel death, again and again and again.

Five times. Ten. A hundred. Each time, the flesh reforms over the bones, and the flames return, terrorizing him endlessly.

Until all at once, it stops.

"Luke?" I whisper.

But Luke is never coming back.

From behind the burning corpse of my old friend, the dark druid emerges, triumphant and smug.

"Unworthy," he taunts, banging the bottom of his staff on the ground. Luke's corpse ignites once more, then burns to cinders.

I rise to my feet, glaring at him with every last bit of

rage and hatred I can muster. "Luke wasn't unworthy. He was innocent!"

"But you are not."

"Then why did you kill him?"

"*I* didn't kill him. *You* killed him. That's what happens, Starla Milan. The Unworthy taint all who enter their orbits, destroying everything wholesome and good in their path." With that dreaded staff, he pushes at the white powdery ash of my friend's corpse. "Is this what you want for your friends? Your lovers? For *them*?"

Blinding pain shoots through my skull, and I drop to my knees, clenching my head to stop my brains from leaking out.

Images appear in my mind, each one more painful than the last.

Baz, his flirtatious grin driving me wild, his mischievous gaze promising me pleasures we've only just begun to explore together.

Kirin, his glasses sliding down his nose as he glances up at me from a book and smiles.

Doc, folding his arms across his chest, glaring at me with that stern but sexy look that drives me more wild by the day.

And Ani, his caramel eyes lighting up as he makes me laugh with some crazy new prank, some impossible karaoke song only he could pull off.

One by one, their smiles fall. One by one, the light fades from their eyes.

One by one, I watch them burn, and all the while, Judgment laughs.

I can't open my eyes, can't shake myself free from this mental prison. Just like with Luke, my Arcana brothers burn and reform, burn and reform. Soon, my parents appear, watching it all happen with sad, disappointed eyes.

You never listen, Starla. None of this would be happening if only you'd listened...

"But this *isn't* happening!" I scream, forcing myself to hold on to some semblance of reasoning. My parents died long ago. Luke has been dead for months. My brothers are alive and well and safe—bond or not, I'd know it in my heart and soul if that were not the case.

"Oh, but it is happening," Judgment says. "Perhaps not on your timeline, or in your realm, but that matters not."

"Stop... stop manipulating me," I grind out, but my resolve is weakening. I still can't open my eyes, and my head feels like it's full of wasps.

I'm losing this battle; my logical protests are nothing in the face of such madness. It shouldn't surprise me. Torture is Judgment's art, and he's had thousands of years to hone his craft.

"A shame, really." He crouches in front of me and leans in close, his foul breath making my stomach lurch. "Your four Arcana mages had such potential. Alas, their devotion to their Star has blinded them. So many talents wasted, so many lives ruined."

"This... isn't... real!" Panting, I shove my hands through

my hair and yank hard, as if I can split open my own skull and empty out the toxic sludge he's put inside. "Get out of my fucking head! Get *out*!"

He doesn't get out though. Doesn't even move, though I can pretty much guarantee there's a damn smile twisting his lips. I can practically hear it stretching across his smug face.

My vision darkens, the heartbreaking images of death and destruction flickering out like an old film reel.

Then, just before it goes black, my Princesses come into view.

Four strong, magickal sisters, their eyes blazing with power. They stand side by side and link arms, forming a barricade in my mind, a literal force field that eradicates the terrifying images of my mages and replaces them with fierce, white light.

My headache vanishes.

I can breathe again.

I can see.

I open my eyes. Judgment's smile slips from his face.

Drawing courage from my elemental sisters, I get to my feet, their magick coursing through me, lighting me up inside and out until I'm surrounded in a bright, protective bubble.

"What is this witchcraft?" he hisses, scrambling to his feet.

"Where I come from, we call it girl power." I lift my hands, feeling the magick crackle on my palms. "So why don't you take that sad little stick and shove it right up your—"

"Unworthy!" he bellows. "All unworthy shall burn!"

His voice reverberates inside my skull, splitting it with a pain that forces me back onto my knees. In my mind, the Princesses stand firm, pushing me onward, but every time I try to get to my feet, the pain knocks me right back down.

Judgment's face twists into another smile, a bright ruby-red flame igniting the tip of his staff.

"And on this night," he shouts into darkness, "the Star shall be forever dimmed."

Grabbing the staff with both hands, he raises it above his head, and I know at once what comes next. I can see it in his eyes—the victory he can already taste.

He's going to bring it down on my head, split my skull in two, and end this once and for all.

On shaking legs, I force myself to stand up.

He may succeed in ending me tonight, but this little star is going out with a bang.

The pain in my head is so intense, my brains must be liquifying. I can't remember how to form words, how to cast a spell. I have just enough energy to meet his eyes. To look into the face of evil and smile.

And to raise my hands and call on the last little flicker of magick inside me.

Judgment's eyes fill with hatred, with darkness, with rage.

He lets out a bone-rattling roar, and with all his might, slams the staff down and...

Totally misses.

It whooshes right past my ear, and suddenly I'm on my ass.

Knocked on my ass, more precisely. My assailant grunts as we hit the ground together, his hands cushioning my head from impact.

I blink up into a familiar pair of pale green eyes, my heart racing. "Kirin?"

"Up, Stevie. Now." He jumps up and hauls me to my feet, shoving me behind him as he spins around to face our attacker. Judgment is already charging for us, his fiery staff raised for another killing blow.

With one hand pushing me backward, Kirin raises his free hand and mutters a spell, calling the wind to life. White light explodes before my eyes, and in a brilliant gust, Judgment is blown backward, chased into the darkness until he's nothing more than a speck of ruby-red fire.

Kirin turns around and grabs my hand, holding tight against the wind.

"Don't let go!" he shouts, and I nod, my hair whipping my face, stinging my eyes. The wind buffets us hard, stealing my breath.

"I can't control it!" he shouts again.

A powerful gust slams us together. Kirin wraps an arm around my waist and pulls me tight, his hold almost painful, but I don't even have the breath to cry out. The wind roars in my ears like a wild beast, plucking us off the ground and tossing us into the sky as if we're no more significant than feathers. Kirin is shouting and I try so hard to hold on, but the wind is too powerful, doing its damnedest to pull us apart.

He screams my name, and in a terrible, horrifying instant I'm torn from his arms, and then I'm falling, falling, falling...

TWELVE

STEVIE

I hit the ground so hard it knocks the breath from my lungs. Blood fills my mouth and stars dance before my eyes, and for a minute I just lie there, flat on my back like an overturned bug, wondering how long the human body can stay conscious after breaking every bone.

I can't feel anything. Just a faint buzzing in my veins. Maybe it's not even real buzzing. Maybe I'm already dead, and I'm just having some *phantom* buzzing as I remember the good old times—like getting blasted to oblivion in the dream realm with...

Oh my Goddess, Kirin!

Breath and memory flood me in a rush. I cough and gasp as I figure out how the hell to breathe again, and memory after memory slams through my mind like a movie on fast-forward.

The very last frame is of Kirin, desperately reaching for my hands as the wind tears us apart...

Still gasping, I roll onto my stomach and push up onto my hands and knees, spitting out a mouthful of blood. My entire body throbs with crushing pain, but I need to find Kirin. I need to know that he made it back here with me, wherever "here" is.

I need to know that he's okay.

Ignoring the desperate ache in my bones and the searing headache, I crawl gingerly across the terrain, calling his name. My voice is faint and broken, but I don't dare stop. Not until he's safe in my arms.

"Kirin," I croak out, spitting out another mouthful of blood. But here in the endless dark, there's no response. Even the wind has retreated, leaving me alone in silence and agony.

Give up, a familiar cruel voice echoes. *Give up and save yourself, just like you did that day at the river...*

Guilt burns and bubbles in my gut, but Judgment is nowhere in sight. It's all in my mind now—another of his artful tricks, like an infection that can lay dormant for years, only to pop up again when I'm at my weakest.

"You're nothing but a scavenger," I pant, reaching up to cradle my bruised ribs. "Show yourself. End this."

But of course he doesn't come. I don't even know if he's still in the realm—not after what Kirin did to him.

I soldier on, inspecting every nook and cranny for the man I love.

You let your own parents die, the voice comes again. *So why not your Arcana brother? You're nothing to him. Nothing but vile filth. Even if you do make it out of this alive, he's never going to look at you the same way. You're weak, Starla Milan. Weak and —*

"Unworthy, got it. You know, for a dark minion and supremely magickal being who's been around the block a few thousand times, you really should've developed a broader vocabulary by now. See kids, this is why it's important to stay in school."

The voice mutters some new insult, but I ignore it now, shoving it aside and taking a deep, cleansing breath. Even here, my healing powers are working their magick; the aches in my body have begun to subside, my vision finally clear.

Slowly I get to my feet, testing my strength and balance. When I don't immediately collapse, I take a few steps forward, gradually picking up the pace.

"Kirin!" I call out, happy to note my voice is stronger too. "Kirin!"

I stop and strain to listen, but there's no response.

But there, a few paces ahead, I spot a dark shape in the distance, its outline softer than the rough boulder behind it.

Human-shaped.

Kirin-shaped.

The tattered remnants of his tuxedo jacket come into focus.

He's slumped on his side, his back against the rock, and he's not moving. Not breathing.

No...

Fear gives me purpose and strength. I break into a limping run.

When I reach him, I fall to my knees again, my vision blurring with tears.

"Kirin," I say softly, running a hand up his arm.

No response.

Please, please wake up. Please be okay...

I slide my fingers beneath his jawline, searching for the faintest beat of his pulse...

There. He's alive. Super fucked up, but alive.

"Kirin, can you hear me?" I reach out for his energy, slowly moving my hands over his body, checking him for injuries. Despite appearances, his physical body seems intact, and his energy isn't giving off any dire warnings either.

I blow out a breath just as a low moan rumbles from his throat.

"Don't," he whispers. "Please don't."

"Don't what? I'm sorry! Did I hurt you?"

"Don't... stop touching me." His eyes blink open, and he smiles up at me, a beacon on the darkest night.

Tears of relief spill down my cheeks. Without hesitation, I take his face between my palms and lean in for a kiss, and when Kirin slides his hands into my hair and deepens our kiss, I laugh, feeling very much like the princess who finally figured out how to break the curse.

* * *

"So how the hell did all this start?" I ask Kirin as we continue our trek through the Breath and Blade lands. Once

I found him, it didn't take long for us to fully heal. Whether it was our own magick, the professors looking out for us from the material realm, or something else entirely, neither of us wanted to speculate.

Besides, we've got plenty of other topics for speculation, including where Baz ended up, why we still haven't been able to locate the standing stones, and what the hell is going on in our subconscious minds to bring this epic, level-ten shitshow to fruition in the dream realm.

"I remember we were talking about your family," I continue, "and then I just... I don't know. All I could see and taste was the river. It's all that existed."

Kirin slides a protective arm around my shoulders, pulling me in closer. "It's just like you said—one minute we were talking, and then you just..." He closes his eyes, his voice pained. "There was so much water, and I couldn't... It just kept coming... It's like you were drowning on dry land."

"It was the river where my parents died. I saw my father. He said... he said he should've just let me drown that day."

Kirin's hold tightens. "It wasn't really him, Stevie. Just a subconscious projection—exactly the kind of thing Lala warned you about."

"It felt so real," I whisper, fighting off a shiver. No matter what happens after this, I'll never be able to scrub that image from my mind—my father's black lips, blood seeping into the water...

"I know it did," Kirin says. "They're just projections,

though. With very real consequences, but still—it's all coming from our own minds. It's why my siblings appeared to me as children. Even though they're adults now, and Casey was an adult back then, I still feel like I was supposed to protect them. You seeing your father like that... It's not surprising. You blame yourself for his death. Whatever you thought he said to you, that was just your own guilt speaking."

"You're right," I say. "But there's something just... off. For one thing, I've been carrying this guilt for years. I've had thousands of nightmares about that day—sometimes with just my father, sometimes with just Mom, usually with both. But no matter how it played out, my parents were never outright cruel in those nightmares. I never felt so... so judged."

Kirin nods. "Yeah, I had the same experience. It's like everything is amped up by a thousand in this place."

"Not only that, but if the whole river thing was *my* subconscious projection, how did you end up there?"

"I was frantic, Stevie. You were literally dying in my arms—drowning—but I knew there had to be more to it than that. So I just... I imagined my worst fear come to life." He stiffens beside me, his fingers dig into my arm, holding tight. "Losing you to that monster... I saw the whole thing play out in my mind. The way he taunts, the bright red flames as his staff ignites..." He rubs at his chest, his voice breaking. "I saw him raise his staff overhead, and I felt the most intense rage and fear inside me... The ground shook, the spires crumbled to dust, and when I opened my eyes again, I was there."

"So your projection brought you into my projection."

"That's one way to put it, I guess."

"Who knew mutual projection could be so fun."

Kirin laughs, but it's not enough to break through the heaviness.

"That night in London," I say. "It's the worst thing that's ever happened to you. And I basically just lived through a funhouse version of two of the worst moments of my life too—not just my parents drowning in the Lost Canyons, but the day my friend Luke was killed in Tres Búhos. After that, I saw you and the guys…"

I close my eyes, letting the whole story spill out. My father and Luke. The fight on the boat. And then Judgment, burning Luke to ash before moving on to Kirin and my brothers, over and over again.

I take a deep breath, but the fetid taste of burning flesh lingers in my mouth and lungs, threatening to pull me right back into that nightmare.

We stop on the pathway, and Kirin cups my face, tilting it up toward his.

When I open my eyes and look into his steady gaze, a calmness washes over me. His energy is all love and support. Friendship. Gratitude.

"Me too," I whisper, a soft smile finally breaking through. Kirin leans down and brushes a kiss across my lips.

"You're not alone. Whatever demons your subconscious throws at you here, I've got your back. Always."

I wrap my hands around his wrists and sigh. "That's just it, though. Personal demons are one thing, but this... Lala told me the Dark Arcana are not part of our subconscious. Their energy exists here, just like we do."

"Okay. So what are you saying?"

"All this stuff from the past... We're not just experiencing our own guilt bobbing to the surface. That's just regular dream stuff, right? But now, it's like someone is getting inside our heads and twisting things around, amping everything up like you said."

"Judgment," Kirin says.

"In his present incarnation, he believes we need to atone for our sins, to cleanse ourselves. In his mind, we're unworthy—that's what he keeps saying. Unworthy and—"

"And we need to burn." Kirin rubs his chest, his eyes glazing with remembered pain. "So this is his way of getting us to atone."

"Somehow he's getting into our heads, rooting around for all the stuff we hate most about ourselves. He wants us to relive and re-experience our most soul-crushing guilt. To let it consume us. Tear us apart."

"If that's his big strategy," Kirin says, "I can tell you right now, it's not going to happen. You, me, Baz... We're in this together. As long as that holds true, we can face whatever demons we..." His words trail off, some new realization making his mouth go slack.

I gasp and we lock eyes, and in that instant I know we're both thinking the same thing.

We're *not* together. That's the problem. We don't even know where Baz is.

Kirin and I just went through hell, and we had each other for support. Baz is completely alone here. I can't even imagine what he's facing. With everything he endured as a kid—witnessing his brother burn another mage alive, sending that same brother to prison, being abandoned by his parents, living with the asshole Kirkpatricks—I have no doubts Judgment will find plenty of fertile ground in Baz's nightmares.

And that's just the stuff he *told* me about. Every time I look into his eyes I catch a glimpse of another ghost, too many to talk about, too many to count, and—though I suspect he's been trying for a long time—too many to outrun.

Judgment floats into my mind again, his cruel laugh, his wooden staff on fire as he slams it into Baz's chest...

Goddess, he's going to make Baz's memory his own demonic playground. And by the time we see our friend again, he won't even remember us. Won't even remember how loved he truly was...

"Baz has so many skeletons," I whisper, my throat tight with emotion. "Facing them alone is..." I let out a heavy sigh, not sure how to finish that thought.

Kirin does it for me, the look in his eyes matching the terror thumping through my heart. "A death sentence, Stevie. We need to find him. Now."

THIRTEEN

STEVIE

It's snowing.

In the middle of the desert.

"Something tells me we're getting close." I slow the pace as we come up over a rocky rise, taking in the vista ahead of us. Labored from our sprint, our breath comes out in thick white puffs.

"Wow," Kirin says. "If it weren't so completely creepy, it might actually be breathtaking."

The world before us is nestled in a thick, white blanket of snow, the stone spires encased in ice. Snowflakes continue to fall wet and heavy on our heads and shoulders, but despite the newly freezing temperature, I don't feel cold.

"There. Just before that next rise." I point to a structure rising up from the ground, its sharply-angled roof completely out of place in the rocky desert.

"Is that…" Kirin narrows his eyes. "Is that a house?"

"Let's go check it out."

Holding hands, we make our way down the icy slope and beyond, gaping at the house coming into view before us. It's not just a house, but a huge Victorian manor, dark gray with white trim and ornate turrets, the entire property surrounded by a wrought iron fence. Just like our winter wonderland, the stately home would probably be breathtaking in another context. Here in the desert of dreams, it's just plain creepy.

Goosebumps that have nothing to do with the cold raise on my arms.

"Do you think Baz is in there?" Kirin whispers.

I wrap my hands around the frigid iron fence and close my eyes, reaching out for a hint of humanity.

It hits me all at once, the pull of his energy so fierce I nearly stumble.

"It's him!" I gasp, tears of relief burning my eyes. "But it's… Something's wrong. It's like he's…" I close my eyes and tighten my hold, trying to tap deeper into the feeling. Almost immediately my stomach knots up, my mouth filling with the taste of bile. It's all I can do to control my trembling muscles. I seriously feel like I might pee myself.

But none of this frenetic energy is mine. It's all Baz.

"He's fucking terrified," I whisper. *And deeply ashamed*, I think, though I keep that bit to myself. I have no idea what we'll find in there—only that Baz doesn't want us to find it at all.

"We have to help him," Kirin says, already wrenching

open the front gate. We're about to head in when something catches my eye—soft light flooding one of the upstairs windows, shadows moving behind the curtains. Before I can get a better look, the room fades into darkness once more.

"Did you see that?" I ask. "Someone's in that front right bedroom."

"Let's go." Kirin grabs my hand, leading me through the gates. "Whatever happens, stick close."

We creep along the walkway that leads up the porch steps to an elaborate front door made of heavy oak inlaid with stained glass panels. Pressing a finger to his lips to shush us both, Kirin twists a brass doorknob.

It's unlocked, the door swinging open on its own, as if in invitation.

Clasping my hand once again, he leads us into an elaborate great room that opens into a huge living and dining room beyond.

Despite its surprisingly modern open-plan style, the interior looks more like a museum than a house where anyone actually lives. All the walls are a pale gray, the window treatments a few shades darker. The furniture is beyond opulent, all dark woods and rich velvets, like something you'd expect to find in a castle in England. Much of it is antique, but nothing is chipped or faded, every piece perfectly restored and displayed.

I glance around, half expecting to see ropes stretched across each area, preventing anyone from getting too close.

The energy feels as cold and empty inside as the snowy landscape outside.

A shiver rolls through me, and I rub my arms to chase it away.

There's no love here. No sense of comfort or safety. Only fear and revulsion. Only pain. Only neglect.

Even the bookshelves feel staged, as if someone went out and bought the most beautiful, expensive editions of all the classics, then tucked them away and made sure no one in the house was ever allowed to read them.

Everything here is just for show.

With a sinking realization in my stomach, I know exactly where we are.

It's Janelle Kirkpatrick's house—a projection of it, anyway. The place where Baz spent his adolescence after his real parents went off treasure-hunting overseas and his older brother went to prison.

When he first told me about it, he'd mentioned how Carly's parents used to fight a lot. But the energy here holds more than just stale arguments and old grudges. There's something sinister at work here, some dark energy seeping out through every wall. Whether that's just part of the dream realm, a Dark Arcana trick, or something else, it's pulsing through the air like poison, so thick I can almost reach out and touch it.

My heart hurts to think of Baz living in a place like this. Carly didn't deserve it either.

"I'm no empath," Kirin says quietly, "but this place has some seriously dark mojo."

I let out a heavy sigh. "It's the Kirkpatrick house. Baz basically grew up here."

Kirin's eyes fill with pain and sympathy as the pieces click into place, and I know we're both thinking the same thing.

My parents died, and Kirin is tragically estranged from his, but we both grew up knowing we were loved. Wanted. Cherished.

Baz and Carly weren't so lucky.

"Obviously there's something here he hasn't dealt with," Kirin says, running his fingers along the spotless, flawless dining table. There are eight chairs surrounding it, but I wouldn't be surprised if no one ever ate a meal in here.

"Let's just hope we can find him before—"

Creaking on the floorboards upstairs cuts off my words. Kirin and I exchange a quick glance, then we're both heading toward the staircase at the far edge of the living room.

Just before we reach the first step, we run smack into a wall.

Invisible, but just as solid as any other.

"What the hell?" Kirin tries again, holding his hands out in front of him.

Same results.

"Let me try something." I press my palms flat against the invisible barrier and close my eyes, trying to get a read.

"Is it the house?" Kirin asks. "Judgment?"

"It's Baz. Some kind of protective energy, almost like a

shielding." I try to separate the threads of energy, to figure out which emotions are strongest. "I'm not even sure he's doing it on purpose."

At this, the jumble of energy beneath my touch turns cold and prickly, almost painful against my skin. Waves of revulsion and shame emanate outward, the wall turning colder with each passing second.

Soon the self-loathing is so intense, I nearly cry out in pain.

Whatever Baz is fighting in there, he doesn't want us to see it. He doesn't want *anyone* to see it. And worse? Even if he survives this monster, he's never going to be the same.

"Any luck?" Kirin asks.

I pull back from the wall and shake my head, turning away so Kirin can't see the tears in my eyes.

"Stevie," he says softly, his hand stroking my hair. "Whatever this is, we'll deal with it. But you have to talk to me. You can sense things that the rest of us can't. So that means you have to translate for us, no matter how scary or painful it is. You have to tell me what's going on."

Kirin's right. I can no more shield him from this than I can shield Baz from whatever he's wrestling with upstairs. We have to face this—all of us. Head on, eyes wide open, or we may as well surrender to the Dark Arcana right now.

I take a deep breath and dash away my tears. Now is not the time to break. Baz needs us, strong and ready to fight.

"Here's what's going on," I say, turning back to face Kirin. "Whatever Baz is facing in there is so fucking terrifying, his mind is putting up physical barriers." I bang on it with my fist, accomplishing nothing but a throbbing hand. "We're not getting through it. We're not getting up those stairs. So we either figure out a way to help him from here, or we're going to lose him forever."

FOURTEEN

BAZ

Footsteps nearby. A creak in the floorboards. The soft snick of the doorknob turning.

With a jolt, I open my eyes. I'm lying in a small bed, staring at a wall covered in black-and-white photographs—a pineapple on a kitchen counter. A close-up of an ornate glass chess piece. A portrait of a teenaged Carly Kirkpatrick baking cookies, eyes squeezed shut in a rare bout of laughter, flour dusting her nose.

I know these pictures. I *took* these pictures.

My mouth turns sour and metallic as I realize I'm back in my bedroom—the one they set up for me when Janelle and her husband took me in.

And I'm shivering with cold.

No, not cold, I realize. *Fucking terror.*

"Honey, are you awake?" Her voice calls to me, the words hissed and slurred as she pushes open the door. Light spills into my dark bedroom from the hallway, and I squeeze my eyes shut tight, pretending tonight will be different.

"Baz, sweetie?"

The sharp tang of alcohol floats in through the doorway. I don't answer her. Just force myself to take deep, even breaths. Pretend I'm asleep.

I'm asleep, Janelle. You don't need to wake me. Your daughter is in the next room. This is wrong. Please, please go away...

My silent plea goes unanswered. She maneuvers her way inside, her shadow sliding along the far wall twisting and bending, turning from woman to monster before my eyes.

Then she shuts the door behind her, throwing us both in darkness.

I hear the familiar pad of her footfalls as she makes her way to my bed by memory. The scent of her perfume makes me gag, and I bite the insides of my cheeks to keep from crying out.

She's warned me before; it will only make things worse.

She lifts my blankets, cold air licking my bare arms and chest. Not for the first time, I wish I'd thought to wear more layers to bed.

Not that it would stop her.

The mattress dips as she slides beneath my blankets, fitting her body against my backside.

My skin crawls with revulsion, but some stupid, childish part of me still believes if I pretend I'm asleep, she'll leave me alone.

I force out a long, slow breath. A soft snore.

"I know you're awake," she teases, her breath hot and sticky on the back of my neck. Cold fingers trail down my bare arm. Across my stomach. "Just like I know you want this."

My mouth turns to ash. Hers turns to metal. Cold, sharp teeth nip at the skin on my neck, my earlobe.

The scared little boy inside seizes my lungs, choking off my air. *I told you so,* he says, and I know he's right. Here, the nightmares are *always* real, and now the monster is in my bed again, clawing and tugging, devouring. Always devouring.

And her words, her promises, her little so-called seductions... Every one of them feels like a threat, and soon I start to believe her.

I *do* want this. Don't I? Why would she be here otherwise? Why wouldn't I scream? Tell someone? Run away?

It's my fault. It's always been my fault. My idea. My punishment.

When it first started, I used to wonder if she'd wake up after—early in the mornings when she was back in her own bedroom and sobriety finally dawned in her mind—and feel guilty or shameful, dirty and broken.

The way she made *me* feel.

But that was always just wishful thinking.

Janelle feels *nothing*.

Her lips return to the back of my neck, leaving a trail of red lipstick marks I'll have to scrub off in the morning with Carly's exfoliating soap. I squeeze my eyes shut, swallow past the burn of shame rising in my throat. Pray it's over soon.

But it never is. Not until she says so.

"Let's get you out of these pants," she says, her breath wet and sticky on my skin as her fingers tug at the back of my waistband. Instinctively I grab onto the front, holding on like a damn lifeline.

"Hmm. Playing hard to get tonight?" Janelle laughs, still working on the pants. "You know what happens when you don't cooperate. And it's wintertime, too. Are you sure you want to play this game with me tonight?"

As if I needed the reminder, the wind howls against the windows, coating them in sleet. An involuntary shudder wracks my body.

Last time I didn't cooperate, she locked me outside and forced me to sleep in the woodshed wearing nothing but boxer shorts. When her husband Charles came home that morning from a business trip and found me curled up in the corner of the shed, my lips blue, my skin raw and red, I couldn't even speak—couldn't even make up an excuse to explain what the hell I was doing out there.

Turned out I didn't need one—Janelle took care of the explanations. By the time Charles led me inside, she was already pacing the kitchen, clutching an empty bottle of vodka she'd polished off the night before.

She said she'd found it in my closet, looking for clues about my whereabouts when I didn't come home from some high school party last night. Said we needed to have a family meeting. That she and Charles wanted to help me, but trust goes both ways, and if I kept drinking and sneaking around, they'd have no choice but to put me in foster care.

When all the lecturing was over, Charles sighed and told me to go shower up and sleep it off. Never said another word about it.

But the disappointment in his eyes left a wound that never quite healed.

"Let go," Janelle warns now. "I'm not in the mood to fight with you tonight."

I roll onto my back, look up into her dead eyes.

"That's better."

"It's wrong," I whisper, hoping like hell it reaches into some motherly part of her brain, some moral part, *any* fucking part to make her stop. "I'm just a kid."

"A kid? Is that what you think?" She grins, bright red lips blazing as she slides her hand down the front of my pants and grabs on tight. "I'm afraid you're *all* man, my sweet."

My gut rolls, shame and revulsion mixing into a familiar toxic stew. "No," I whisper. "Please stop. I just want you to—"

Baz, we're here! We're coming!

A strange, disembodied voice cuts off my thoughts, an echo of a memory I'm not even sure I really heard.

"*What* did you say?" Janelle asks, her tone mocking. "You want something from *me*? Something more than what I've already given you? A home, an education, financing to keep your brother alive after you had him locked away in that terrible place... Really, Baz. I've never met anyone so ungrateful. So—"

"Shh." I press a finger to her lips and strain to hear it again, to hear anything above the slamming of my heart in my chest, the rise and fall of this vile woman's breath.

Something about that disembodied voice felt familiar. Kind.

Do you hear me, Baz? It calls again. Louder this time—no, I'm not imagining it. It's a woman's voice. *We're right here with you! Don't you dare give up!*

Janelle sidles closer to me in bed and purrs, parting her lips and sucking the tip of my finger between them.

The otherworldly voice fades into oblivion.

I snatch my hand away and close my eyes, wishing I could bring that voice back and make Janelle fucking disappear instead.

"Don't do that," I snap, wiping my finger on my pants, but my command falls on deaf ears. Janelle does whatever the fuck she wants. Tonight, last night, tomorrow night, *every* night.

Her house, her rules—a fact she never lets me forget.

"Hmm. Someone is in a mood tonight," she teases, but her tone is anything but. She's well past annoyed now, sliding dangerously into pissed off she-wolf territory. "Maybe I should've brought drinks."

"No drinks." My mouth sours at the thought. Vodka and orange juice—her favorite drink, and her favorite trick. Get me drunk, then convince me none of this ever happened. That it's all in my fucking head. That I need help

—serious help. That she's worried about me. That Charles will be so upset to learn that I'm making up such terrible stories.

Rage boils in my blood. I feel like I'm on fire from the inside, and if I don't destroy something soon, I'll explode.

Fight it, Baz. Whatever it is, fucking fight it!

It's another voice—definitely male. Familiar. The tone, the urgency… It's someone I know. Someone who cares.

Your brothers are here with you, he calls again. *We are the Keepers of the Grave, and we are with you.*

Keepers of the Grave?

It feels so familiar, like a dream I just can't quite remember.

Baz! It's the woman this time. *You still owe me a rock-climbing date. Don't think you're getting out of it!*

The words make no sense, but whoever it is, I believe they know me. They're here to help me.

My heart leaps, hope mixing with the rage in my veins, but…

No. It's fucking impossible. Who the hell would be here to help?

My brother is in jail. My parents are who-the-fuck-knows-where. The woman who signed up as my de-facto guardian is lying right next to me, her cold feet sliding down my calf, her every touch making me wish I could boil myself alive.

No one is coming to help me. No one gives a shit.

With this monster, I'm on my own. Always.

"Does this mean we're done with our little tantrum?"

Janelle slides her leg across mine, her hand seeking me once again. Stroking. Burning.

"I hate you," I grind out.

"Shh." She nuzzles my neck. "We both know that isn't true."

Hold on, Baz! The woman calls again. *We're not going anywhere, so you just hold on!*

Suddenly, Janelle freezes, her breath hitching.

She heard it that time. She fucking heard it.

I pull back and look into her eyes, and for the first time since she started making these nighttime visits, I see something new there.

Fear.

The voices are real. And whoever they belong to, she's fucking scared of them.

With newfound courage, I push her away, bolt upright in bed.

"Hello?" I call out. "Who's there?"

"Baz!" the woman calls out. No longer an echo, her voice is suddenly loud and clear. "Kirin, it's him! He hears us!"

They're standing right downstairs.

"The barrier's still in place, Stevie," the male voice replies. "We can't get to him."

Kirin... Stevie...

I know those names. I know those people.

I gasp, and everything crashes through me in a flash. Memories. Images. A timeline condensed down to this very moment, to this very place.

This isn't Janelle's house. I'm not a fucking kid anymore. This is the dream realm. It isn't fucking real. Ford wasn't real.

And this monster in my bed... This bitch isn't real either.

"We're done here," I say flatly, wrenching myself from the bed. She looks up at me with wide, confused eyes, but now that I see through the charade, she can't fuck with me anymore.

"You're making a terrible mistake," she warns.

"Yeah, well. Welcome to my life." I try to think of some final parting words, something cold and biting, but I don't even give a shit anymore. I'm done with her. Done with all of it.

I turn my back on her, reaching for the bedroom door-knob and the freedom waiting just on the other side.

But when I wrench it open, it's not freedom I find standing before me.

It's a Dark Arcana asshole dressed in a stained white robe, his mouth and chin black with blood, eyes glowing with pure rage.

Judgment.

I barely have time to get my fists up in front of my face when the son of a bitch jabs me in the gut with his staff, dropping me to my knees.

"Unworthy," he hisses. "All shall burn."

He swings in a wide arc, clocking me in the temple.

Stars swim before my eyes. Without warning, he nails me again. My vision turns black at the edges.

"Burn!" he roars, and the staff ignites, bright red flames cutting through the darkness in my head. A harrowing, all-consuming pain tears through my brain, unlocking a flood of vile memories.

My brother, his coal-black eyes after he burned a mage alive.

Janelle, the first night she slipped into my bedroom and every night after. Her red lips. Her searching hands. The poison she spoke, her words like a spell that destroyed my heart, one whisper at a time.

All I want to do is end this.

I grab the end of the staff, bring it close to my face. One more inch, and I'm done. I can burn it all away. Ford's violence, Janelle's touch, the memories, the pain, the disgust, the hatred—all of it.

It's what Judgment wants. I can see it in his sneer, in the way his eyes light up as my spirit dims.

All I want to do is give up. I can almost taste it, the sweet relief of death.

But one thought, flickering like a candle in a forgotten basement, yanks me back from the brink.

If I give up now, if I let this fear take me, I'll never get to hold Stevie in my arms again. Never get to tell her I'm in love with her…

"Do it," Judgment whispers, looming over me like a specter.

"Fuck… you." I push the staff away hard enough to throw him off balance. The pain leaks from my head like blood from a wound, and I'm on my feet again, ducking and bracing for a fight. But Judgment recovers faster than I do, and in a swift blur, he jabs the business end of the flaming staff straight into my chest.

My bare flesh melts clear to the bone, the pain like nothing I've ever endured. Tears spill unbidden as I gasp for air, but I refuse to go down on my knees again. Refuse to lower myself. Refuse to give in.

"Baz! Don't you dare stop fighting!" Stevie shouts from downstairs, as if the little witch knows exactly what I need to hear right now. "I swear to fucking Goddess, if you don't come down here in one piece, I'll beat your ass myself! And I'm super pissed off right now, so don't press your luck!"

"What she said!" Kirin shouts.

I crack a smile despite the searing pain, my heart damn near exploding in my chest.

That's my fucking girl down there. My girl and my brother. And I'm not letting them anywhere near this shit...

Hope and rage twine inside me, giving me new life.

"You want some of this?" I glare at Judgment, ignoring the burn of his staff, the fury in his eyes. "Do your best, you son of a bitch. You don't stand a chance. Not anymore."

He lifts his staff again as if to strike, but the flame immediately flickers out, and so does the fire inside him. His face goes slack. His shoulders slump. He has to grip the doorframe to avoid falling on his ass.

I take a step toward him. Glare at him with everything I've got. "We're done here."

With a final, whispered threat, the monster before me vanishes.

The monster behind me, on the other hand, is still hanging around like a rash you just can't cure.

I turn around to face her. Hope like hell I can figure out how to make her vanish too.

"Now that looks like it hurts," Janelle coos, her eyes trailing down my wounded chest. She juts out her lips in a pathetic pout. "Let Mama kiss you and make you all better."

She grabs my face, pushing up on her toes to mark me with her bright red mouth.

Her sick smile is all it takes.

The toxic rage inside me ignites.

With a roar torn from my darkest depths, I punch a hole in her chest and rip out her stone-cold heart. It's as black as pitch, as shriveled as a raisin.

Her body hits the floor with a soft thud, blood seeping into the carpet beneath.

This was the mother of my friend. This was the woman who took me in after my own parents couldn't be bothered.

But as I watch the black pool of her blood spreading out around her lifeless body, I've only got one thing to say to her.

"Rot in it, bitch."

FIFTEEN

STEVIE

At first, all I can see is the blood.

His hands and arms are covered in it, a thick, wet layer glistening on his skin like garnets in the moonlight.

The rest of him comes into view slowly as he descends the stairs and walks toward me. The dark swoop of his hair. Childishly small pajama pants. The swagger, still there despite the obvious wounds.

And last, as the invisible energy shield drops away and he stops to stand before me, those smoldering red-brown eyes.

"Baz," I breathe, tears of relief stinging my eyes. I take his face in my hands, searching every inch of it. I've never seen him so drained. "You're hurt."

"Nothing I won't survive." He grabs my wrists and pulls my hands close, pressing a kiss to each palm, leaving my skin stained with blood. Before I can force him to sit down and let me check him over, he asks, "Where's Kirin?"

"Right here." Kirin comes out from the kitchen with a wet towel and bottle of water. Passing both to Baz, he shakes his head in disbelief. "Goddess, you look like hell."

"I earned it, brother. Believe me." Instead of drinking the water, Baz dumps it on his head and hands, wiping off the worst of the mess with the towel, then tossing it all on the floor behind him. It hits the hardwood with a *thwack*.

"Do you want to… ah…" Kirin scratches the back of his neck. "Talk about it, or—"

"Nope."

"Fair enough." Kirin's clearly relieved to skip the trip down Baz's bad memory lane. Still, he pulls Baz in for a hug, holding on a little longer than usual this time. I expect Baz to pull away, to shake off the extra affection. But instead, he returns the embrace, resting his head on Kirin's shoulder and letting out a deep sigh.

The sight of it makes my heart heavy. Not just with sadness for what we've already endured here, but with hope. With love—so much love for both of them, I'm practically bursting with it.

Goddess, I'm so blessed to have these men in my life…

After a long beat, Baz claps Kirin on the back, then finally turns to face me again, forcing a flirtatious grin. Maybe it's a mask, maybe it's a coping mechanism, but right now I'll take it. It's been far too long since I've seen that look in his eyes, and right now, the memories of everything we've shared together—every stolen kiss, every blissful night between the sheets—is just enough to keep me going.

And to keep him going too.

"Interesting outfit, Little Bird." Baz looks me over slowly, his gaze burning a hot path down my shortened dress, lingering on my bare legs. "Put that together yourself, did you?"

"Sure, I do what I can." I fluff my hair, losing a few more hyacinth flowers in the process, but Baz isn't returning my teasing smile. He's staring at me like he wants to eat me.

Liquid heat pools between my thighs, and for a moment I forget where we are, what we came here to do.

"Just so we're clear," he says, sliding his hands down my backside and pulling me close, "the minute we get out of this mess, you're getting ravaged."

"Is that so?"

"Put it in your calendar." He makes a checkmark in the air. "Ravaging, Saturday, nine a.m. Ravaging again, ten-thirty. Noon is booked up too. In fact, you should probably just block out the whole week."

"Are you going to wear those pants?" I lift a brow, biting back a laugh at his own super-special outfit, which at the moment consists of nothing but a pair of *really* tight PJ pants.

"The zombies glow in the dark," he says.

"I bet they do."

"So, about this ravaging…"

"I'll think about it."

"Less thinking. More…" His mouth descends on mine in an instant, capturing me in a fevered kiss I feel all the way to my toes. Visions of our meadow flicker in my mind, heat cresting between us as he slides his tongue into my mouth, tempting me with every stroke.

Goddess, I missed the taste of him. We're not even naked, and I already feel like I'm about T-minus five seconds to a hot, screaming—

"Yes, and I'll just be over here," Kirin says loudly, "watching you two make out in the middle of a nightmare house in the desert. No, no, don't worry about me, it's fine. I've got plenty of thoughts to keep myself occupied, and the visuals you're providing are just spectacular."

Baz breaks our kiss just long enough to give Kirin a sly grin. "You're welcome to join us, brother. We can make a sexy Stevie sandwich."

Hot lips flutter over my neck, and I let out a tiny whimper of pleasure, my body melting against his chest as the images come unbidden…

Mmm, what I wouldn't give to be the meat in their sexy sandwich…

"Yes, well…" Kirin lets out a laugh that turns into an adorably nervous cough. "Maybe some other time."

"No time like the present," I tease, and Baz quirks an eyebrow, his smile widening.

"The plot thickens." He arches his hips ever so slightly, just enough to give me a preview of the situation unfolding behind his teeny-tiny zombie pants. "And by plot, I mean—"

"Yes, I know exactly what you mean, and on that note, wow! Would you look at the time?" I laugh, breaking out of our heated embrace. My throbbing core might disagree, but as much as I'd love a red-hot, joint make-out session with the Devil and the Tower in the realm where all things are possible... Right. *Sooo* not the moment.

I turn around and readjust my dress, trying to talk my lady bits off the ledge and remember why we're here.

The answer seems to hit us all at once, a dark, heavy melancholy that sweeps in through the front door and blows across the living room, ushering in the cold.

I let out a deep sigh. Our flirty, joyful reunion was entirely too short.

"So what's next?" Baz asks, the heat in his eyes a distant memory now.

Resigned, I drop onto the couch, trying to figure out the best play. "We need to find the stone cathedral. The sword *should* be there."

"Maybe it's in here somewhere," Kirin says, inspecting a collection of glass chess pieces arranged on an ornate marble pedestal. "Hidden in plain sight."

"Trust me, it isn't," Baz says. "We should go. Now."

Kirin picks up the king piece for a closer look. Seems expensive. The whole *house* seems expensive, every piece of furniture, art, and decor custom-made to announce its utter opulence.

"What *is* this place, anyway?" Kirin asks.

"Someplace better left forgotten." Baz removes the King from Kirin's hands and sets it back on the pedestal, his energy turning chilly.

"Far as I care, this place can burn," Baz says. Then, without warning, he grabs the King again and whips it at the fireplace, shattering it into dust. The Queen follows, and then the rest of the set. A vase. A chair. A framed mosaic of the desert and a ship's clock from the mantle.

Piece by elegant piece, Baz destroys nearly everything in that living room, smashing and tearing, pulverizing, crushing. When the walls have been stripped bare, when the furniture has been demolished, when there's absolutely nothing left to break, he drops to his knees and unleashes a roar from the very depths of his soul. It rattles the very foundations of the house, shaking with fury, with rage, with pure agony.

My heart feels like the chess pieces, chipped and shattered. I don't know what's happening, can't see the demons that haunt him, don't know how to read the wild torrent of his energy. I don't know how Kirin and I can help him—how anyone could.

I've never felt so lost and helpless before. Not even when my parents drowned. At least on that day, I knew what was coming for them. Knew I didn't stand a chance against that powerful rushing water. The sharp rocks beneath.

But here, Baz fights an invisible enemy Kirin and I can only guess at.

So together we stand behind him in silence, holding hands while our brother falls apart on the floor, trusting he'll come back to us when he's ready.

I don't know how much time passes, but eventually he gets on his feet again. Turns to face us.

His eyes are red and glassy, his face aged a hundred

years since I last saw him on Academy grounds. All I want to do is run to him, to figure out a way to put him back together again.

But before any of us can move, a deep rumble rolls up from the ground.

And all around us, the house of Baz's tormented childhood collapses.

Baz and Kirin dive at me, knocking me to the ground and shielding me from the worst of the debris. But as terrifying as it is, the quake is over almost as quickly as it began. By the time the dust settles, nothing of the house remains.

In its place, surrounding us in a perfect circle, seven sandstone slabs rise from the snow-packed earth, each topped with a perfect stone sphere.

The cathedral.

SIXTEEN

STEVIE

The moment we step outside, the snow melts away, revealing a mirror image of the stone circle we discovered in the real Breath and Blade lands back on campus.

It's exactly where we need to be—exactly where we've been trying to get to ever since we entered the dream realm with Professor Broome's spell. But despite the small victory, something tells me our battles are far from over.

"What now?" Baz asks, reaching for my hand.

I squeeze him back, then force a smile. "Now? We head underground and search. Rather, you two search, and I stand off to the side offering helpful suggestions and looking cute."

"Can you be naked?" he asks hopefully. "Everyone knows helpful suggestions go down better with nudity. Clinically proven. Pretty sure they've done studies."

"Pretty sure you're making that up," Kirin says. Then,

turning to me with the same juvenile hope in his eyes, "But the man has a point. So... can you?"

* * *

Much to their dismay, I don't strip out of my sacrificial gown before leading them to the opening at the other side of the circle, but I do wiggle my ass a bit as consolation.

"Thank you," Baz calls from behind.

I turn to grin at him over my shoulder. "Just doing my part to help you through the hard times."

"I think you're *causing* the hard times," Kirin says, but they're both laughing, the mood about a thousand pounds lighter since we finally arrived at our destination.

It's only a matter of time before we get that sword. Before we're back home with our friends. Before we can put this nightmare realm behind us.

For a little while, at least.

The entrance to the underground is just like it was that day Kirin and I found it back on the material realm—a dark hole at the base of one of the standing stones, hidden behind a large boulder. A narrow stone staircase leads to the chamber below.

"Going down." I call up my witchfire, casting silver light into the darkness. Slowly, the three of us descend into the vast space, giving ourselves a moment to let our eyes adjust.

"Holy shit," Baz says, holding up his hands. Familiar silver-blue magick sparks and crackles in the air, like tiny fireflies dancing around his fingers. "This place is fucking incredible."

"It's exactly like it was back home," I say. "Every detail."

"That's a good thing, right?" Baz asks.

"So far, yes. Now we just have to follow the magick and hope for the best." I close my eyes, casting for a hint of the sword's energy.

"Anything?" Kirin asks.

"I can definitely feel it. The signature is even stronger than before." My palm tingles, my arm tensing with the weight of the sword as if I'm already holding it.

Excitement fizzes in my chest.

We're so close.

"Do we need to do the Tarot spell again?" he asks.

Last time, we used a Seven of Swords spell to coax the sword out of its magickal hiding place.

"I've got it." Keeping my eyes closed, I visualize the sword, feeling its weight, its power, hearing the blade sing as it cuts through the air. I picture the Seven of Swords card in my mind, then repeat Kirin's spell three times, just as he did at the real stone cathedral back home.

> *Magick of air, magick of mind*
> *You know what we seek, so help us to find*
> *Protection we offer, guidance we ask*
> *Let that which is hidden now be unmasked*

Within seconds, the ground begins to rumble, and I let out a happy giggle.

"Stevie," Kirin whispers. "You did it."

"Look," Baz says.

I open my eyes and watch as the stone pedestal rises from the rock, glowing with silver-blue light. There's a deep groove carved into the top slab, just as I expected. But unlike the version we saw back home, this groove isn't hollow.

Fitted inside, perfect and whole and real, is the Sword of Breath and Blade.

"It's magnificent," I breathe, tears glazing my eyes. The silver blade pulses with magick, and the witchfire glows brighter in my palm, as if it's answering the call.

For a long moment, none of us speaks, each lost in our own reverie over the ancient artifact. For so long it was just an idea, a legend we read about in the lore books, the magickally buried treasure we worked so hard to reveal.

But it's no longer a legend. No longer a mythical weapon crafted by the First Fool and his great sacrifice to our kind. Seeing it here, unearthing it from the dream realm, we've just brought the legend to life.

It's a part of our shared history as witches and mages, our legacy as the Arcana and protectors of all magick, and its power is undeniable.

I reach my hand out and hover over the blade, testing the magick that emanates from every inch. "I can't believe we—"

Movement near the guys snags my attention, and I look up to find my Princess of Swords standing between them, arms folded over her chest, glaring at me as if I'm the biggest idiot she's ever encountered. On her shoulder, the black raven caws.

Apparently he thinks I'm an idiot too.

"What's wrong?" Kirin asks.

"We've… got company." I acknowledge her with a smile and a slight bow. "Princess of Swords. Always lovely to see you."

The guys stiffen.

"Don't worry," I say. "You're not the ones she's mad at tonight."

The Princess continues to glare.

She doesn't speak. Doesn't need to. The sharpness in her eyes says it all.

I unleash a sigh. As much as I'd love to stand here admiring our find, she's totally right.

The realm isn't safe, and we've more than overstayed our welcome.

"We found what we came here for," I tell the guys. "Time to collect it and go home."

"Couldn't agree more." Baz claps his hands together, then glances between Kirin and me. "So, which one of my favorite air-blessed wonder twins is going to remove that blade?"

"Kirin," I say firmly, at the same time Kirin blurts out my name.

The Princess rolls her eyes and tosses up her hands,

shooting me a final icy glare before vanishing into the darkness.

"Okay, I guess we're on our own with this," I grumble. Then, turning to Kirin, "I think you should try first. You're the more experienced mage, and my air magick is still pretty unstable."

Kirin shakes his head, taking a step back from the pedestal. "Stevie, we both know this sword was meant for you. It's connected to your elemental affinity—her appearance just now was a clear sign of that. And your sense of it is so much stronger than mine."

I open my mouth to argue, but as soon as I do, the sword's magick pulses through me again, stronger than before. It's clear and perfect and fills me with a deep sense of knowing. Of connection.

Every last one of my doubts disappears.

Kirin flashes a knowing smile and gestures toward the pedestal. "As I was saying…"

Taking a calm, steadying breath, I reach for the sword, wrapping my hand around the grip and lifting it out of its stone groove.

The magick zips down my arm, a bolt of warmth and energy so intense it makes me gasp. I feel it connecting with my magick, bonding, merging. Suddenly it's as if I was born with it. As if I've never been without it.

The Sword was meant for my hand, for my magick. I don't know how I ever doubted it.

With a wide smile and a full heart, I raise my blade up

high, and look up into the proud, happy faces of my brothers…

And another, his wild blue eyes taking shape in the darkness, a small wand held tight in his fist.

My heart drops into my stomach. I'd recognize the madness in that gaze anywhere.

"Clever little witch," the Dark Magician sneers. "Just like her clever little mother." He steps fully into the light, aiming the wand directly at me. "Now, would you prefer to relinquish my sword before or after I remove your head?"

SEVENTEEN

STEVIE

Kirin and Baz are a blur in my periphery as they charge straight for the Magician. But he's more than ready for the attack, raising his free hand and dispensing a powerful blast of magick before they even get close.

It takes me a few beats to process what just happened. To realize that the Magician never once took his eyes off me, and Kirin and Baz are in a crumpled heap on the ground at his feet, unconscious.

The fact that I can still sense their energy is the only reason I know they're alive at all.

"Sword. Now." The Magician creeps toward me, his fingers already reaching out for the weapon, the sickly yellow glow of his magick emanating from his palm. In the other hand, he grips his wand, still pointing it at my face.

I have no idea what kind of damage he can do with that thing.

Terror seizes my limbs. It's all I can do to hold my sword

upright as he stalks toward me, leaving Baz and Kirin behind like discarded trash.

The thought ignites fresh anger inside me, and I hold on to the feeling, using it to fuel my courage.

"Don't take another step." I point the tip of my blade at his chest. "I've got a magick sword and a *killer* resting witch face, and I'm not afraid to use them."

He chuckles, an act that only makes his eyes look crazier, but my words seem to have some effect. He backs off, slowly lowering his weapon.

I'm not stupid enough to lower mine.

For the moment, we're at a standstill.

It's the first time I've seen him up close, the enemy we've feared since my very first vision, and all the lore books and speculation that came after. He's got a dingy white beard and mustache, and he's dressed exactly as I remember, in a long gray tunic and raven-feather cape. His belt is laden with spell pouches, amulets, and desiccated animal parts—all the tools of the trade.

Crazy eyes and grunge couture aside, he looks like somebody's drunken grandfather—a little rough around the edges, with an obvious tendency toward hoarding, but not exactly a deranged mastermind bent on seizing control of magick and killing anyone who stands in his way.

Then again, I thought Professor Phaines looked like a grandfather too. That blindness nearly got me killed.

I won't be making that mistake again.

I tighten my grip on the sword, the magick heating my palms. Warmth rises inside me, and I feel the presence of my Princess of Swords, but I don't dare turn around to check.

I'm not taking my eyes off this motherfucker.

The motherfucker in question lets out a grunt, then shifts his gaze, the look on his face morphing from batshit crazy to pure, uncut adoration.

At first I wonder if he can see the Princess too, but no. It's not my super-hot elemental affinity that's got him so entranced.

It's the sword. It's captured his complete attention. The dude is practically hypnotized.

I lower it ever so slightly, then bring it back up, his eyes tracking the movement like a dog hoping for a piece of meat.

Goddess, each one of these Dark Arcana nutjobs is more unhinged than the last...

"*Mine,*" he says. He's practically salivating.

"Well, you know what they say about possession. Nine-tenths of the law, finders keepers, all that jazz."

"Mine," he repeats, his eyes glazed with cult-like devotion as he resumes his slow steps toward me. "I am the ancient one, the legacy. It's *always* been mine. My birthright. My—"

"Precious, I get it." I point at his chest again. "But here's the thing, Gollum. Unless you want me to add your dick to the collection of shriveled old things dangling from your belt, I suggest you back the fuck off."

He laughs again, that same unhinged chuckle. "You're either very brave, or very stupid, little Star."

"Or both. Did you ever think of that? Goddess, men are so reluctant to give women credit where credit is due."

"I warned your mother this day would come. But don't worry—I'm sure she's waiting on the other side."

"Great," Baz says. "When you get there, you can tell her all about how you got your ancient legacy ass kicked by a bunch of Academy students who haven't even taken midterms yet."

The Magician whirls on his heel and raises his wand, but he's too late. Baz and Kirin are already back on their feet, chanting a combination air-and-earth spell that has the ground trembling, the massive rock ceiling cracking overhead.

"Now!" Baz shouts, and before I can take another breath, Kirin rushes at me, shoving me toward the staircase.

Pieces of the ceiling fall to the ground, an explosion of sharp stone and debris.

"Baz! No!" I try to push my way back into the chamber, but Kirin's got me in a vice grip on the stairs.

"He's right behind us," he says, just as the walls begin to crack and crumble. "Move! Now!"

"We're not leaving him!" I peer over Kirin's shoulder into the dusty air, searching for signs of life. There, across the chamber, Baz stands with his arms raised, his magick all that's keeping the entire chamber from imploding.

I gasp, my eyes finding his across the storm of rock and rubble.

He flashes a devious, devastating smile I feel all the way down to my bones.

"Fly, Little Bird," he says. "Fly."

The rocks come down between us.

And Kirin scoops me into his arms and bolts up the stairs, charging out into the misty night mere seconds before the entire chamber crumbles into dust.

EIGHTEEN

STEVIE

I bolt upright with a gasp, the world spinning, my whole body feeling like it was turned inside out.

"She's awake!" someone calls out. "Cass, Stevie's awake!"

There's a shuffling sound, and then someone is kneeling behind me, warm hands on my bare shoulders, easing me back onto a blanket.

Where the hell am I?

"Stevie? Can you hear me?" Fingers stroke my forehead, my hair. "It's okay. Just breathe."

I know that voice… That touch…

I blink my eyes, waiting for the world to come back into focus. When it finally does, the first face I see is Ani's, upside down and hovering over me, watching me with those warm, caramel eyes. He squeezes my hand and smiles.

"Ani?"

"Good morning, beautiful," he says.

Tears glaze my eyes, and a smile of relief stretches across my face. "Goddess, seeing you is like seeing the sun rise after an eternity in darkness."

Ani leans down and kisses my forehead. "I bet you say that to all the guys."

The guys...

With a jolt, memories come rushing back, slamming through my head with the force of a sledgehammer.

The dream realm... Kirin and Baz...

"Kirin!" I gasp, turning to see Kirin lying next to me, blinking awake just as Professor Broome kneels down next to him. I can sense Baz on my other side, his heat emanating from beneath our shared blanket.

Professor Broome reaches out to check Kirin's pulse. "Slightly elevated. Temp feels a bit high too."

"I'm fine, really," Kirin says, gently shaking her off. "I'm okay. Casey and Janelle?"

"On ice, thanks to Ani." She gestures a ways behind her, where it looks like Isla, Nat, and Professor Maddox are keeping watch over a very subdued Casey and Janelle.

"Unharmed," she adds hastily. "And a story for another time."

"Good... good to know." Kirin's voice is heavy with exhaustion, but his energy is one of pure relief, and when he meets my gaze and smiles, a weight evaporates from my chest.

We're here. We're back.

Reaching out to squeeze his hand beneath the blanket, I

turn my head to the other side to check on Baz, expecting to see his devious red-brown gaze, his maddening smirk.

But his eyes are closed. He's not moving.

Beside his prone body, Doc kneels down, his brow pinched with worry. "Baz, can you hear me?"

"What's wrong?" I try to sit up, but the world starts spinning again.

"Stevie, just try to relax," Ani says gently, urging me back down.

"What's wrong with Baz?" I press. "Why isn't he awake?"

"He just needs time," Doc says, taking Baz's hand. "Just give him in a minute. Just another minute." Worry pulses through his energy, infecting me. "Come on, Baz. Come back to us. Wake up."

My heart kicks into panic mode, and I look back at Kirin. The terror in his eyes unlocks another barrage of memories...

The Dark Magician. The chamber. The collapse.

"He was supposed to be right behind us," I say, fighting to keep my voice even. "You said he was right behind us!"

"I know, Stevie. I... He must've gotten caught up in the rocks." He squeezes my hand tight. "But it's Baz. Of course he'll find a way out. I know he will."

I nod, wanting more than anything to believe him. And in that moment, as my memory crawls back to those final moments in the chamber, a new realization shoots through me like an electric shock.

"Kirin." I sit up, adrenaline chasing away the last of the

dizziness. Beneath the blanket, my hands pat the ground, frantically searching, searching, searching…

Nothing.

"The Sword…" I look all around, but it's not here. If I'd brought it back with me, it would be in my hand.

Disappointment mixes with anger in my gut.

"It didn't work. My dream retrieval, all our grand plans, our theories… Goddess, we just went through hell and back, and what do we have to show for it?"

"It doesn't matter, Stevie." Kirin brushes his knuckles over my cheek. "We'll figure something else out. Right now, the most important thing is that you're safe."

"But Baz…" I turn back to him and reach for his hand, briefly meeting Doc's eyes.

Doc shakes his head, his mouth pressed into a grim line. "He's still not responding."

"He should've woken up by now," I say. "Why isn't he moving?"

Professor Broome shifts to the other side to check on him, nudging Doc out of the way. Kneeling, she presses both palms flat against his chest and closes her eyes.

Through her soft mutterings, Baz lies completely still, his breathing shallow, his skin as pale as the moon.

Professor Broome curses, pulling her hands back.

"What's happening?" I ask.

"His soul is trapped."

"What does that even mean?"

"Traveling through any realm—the astral, the dream realm—it's the soul that wanders, while the physical form remains here," Professor Broome explains. "They're connected by an invisible cord. If that cord becomes severed, it can be quite difficult for the soul to find its way back."

I cling to that d-word like a lifeline. "*Difficult*, but not impossible, right?"

"Stevie..." Professor Broome lowers her eyes and brushes the hair from Baz's forehead, her touch tender. "No, it's not impossible. But it *is* unlikely. Not only did the soul cord become severed, but your connection to him was also lost."

I squeeze his hand tighter. "But that's impossible. I'm right here."

"The three of you entered the realm together in a shared dream," she continues. "And only two of you returned. So your connection—the bond that was supposed to safeguard you in the realm and guide you back home together—is severed. Baz has everything working against him right now, and very little chance of—"

"No. I refuse to accept that," I say, my throat tight. "He doesn't deserve to be stuck there. He was trying to help us. He stayed back so Kirin and I could get out. We were—"

"Let's just focus on trying to get him back, then." Professor Broome reaches across Baz and gives my arm a quick squeeze, apparently accepting that I'm not giving up without a fight, soul-travel rules be damned. "You can tell us the whole story later over drinks," she continues, her tone lighter. "I, for one, am going to need something stiff."

She winks, an obvious attempt at making me feel better.

I have to admit, it works. 'Later over drinks' implies there's going to *be* a later. A future. A moment after this one where Baz is back, and this moment becomes a distant memory we can all laugh about.

Remember that crazy night? Holy shitballs, guys…

"What do we do?" Doc asks.

"He needs heavy grounding," Professor Broome says. "An earthly connection strong enough to permeate his physical senses, overcome the loss of the cord connection, and pull his soul back to this realm."

Earlier tonight, Professor Broome had us remove our protective jewelry before the ritual, but now Ani retrieves Baz's hematite bracelet and fastens it around his wrist. I offer up my Eye of Horus necklace, hoping the extra grounding power will help.

But Baz remains still.

"We need more," Professor Broome says. "We're not getting through yet."

Isla hands over her necklace, then heads over to the other group to borrow their grounding jewelry as well.

Baz is fully adorned—neck, wrists, anklets, several hematite stones placed on his bare chest.

Appealing to his earth magick affinity, Ani gathers rocks from the area, piling them at his head and feet. We attempt grounding spells, way-finding spells, homecoming spells. Professor Broome whips up several potions from the contents of her bag of tricks, but nothing works.

Trying not to lose hope, I think of his affinity, the power of earth, the corresponding Tarot sign of Pentacles.

Pentacles... material realm... pleasures... sensuality...

That's it.

"I know what to do," I announce. Without further explanation, I lie back down and slide closer to him beneath the blanket, pressing my naked body against his. The others are gathered close, but there's no time for modesty now. After everything we've tried, this is our last hope; even a second's hesitation could condemn him to a fate worse than death.

"Come back to me," I whisper, kissing his mouth. His jaw. His ear. "I need you here with me."

Heat crests between us, his body already warming at my touch. I press closer, sliding my hand across his abs, kissing his neck, visualizing the moment when he wakes up and sighs my name.

Between the urgency and the fact that everyone is watching, nothing about this feels sexual, but the raw sensuality of it is hard to deny. That's the whole point—connect him to an earthly pleasure. An intense, life-affirming, earthly pleasure to light his path back home.

"Come home, my Cernunnos," I whisper, kissing my way back to his mouth. Images of our meadow flicker in my mind, the scent of wildflowers invading my memory. "Baz, please. We're all right here waiting for you."

The breeze stirs, as soft as a sigh...

No, not the breeze. An actual sigh.

A deep breath.

A shocked gasp, and suddenly Baz shoots upright, scattering the hematite and rocks.

He stares ahead, his whole body trembling.

All of us are holding our collective breaths.

"Baz?" I whisper, sitting up and touching his shoulder. "Baz? Can you hear me?"

Slowly, he turns to look at me. His brow is furrowed, his eyes wild, his mouth parted as he struggles to slow his breathing.

But then his eyes light up, and he takes my face between his hands and kisses me fiercely, and the entire group whistles and cheers.

We did it. We brought him home.

He finally pulls back to look at me, his gaze sweeping down to my lips, then back up to my eyes.

"Don't cry," he whispers, swiping my tears with his thumbs. His vulnerable smile melts my heart. "Please, Stevie. You're killing me."

"Goddess, Baz. I thought we lost you. I thought I'd never—"

"Shh. I'm okay. We're all okay." He silences me with another kiss, then pulls back to look at Kirin. They share a quick nod, but the look in their eyes tells me just how much they care about each other.

Just how much we all came close to losing tonight.

"What even happened?" I asked him, still processing the fact that things went so sideways tonight. "Why didn't you come back with us?"

"What can I say? The place was starting to grow on me." He cracks another smile, all traces of vulnerability gone. "I figured I'd stick around, take in some of the sights, have a little fun."

I know he's kidding, forcing the jokes to cover up the fact that he practically died—*worse* than died—but still. I can't find the humor in it. Not tonight.

"Fun?" I snap. "You call that *fun*?"

"Like fucking Disneyland, baby." Still grinning, he folds back the blanket, giving us all a show.

For once, it's not his rock-hard abs—or rock-hard anything else, for that matter—making my heart skip.

There, sitting proudly on his lap and gleaming in the moonlight, is the Sword of Breath and Blade.

"Holy shit on a shamrock," I breathe. "Is that—"

"Yeah, I think maybe you dropped this on your way out?" He lifts it from his lap and hands it over, but apparently the surprises are just beginning. "Oh, I picked up another little souvenir too."

With two hands, he lifts the object from his lap. About the size of a steering wheel, grooved and blackened with age, but there's no doubt in my mind what it is.

"The Pentacle of Iron and Bone," I whisper, allowing myself about ten seconds to admire both objects, to revel in the fact that we actually—against all odds—pulled this off tonight.

Then, before anyone else can utter a word, I turn to Doc and say, "We need to cloak them. Right fucking now."

"Get Professor Maddox," Doc tells Ani. "Quick."

Ani's gone and back in a flash.

Professor Maddox takes one look at the majestic objects in our hands, then she and Doc get to work, calling on their water and Moon magick to cast a powerful illusion spell.

"It's only temporary," Doc says when they're done. "We've managed to essentially jam the magickal signature —to anyone who comes looking, these will look like useless props. But we'll need to do something more permanent to keep them out of enemy hands for the long haul."

"Add it to the list," Ani says, glancing back at the prisoners.

"First things first," Doc says, hands on his hips, his eyes stern.

I wait for him to say something profound and leaderly, something about how it's time to dig deep and shore up our courage and prepare for the long, hard road ahead. But then out of nowhere he just grins and says, "Group hug?"

Everyone cracks up at that. But before the love fest can begin in earnest, I make Doc go find me some clothes— preferably something warmer than the skimpy karaoke outfit I first showed up in. Ditching the blanket, we get dressed quickly, then bring it in for some much-needed hugs with the whole group, our embrace a wordless promise that we'll always have each other's backs.

It's a balm on our weary souls, and an infusion of energy for the long night still to come.

NINETEEN

STEVIE

With everyone relatively safe and accounted for, including the two formerly gun-toting witches who may or may not be working for the dark side, it's time to talk strategy. Sleep is a seductive mistress, but for now, we need to power through our exhaustion and figure out our next steps. One slip-up, one careless mistake, and we'll draw the Dark ones right to our doorstep.

There's a good chance we already have. But considering the crazy impossible odds we've already faced down tonight, I'm choosing to believe luck is on our side.

Doc puts the two traitors in the protective custody of Professors Broome and Maddox, with Nat and Isla assisting on the trek back to campus proper. Professor Maddox offered up the basement of her store, Time Out of Mind, where they'll be secured physically and magickally until Doc can figure out how to question them.

After the professors whip up a protective potion and

spell for us to use on the Arcana objects, Doc sends them on their way, promising to check in with them after the five of us deal with the sword and pentacle.

As much as I'd love to keep that blade under my pillow at night for just such an occasion as slashing some Dark Arcana nightmares, it's not safe. Until we can retrieve the wand and chalice, and figure out what to do with the whole creeptastic set, we need to hide the sword and pentacle and protect it with the strongest Arcana magick we can muster —something to keep the Magician and his evil cronies totally off our scent.

We all agree the Fool's Grave is the best place.

Plan set, we take a few more minutes to collect the rest of our things, scanning the area to make sure we leave no trace behind.

I follow after Baz, eager for even a few minutes alone, desperate to know what happened back in that cathedral.

We head just out of earshot, keeping the others in view.

Before I can ask a single question, he gathers me into his arms and kisses me.

"I have never been so happy to see another human being in my life, Little Bird. Goddess, you're a miracle."

"Me? You're the one who brought back those souvenirs. I had no idea you could dream-retrieve."

"Neither did I."

I wait for him to say more, but he just releases me, lowering his gaze to the ground and kicking at a rock. He's still smiling, but his energy feels unbalanced, like he can't decide whether he feels relieved or terrified.

"How did you find the pentacle?" I ask.

"After you found the sword, an idea started worming into my mind. I knew it had to be in the Forest of Iron and Bone, but I had no idea where, and no idea how the hell we'd get there before we woke up."

"Everything was so unstable there."

"Exactly. But then, as you were squaring off with the Magician and Kirin and I were figuring out how to deal with him, the idea came to me. As long as my earth magick followed the same rules in the dream realm as it did back home, I could probably use the rocks to do a teleportation spell. So once I was sure you and Kirin were safe, I rained all hell down on the Magician, grabbed the sword you dropped, and magicked myself the fuck out of there, straight to the Forest of Iron and Bone."

"But how did you survive that collapse? You were all the way across the chamber. Baz, I saw the ceiling come down."

"Me and rocks… Well, let's just say I know how to keep myself safe underground." He kicks at the rocks again, blowing out a breath. "Anyway, once I was out of immediate danger, I set out to finding the pentacle, knowing I'd have at least a little time before the pancake formerly known as the Magician resurrected and tracked me down."

"Where was it?" I ask. "The pentacle, I mean. How did you find it?"

"I blocked out everything else, closed my eyes, and asked for guidance on finding the most spiritually intense place in the forest. The answer came to me in a flash, along with an *actual* guide." At this, he finally meets my gaze again, darkness and rage leaking into his energy like ink spilled in water.

And I know, in that moment, exactly where he found the pentacle.

"The petrified tree," I whisper. "The one where he... Professor Phaines..." I close my eyes, the remembered taste of blood filling my mouth. What he did to me there...

"Stevie, it's okay." Baz's touch on my face pulls me back, and I open my eyes, the old memories fading. "I'm sorry. I didn't want to tell you."

"It's okay. I mean, it kind of makes sense. Phaines picked that tree for a reason, right?"

"He must've sensed the power there, even if he didn't know exactly why."

"And the guide?" I ask, eager to move on from Phaines. "You said an actual guide came to your aid. Was it Lala?"

"Not... exactly." A smile softens his face, his eyes drifting skyward. I follow his gaze to a bright white mass taking shape in the darkness, floating down toward us like an angel.

"Oh my Goddess," I breathe. "Really? He helped you?"

"*You* helped me," Baz says. "You're connected to him. He sensed your need, your desire to find me and get me home safe."

The snowy owl is majestic, shimmering overhead as he slowly descends.

"Oh, my sweet friend." An echoing laugh escapes my

lips as I hold up my arm in invitation. "You have no idea how happy I am to see you."

"I said the same thing in the realm," Baz says. "Excellent wingman, no pun intended."

My beautiful familiar settles on my arm. He's heavier than I remember, but I welcome the ache in my muscles, the sharp bite of his talons on my skin. It's a reminder that we're never alone—that he's always watching over us. Not just me, but everyone I care about.

I stroke his head, the feathers soft and silky, and wonder how much he can understand me. Between my classes, magick lessons from Kirin, the prophecy work, the constant threat we're all facing, romps through the dream realm... I've had zero time to work on our bond. Kirin believes it will strengthen the more I use my air magick, but I'm still pretty green on that front too.

Closing my eyes, I envision the Ace of Swords and try to summon the wind, but all I manage is a quick breeze. When I open my eyes and meet his golden gaze again, I swear the owl is laughing at me.

"If you've got a better idea," I tease, "I'm all ears."

Crickets.

Goddess, I must look insane. The thought makes me laugh again, imagining what Jessa would say if she could see me now, standing in the middle of the Towers of Breath and Blade with a big-ass bird of prey on my arm like some kind of warrior goddess of old.

"Thank you," I whisper.

He shifts along my arm and nuzzles my neck. And then he's off once again, soaring back up into the night.

I watch him disappear, trusting that he'll be back.

A heavy sigh escapes, and I turn back to Baz, doing my best to rein in a surge of anger. "You should've told us your plan. We could've gone to the Forest together. Or just... I don't know. Figured something else out."

"There was no time. Once Kirin and I decided on the best way to get you out of that chamber, it was all we could do to make it happen before that asshole took you down."

"We all knew the risks going in there, and we took them together. We were supposed to *stay* together. We agreed—"

"Yeah, we did. But trust me when I say this: you can talk me into just about *anything*, Little Bird." He hooks a finger under my chin, all humor gone from his eyes. In its place is a love and protectiveness so fierce it makes my heart skip. "But here's the thing about the realm. If you die there, you die here. I wasn't about to let you die. End of fucking discussion."

"I wasn't about to let *you* die, either, you dumb shit!" I shove him hard, no longer able to hold back. We almost lost him tonight, and he thinks that's the end of the discussion? "We made an oath, Baz. We're brothers!"

He shakes his head, totally resolute. "Doesn't mean I have to let you die for me."

"Yes, it does. It means *exactly* that. Why can't you see it? Why does everything with you have to be so—"

He grabs my arms and hauls me in close, stealing a kiss so ferocious he draws blood. By the time he breaks it off, we're both panting, our lips swollen, our eyes wild with anger and passion and everything in between.

For a long moment, we glare at each other, hearts beating madly, tension sparking between us.

But then Baz lets out a resigned sigh and reaches for my hands, slow and soft this time, his touch as warm and gentle as his smile.

When he speaks again, there's no more anger, no more resistance. Only a sweet, tender honesty that melts my heart into goo.

"Because I love you, Starla Milan," he says simply. "It's as simple and as complicated as that."

TWENTY

STEVIE

"You ready?" Baz takes my hand, brushing his thumb across my skin, and I nod. Linking my arm with Kirin's on my other side, I pull them both a little closer, focusing on their warmth, their familiar scents, the feel of their protective presence. After everything we've just been through together, I don't want to let either of them out of my sight.

Doc and Ani gather around us, each carrying one of the objects. Baz calls on his earth magick, the air turning a deep, sparkling purple as it sweeps us up and brings us to our destination.

We step out into the Petrified Forest of Iron and Bone, Baz's spell leaving us inside the narrow passageway that leads to the sacred cave known as the Fool's Grave. We walk the path in silence, each of us undoubtedly contemplating the craziness we've just survived... and the craziness yet to come.

Despite the close quarters, I keep my brothers at my

sides, all my senses tuned in to our surroundings, scanning for a disturbance. Yes, we cloaked the sacred objects back at Breath and Blade, but how can we be certain the spell is strong enough? What if—in those first few moments after Baz's return—the Magician picked up on the relics' magickal signature?

For all we know he's already waiting in the shadows, watching. Biding his time until he can make his next move.

A shiver rattles my bones, and Kirin and Baz instinctively move in closer, their protective energy wrapping around me like a blanket as we enter the cave. Every few minutes, Baz squeezes my arm and smiles at me, and my heart skips, a sweet reminder of his earlier words—a confession I haven't even had time to process yet.

Because I love you, Starla Milan. It's as simple and as complicated as that.

I smile back at him, hoping he knows how much it means to me. How much *he* means to me.

Pushing through our exhaustion, we make our way into the inner cave to perform the Keepers of the Grave ritual, slicing our palms over the now-familiar altar and chanting the sacred spell. After we sign our names in the Book of Reckoning, Doc places the King of Swords Tarot card inside the book and recites the last spell of our opening rite:

> *Let our thoughts be true, our messages clear*
> *Both words and intent are recorded here*
> *Leave nothing unwritten, no secrets to bear*
> *Among brothers in blood, all things are shared*

The Tarot card glows, the book ready to record our meeting for posterity, but it's a long moment before any of us speaks again.

They're leaving it to me, I realize. To share everything that happened inside the dream realm—all the things we didn't have time to talk about back at the Towers of Breath and Blade.

Taking a deep breath, I do my best to fill them in on my experiences, starting with my visit from Lala—namely, the fact that she hid the objects in the realm, and what it means now that we've brought two of them out. I skip over the whole death-by-suicide thing, though. Hearing that particular prophecy would drive them insane with worry, and for what? That particular little fortune is *never* going to happen.

"The High Priestess," Doc says, his eyes full of wonder. "I always sensed a mystical connection to Lala, but I had no idea just how mystical it really was."

"We should've known," I say, thinking back to the first time I met her. "There's no way a normal person could make tacos that good. Even a witchy normal person."

This gets a small smile, a spark of warmth in the dim cave that bolsters me for the next part.

Slowly, taking strength from Kirin and Baz, I tell Doc and Ani about my terrifying run-ins with Dark Judgment, the visions of my past shames, and my theories on how he's twisting our guilt and fear to his own ends.

Kirin and Baz fill in the gaps with their own experiences, though Baz is vague on the specifics, including the fact that the house where we found him was a projection of Janelle's. His energy is so guarded—it's no wonder his subconscious put up that force field in the realm.

I'm beyond worried about him. Of the three of us, he's acting the least affected by our experience.

Which tells me he's feeling the exact opposite, whether he's ready to admit it or not.

Doc and Ani ask a few questions, but in the end, we all decide it's best to just bury the objects and call it a night. The sun will be up soon, and Doc and Ani still want to check in on the prisoners at Time Out of Mind before trying to catch at least a few hours' sleep.

As for Kirin and Baz, they might not realize it yet, but they'll be accompanying me back to my suite for a slumber party. There's no way I want to be away from them tonight. Or tomorrow for that matter. In fact, I'm thinking this will take a good month at least.

Doc leads us to a small antechamber behind the main cave area, and we place the sword and pentacle on the ground. Powerful magick emanates from both of them, making my palms tingle, calling to that deep and ancient part of my Arcana soul that knows the sacred objects are part of my legacy. Part of *our* legacy.

By their awed expressions, I know the guys feel the same way.

It's a shame we have to hide them like this—more secrets buried, more parts of ourselves denied.

But I also know it's for the best. Our lives are at stake here. Magick itself is at stake.

"Stevie, are you ready?" Doc asks, and I let out a final sigh of regret, then nod.

Kneeling before the objects, I place a card at each cardinal direction, just as Professor Maddox instructed us—the Princes from each of the Tarot suits, four brave knights to serve and protect these most sacred artifacts.

Cards in place, I remove a small vial of dark, silvery liquid—a potion Professor Broome created for us.

"Even if their magickal signature has already put the Academy on the Dark Magician's radar," I explain, "the objects will be safe here. Aside from the five of us casting the spell, anyone who comes within a mile of the Fool's Grave will be magickally turned around, wandering and confused for days."

I unstopper the vial and pour the contents in an unbroken circle around the objects, just as Professor Broome instructed. The silver liquid bubbles as it hits the ground, glowing bright white when the circle is complete.

Vial empty, I rise and join hands with my brothers, the five of us forming a circle as I recite the final spell:

> *Arcana princes, one and all*
> *We beseech you, hear our call*
> *Sword and pentacle are protected*
> *When our foes are misdirected*

After the third recitation, the glowing white circle turns into a dome, enclosing the Princes and the objects inside.

"Assuming we did the spell right," I say, "we're the only

ones who can see or sense the objects, and the protective shield can only be opened with our blood."

"Any of us?" Ani asks.

"All five. The professor said it won't work otherwise."

He nods, and the five of us continue to stare at the glowing dome, at the objects inside.

"Does anyone else feel like we're just moving chess pieces back and forth across a board for all eternity?" I ask.

No one replies. There's no need; their heavy sighs are enough.

But it's not just the futility of it all that's getting to me. Something else is nagging at the back of my mind, and has been ever since Baz brought the objects back. Maybe even since we first figured out they were in the dream realm.

"Guys, something about this isn't adding up," I say, the nagging intensifying. "This stuff was hidden in the dream realm for decades. And before that, hidden on campus for what—centuries? And none of the Dark Arcana could find it. Nor could the scholars or even the most experienced treasure hunters who've made *careers* out of tracking down legends like this. Yet I'm here at the Academy for a couple of months—total newbie, no magickal education, no knowledge, basically just a girl who loves tea—and I manage to put the pieces together? Then we just march in there and bring them out?"

"I wouldn't say we just marched in there," Kirin says. "It was hell."

"It was, but we survived it," I say. "Right?"

"You're saying it was too easy," Doc says, confirming my exact thoughts.

"You don't think so?"

"We're intrepid magickal adventurers," Ani says, hopeful as ever. "Maybe something's going our way for once."

"Said no intrepid adventurer, ever." I walk around the dome, peering down at the objects that have consumed our thoughts for so long. "I don't know. Maybe we should've let sleeping dogs lie."

"No. I stand by our decision to pull them out of the realm," Kirin says. "We don't know how long they would've remained hidden there, especially with the Dark Arcana gaining power. Lala confirmed as much."

"Kirin's right," Doc says. "At least now we know where the sword and pentacle are, and we've hidden them with powerful magick. We'll do the same when Ani and I locate the wand and chalice."

"What?" I gasp. "Doc, no." Fear grips my chest, making it hard to breathe. The idea of going back to the realm... of subjecting Doc or Ani to the pain that the rest of us already endured...

"It's the only way, Stevie," Kirin says, his touch on my shoulder reassuring. "Ani's got the best shot at connecting with the wand, just like Doc does with the chalice." He glances over at Doc, then back to me. "But we don't have to go tomorrow. Or even the day after that."

Doc shakes his head. "The longer we wait—"

"We need time to regroup," Kirin says firmly. "Now that

we have a better idea of what we're dealing with in there, we can come up with a solid plan of attack, including better failsafes for coming out of the realm." He squeezes my shoulder, his tone softening. "But Stevie, Doc's right. We do have to go back. And we can't put it off too long."

I cover his hand with mine and nod.

"One week," Doc says. "We'll take one week to prepare. Next Friday, we go back in."

On that ominous note, we head back to the altar, pack up the Book of Reckoning, and slip out into the night, making our way out of the rocky maze.

When we finally reach the open forest again, I turn my face skyward and close my eyes, letting the cool night air wash over me. The sound of crickets is a lullaby, and despite the crazy night, I smile, grateful for such a simple pleasure.

"Before we head our separate ways," Doc says, calling my attention back to the group, "there's another important matter I wish to discuss with everyone."

My stomach twists, but when I meet his gaze, I see only a happy light shining back. Doc winks, and my mood improves exponentially.

"I know we've got much bigger problems on the horizon," he says to the group, "but I don't want to lose sight of the joyful moments, either. To that end, I would like to invite you all to celebrate Harvest Eve with me on Tuesday. Stevie, please extend an invitation to Isla and Nat as well."

"Really?" I beam at him, tears pricking my eyes. This was going to be my first Harvest Eve in years without Jessa;

I'd kind of put it out of my mind, too afraid to face it alone. "Harvest Eve was always my favorite. Jessa and I used to go all out."

"Does that mean it's a yes?" he asks, his tone hopeful.

"More than a yes," I confirm, already picking out the perfect Harvest Eve outfit in my mind. "It sounds fun."

Doc smiles, but the guys let out a collective groan, and his good cheer falters.

"Wait, what's wrong with Harvest Eve?" I ask.

"Are you... cooking again?" Baz asks Doc, making air quotes around the word 'cooking.'

"Doc cooks?" I ask. "I had no idea."

"Sure, he... cooks." Baz makes the air quotes again, and Ani and Kirin crack up.

Doc glares at them. "Don't all rush to my defense at once, you ungrateful trolls."

"We got food poisoning last time, Cass," Baz says. "In case you forgot."

"You can't prove that was my fault."

"The turkey was still frozen inside," Baz says. "Generally a good indicator that something about the bird ain't right."

"Let's not even talk about the deviled eggs," Ani says, clutching his stomach.

"What was wrong with the eggs?" Doc asks.

"Probably nothing," Ani says. "Until you left them out in the sun for four hours."

The guys can't stop laughing, but poor Doc just shakes his head, his holiday plans clearly foiled.

"Hey." I reach out and grab his hand. "I would love to come to Harvest Eve, Doc. No matter what's on the menu."

"Really?" He smiles, his eyes filling with new light. He squeezes my hand, and a little spark of heat zips between us, making my heart skip.

"Traitor," Ani teases.

"You're making a huge mistake," Kirin says.

Baz shrugs. "I hope you have decent health insurance, Little Bird. Because otherwise—"

"Oh, for the love of the elements," Doc grumbles. "Save your concerns. The event will be catered this year. Those who choose to join Stevie and me will be treated to the finest French cuisine Arcana Academy has to offer."

Baz lets out a low whistle. "Sounds a little fancy, Cass. You sure about this?"

"I've already made the arrangements with Café Marchande," Doc says. Then, pointing a finger at Baz, "But that is in *no* way to be taken as an admission of guilt."

Baz grins. "In that case, I'm in."

I look up at Doc again and smile. "We're *all* in, Doc."

TWENTY-ONE

BAZ

"Please don't go, Baz," Stevie whispers. "Not yet."

Standing in the middle of her bedroom, she nibbles her bottom lip and looks up at me, her eyes impossibly bright after our wild, sleepless night in the realm.

We've just been to hell and back, but you wouldn't know it to look at her. Freshly showered, dressed in a silky little white robe, skin smelling like summer... Goddess, she's fucking devastating.

And she knows exactly what to say to make me come undone.

She *owns* me, body and soul. All I want to do right now is crawl between the sheets, take Stevie into my arms, and sink deep inside her, erasing the memories of that horrid realm, one sinfully-hot kiss at a time.

I don't even care that Kirin's here too. Not if that's what my girl wants. Sharing her, loving her, giving her what she needs, what lights her up inside... That lights *me* up too.

And I can tell every time Kirin looks at her he feels the exact same way. Doc and Ani too. There's no getting around it—we're a package deal now.

The thought should make me hot with jealousy. Instead, it brings me comfort.

They're my brothers. My family. Each and every one of them, and there's nothing I won't do for them.

But as Kirin enters the bedroom and passes her a cup of hot tea, a shy smile on his face, I know I'm no good for either of them right now—for any of my brothers. No matter how badly I want to stay tonight, my mind is about to go rogue. I can feel it happening, my grip on reality unraveling like a thread pulled on an old sweater.

If that romp through the realm proved anything, it's that my demons are far from under control. No matter how many miles and years I put between me and my past, those monsters always manage to find me. And after tonight, I have no idea what they're capable of.

"Baz?" she whispers, hope lingering in her smile.

I hate that I'm about to crush it.

But I can't stay. Not like this.

"I just... I need a little time to regroup." I reach for her face, allow myself the simple indulgence of brushing my thumb over her soft skin. "Hot shower, long nap, a few rounds of Candy Crush... I'll be good as new before you know it."

Her smile falls, damn near taking my heart with it. "After what you went through tonight, I'm not sure 'good as new' is on the menu just yet."

"I had a rough re-entry is all."

"All the more reason for you to stay." She grabs my hands, holding tight. "I hate the idea of leaving you alone right now. None of us should—"

"My suite is right downstairs," I remind her, forcing a little confidence into my voice. "Kirin will stay with you for now."

Kirin catches my gaze and nods, but it's clear he's not buying my act either.

Both of them can see right through me. That's the worst part.

They always could.

"Whatever it is," Stevie whispers, "we'll work through it. You're not alone, Baz. I've got your back."

I pull her in for a hug, bury my face in her hair. It's nearly impossible to speak around the damn knot in my throat. "I know, baby. I know."

"And I know how to rock a sword," she teases. "Also a selling point."

"Don't I know it."

Yeah, Stevie may be a natural with that sword, and I swear just thinking about the way she threatened that Dark Arcana dickhead tonight gives me a major fucking hard-on.

But the demons on my ass aren't the kind you can take down with threats and a magick sword. They're the kind that infect the mind, invading every last place inside until they've got you convinced the only monster worth killing is you.

That torment, that agony… I'll never let her see it in my eyes. Never.

"Get some rest." I try to dislodge from our embrace, but she's still holding tight.

"Please stay," she says again, her voice equal parts satin and steel.

But deep down, she knows I'm leaving.

Deep down, she knows I'm already gone.

Back in my own suite, the ice-cold shower makes my dick shrink, but does nothing to chase the damn ghosts from my head.

Naked and dripping, I stand in front of the bathroom sink and glare at the mirror, trying to find one familiar thing about the asshole staring back at me. I'm almost embarrassed that Stevie saw me like this at all—confused and weak, broken, barely keeping it together. My eyes are bloodshot, my mouth drawn tight, jaw clenched.

I hate that Janelle turned me into this.

Crazed or not, I still wish they'd have let me kill her.

In the dream realm, Janelle had claws and teeth. But here in the material realm, she needs neither; the memories of what she did to me are more terrifying and vivid than any monster my subconscious could serve up.

Every time I close my eyes, I see her.

That awful red lipstick staining my pillowcases, my skin. Her laughter as she caught me in the laundry room a hundred times over, frantically scrubbing the evidence from my sheets, so sure her husband would come home from some business trip and discover what'd happened. That she'd make good on her threats to tell him I attacked her, forced her. That she'd tell him I liked it. That he'd take away everything they'd given me, and my parents would find out, and Carly would be devastated to discover the boy she thought was her best friend was nothing more than a sick, filthy little bastard.

But every time I open my eyes, I see my own shame. My cowardice, staring right back at me, daring me to take a stand.

How can I be the man Stevie needs, the man she deserves? Earth magick was a temporary solution to get us out of a jam tonight, but it's going to take a lot more than dropping a few rocks on someone's skull to truly defeat the Arcana. How am I supposed to stand in solidarity with my brothers against the darkest enemy we've ever faced when I can't even get over some shit that happened when I was a stupid fucking kid?

Rage burns a path clear down my throat, right into my gut.

I slam my fist toward the mirror, stopping just before I smash the glass. All I want is to shatter it, to slice my hand to ribbons, to feel the pain of something else for a change. But I hold back.

Denied its outlet, the rage inside boils. I'm fucking *trembling* with it, half a heartbeat from tearing the mirror from the wall, when a searing pain lances my chest.

I sputter and gasp, stumbling backward as I frantically claw at my own flesh. I barely manage to get on my feet again when I see it in the mirror, a beacon to my secret shame.

There, blazing red with blackened edges, the mark shines bright over my heart.

Roman numeral twenty—XX. The mark of Judgment's wand.

As quickly as it appeared, the mark vanishes before my eyes, my skin instantly cooling.

The pain is gone. The rage. All of it.

All that remains is his voice, the final threat he uttered in the realm seared into my memory for eternity, echoing through my skull.

The unworthy shall burn, burn, burn.

I will come for you, boy. One night, I will come.

And when you hear my clarion call, you will beg *me to set you aflame.*

To set you free.

TWENTY-TWO

CASS

Dawn has just touched the frost-covered window panes when I bang impatiently on the front door, scaring a few ground squirrels out of the bushes.

"We need to talk, Anna," I call out. "Now."

My patience for the headmistress is already well past thin. Add that to the fact that I'm here on her doorstep this morning instead of back at Stevie's suite... Goddess, I hate that I had to leave her side. When she finally returned to us from the realm last night, it was all I could do not to break down. And in that moment—and every moment since—it's been all I can do not to gather her in my arms and kiss her senseless...

Stop fantasizing about things you can never have, Professor.

I bang on the door again, so hard the decorative window pane at the top rattles. Seconds later, I finally sense Anna's presence. She's lingering just on the other side, but she makes me wait a few more beats before wrenching open the door.

Dressed in a dark gray pantsuit, her hair pulled into a severe bun, our illustrious headmistress looks even more uptight and terrifying than usual.

That might work on troublesome students or a donor unwilling to part with his cash, but the effect is lost on me.

With what I've come here to say this morning, I'm not the one who should be afraid.

"Cassius Devane," she snaps, a bit of her composure cracking. "I've been trying to reach you for hours. Where on *earth* have you been?"

"That's not the question you should be asking." Uninvited, I step inside the doorway, forcing her to take a few steps back. "The question you should be asking is, 'What can I do for you, Cassius?' Followed by the proclamation, 'Whatever you need, I will move heaven and earth to make it happen.'"

I loom over her in the doorway, but she doesn't flinch. With Anna Trello, it's always a contest of wills—one she typically wins.

Not today.

"You obviously have no idea what's been going on here," she barks, doing her best to intimidate me despite the fact that I've got several inches of height and a whole lot more anger on her. "There was an explosion at a campus bar last night—no injuries, thank the Goddess—but Casey Appleton has not been seen since dinner. Janelle Kirkpatrick is also missing. The students are absolutely frantic over the explosion, which only fuels their speculations about the dangers unfolding just outside our walls. Our country is in total lockdown, Cass. The government is waging an all-out war against witches and mages at every turn. Despite all of this, you have the gall to grace my doorstep this morning, looking and smelling as if you've been cavorting with... with *townies* all night?"

She glares at me as if she's daring me to deny her accusations, chin jutting out like some haughty aristocrat.

"Are you finished?" I finally ask.

"I beg your pardon?"

I hold up a hand to stop the next diatribe. "I'm here because I need a secure, off-campus location—cloaked if possible, warded at a minimum—with a basement and an SUV onsite. No questions asked."

Anger rises from her toes to her eyeballs, turning her face the color of an overripe tomato. "What could you possibly need all that for? And what makes you think I have access to something like that?" She turns and heads into her living room, muttering all the way. "Unacceptable. Absolutely appalling behavior from an esteemed—"

"Anna?" I follow close on her heels. "Exactly what part of 'no questions asked' is confusing for you?"

"You come here making demands that are—"

"Well within your power to meet. In fact, I understand the Academy's very own Red Sands Canyon community is lovely this time of year. And as the rampant militarization of our country makes it quite impossible for wealthy donors and dignitaries to visit us at this time, I'm sure there are plenty of vacancies, aside from our APOA guests. And Mrs. Kirkpatrick of course. Oh, that reminds me." I tap my chin, my voice dripping with condescension. "I'm going to need a home as far away from the others as possible. I'm sure you of all people understand the need for privacy and discretion, particularly since popular bars are exploding on-campus and we're still no closer to installing the additional security equipment we discussed weeks ago."

Anna clenches her teeth, shoulders nearly shaking with rage. "I will *not* have you stand here and lecture me about privacy after barging unannounced into *my* home. You *know* I care deeply about our students and faculty. I'm still working on procuring the funds for the security upgrades —that's not off the table. As I've told you before, these things take time."

"All the same, I require off-campus housing at this time."

"Do you have any idea how many strings I'd need to pull? How much I'd be risking?"

I smile, raising my hands in mock concession. "I assure you, Anna. I wouldn't be asking if it wasn't important. It's just... Well, I can't get into specifics, but this is a matter of urgency that affects us all. And when it comes to protecting the students and faculty you care so deeply about, I assumed you wouldn't want me taking chances. Was my assumption incorrect?"

She doesn't reply.

"Then it's settled." I glance at my phone. "You've got one hour. Shall I wait? Is there coffee? I'm quite exhausted after my night of—how did you put it? Cavorting with townies? I could use a pick-me-up."

Anna huffs. "Apparently you missed this lesson, but civilized people do not march into homes and make demands. We arrange meetings, exchange discourse, make compromises, come to mutually beneficial agreements."

"Right. And how many students have been attacked while you've been arranging, exchanging, and compromising to your mutual benefit? Wait... Does the exploding bar count as an attack, or was that just a mundane gas leak? I'm already losing track."

Ignoring the digs, Anna storms off into the kitchen, leaving a few slammed cupboards and drawers in her wake, and I blow out a breath of relief. I've got her where I want her, even if it ends up costing my job.

One thing I'll say about Anna—she knows when she's lost the battle, even if she's planning to win the war.

I take a seat on her couch, doing my best not to worry about Stevie and the others. She's supposed to be recuperating with Baz and Kirin while Ani and the professors entertain our *less* savory guests at Time Out of Mind. That's a temporary solution, though. Professors Maddox and Broome—as smart and powerful as they may be—are not mentally prepared to do what needs to be done.

A basement in the middle of a popular student shopping center isn't the right location, anyway. For this job, I need somewhere far off the beaten track.

A place where no one will be able to hear them scream.

Five minutes and several broken dishes later, Anna returns with a fresh cup of coffee.

"Is this your idea of a peace offering?" I ask.

Glowering, she hands over the mug, then settles into the armchair across from me. "These demands are a bit outlandish, Cassius. Even for you."

"Yet here we are." I sip the coffee, then offer a smile, my eyes never leaving hers. "Fifty-three minutes to go, Anna. Tick-tock."

She crosses her arms over her chest. "And if I refuse?"

"Oh, I hope you *do* refuse." I lean forward on the couch, letting her see the unwavering seriousness in my eyes. For all the power games, all the theatrics, this a point I will absolutely *not* negotiate on. "Because if my request isn't met within the specified time frame, I will take Starla Milan, along with her mother's research, and we will disappear from this place forever."

I hate using Stevie as a bargaining chip, but she's the only one Anna truly cares about. Whatever Anna's twisted reasons, that's been clear from the start. And if my interrogation doesn't go as planned—if we can't get the answers we need from whoever's camping out inside Casey and Janelle, or if the Dark Arcana track us down to campus and start their bitter war before we can retrieve the other objects —I will *not* leave Stevie's or my men's lives to chance.

The Brotherhood may be charged with protecting magick, but in the end, we protect one another first and foremost.

Anna's face turns milk-white. "You wouldn't *dare*."

"Oh, headmistress. After all these years, I really hoped you knew me better." I drain my coffee, then pull out my phone, glancing at the time. "I suggest you make whatever calls you need to make to get those strings pulled. You've got forty-nine minutes now. Oh, and I'm going to need another coffee, if you don't mind. And maybe a pastry?" I flash a grin as I pass her my empty mug. "I've got a long day ahead of me."

TWENTY-THREE

STEVIE

Kirin and I try to hold a conversation, but I'm not sure either of us gets a full sentence out before collapsing on my bed and drifting into a soundless sleep. By the time I feel him stirring next to me, the sun has risen and set, night falling once again.

I grab my phone off the nightstand to check the time—nine-thirty p.m.—and catch up on the texts I missed. Doc letting us know things are being taken care of. Ani with some Baby Yoda GIFs that make me smile. Isla and Nat checking to see if we want anything from Smash. I reply to let everyone know we're okay, then check the final text.

Baz, just five minutes ago.

Still dog tired. Gonna hang at home tonight, but I'll check in again tomorrow. You 2 crazy kids have fun.

I hit the call button, but it goes straight to voicemail.

Rest up, I text back instead, doing my best to keep things light. *I'll be waiting for you in the morning with tea and pancakes. Naked pancakes, if you're lucky. :)*

I stare at the screen, waiting for the little dots to appear, waiting for the usual flirty banter or innuendo or even the slightest smiley-face indication that he's okay.

But after a full two minutes, nothing comes.

Biting back a sigh, I turn over to check on Kirin, surprised to find him already awake and watching me intently.

"Baz?" he asks softly, and I nod, holding up the phone to show him. "It doesn't even sound like him. Not really. I know it's just a text, but he just seems so... so down."

"He's been through a lot, Stevie. Whatever he dealt with in the realm, we need to let him work through it on his own."

"I feel like we're abandoning him."

"We're just giving him a little space."

I nod, but I can't hide the worry in my eyes. Not from Kirin.

"Tell you what," he says. "You stay here and relax, and I'll make us breakfast in bed."

The sweetness and sincerity in his eyes finally coax out a smile. "Kirin. I think it's a little late for breakfast in bed."

"Brunch, then." Kirin crawls out of bed wearing nothing but sweatpants, the muscles of his broad chest rippling as he talks about cooking for me, like the sexy man-servant of my dreams. "Do you have eggs in the fridge? I do a killer Greek omelet."

"It's nine-thirty at night. Might as well call it dinner."

"Call it dunch and you've got a deal."

* * *

True to his word, Kirin and his killer Greek omelets do not disappoint, and it's not long before we've demolished the entire tray full of deliciousness.

"So that was dunch?" I say, giving my stomach an appreciative pat. "I'm definitely a fan."

"I should've made dessert though," Kirin says, setting the tray of empty dishes on the dresser before joining me back in bed. "Now I'm craving something sweet."

"Can I interest you in some chocolate body powder? It's all I've got on hand at the moment."

Kirin's glasses slide down his nose, his jaw dropping. "Wait. Seriously?"

"Top drawer, nightstand. There's a whole pouch of goodies."

I watch with a satisfied smirk on my face as he rifles through the drawer and pulls out the gossamer pouch, peering inside it. "Chocolate body powder—oh, vanilla too, good, good. Lavender massage oil. Feathers, okay then. And... wait. Warming personal lubricant?"

"Hey, a girl needs to be prepared for anything."

He swallows audibly, nearly dropping the pouch. "What exactly are you preparing for here? The sexpocalypse?"

"No one wants to be caught without the essentials at the end of the world, Kirin." I crack up, taking great pleasure in his awkwardness. "Professor Broome gave it to me with my birth control potion. She said, and I quote, 'all witches and mages should be encouraged to freely explore their sexuality and sensual pleasures.' Apparently, she's like the magickal Dr. Ruth. She's got a whole stash of goodies in her office."

"Good to know." Quickly looking away, Kirin sets the pouch back in the drawer. "What else have you got tucked away in this drawer of iniquity?"

"Hey perv," I tease, reaching over to smack him on the butt. "Make an appointment with Professor Broome if you want in on the fun."

"No need. This is purely academic curiosity, I assure you." Laughing, he pulls out a small bottle of silvery, milky liquid and holds it up. "Let me guess. Body paint?"

"That's the dream potion I made in Broome's class when I wanted to connect with the Dark Arcana. Silversword root, witch's cauldron, and moonstone elixir. But trust me—from now on I'm sticking with the anti-dream stuff."

I lean across him and fish out another bottle, unscrewing the cap to show him the black, viscous contents. "Professor Broome gave it to me last night. She said it would encourage a deep, dreamless sleep."

"What's in it?"

"Don't know, don't care. As long as it doesn't take me back to the realm."

"Are you going to try it tonight?" he asks.

I close the bottle and set both of the potions on top of my nightstand.

"I'm not ready for a deep sleep just yet." I snuggle

closer, resting my cheek on his bare chest, my fingers drawing slow circles over his stomach.

Kirin's breath hitches, his eyes lazily drifting closed.

"I was kind of hoping we could do… something else?" I offer.

"Well, sometimes when I can't sleep, I like to review the elemental, herbal, and planetary correspondences in my head. If that doesn't work, I might do a little light reading on the parallels between quantum physics and magick, or on academic applications for mental spellwork."

I bite back a laugh, tracing my fingers up his chest. "That all sounds *super* awesome, Genius Boy. Really great tips for all the special nerds in your life. But that's not exactly the something else I had in mind."

I don't bother waiting for the gears in Kirin's mind to translate my innuendos. Instead, I lean over and remove his glasses, then claim his mouth in a soft, seductive kiss.

He moans against my lips, opening his mouth to deepen our kiss, his hands sliding into my hair.

But the longer he kisses me, the hungrier I am for more. Not just kissing. Not just touching.

All of it.

I break our kiss and sit up to pull off my T-shirt, my body bare except for a pair of black lace underwear. Kirin's gaze turns eager, slowly drinking me in as his hands slide up to cup my breasts. His thumbs brush over my stiff peaks, and I gasp, arching into his touch, my body already winding tight with anticipation.

He lowers his mouth to my nipple, teasing it with his

tongue before sucking it between his lips, his own moan of pleasure vibrating against my skin. Goddess, his touch, his hot mouth, everything about him is making me wet.

I slide my hands into his hair and tug, slowly urging him back to my mouth. He kisses my lips, my jaw, my throat, blazing a trail of heat and seduction straight back to my lips...

And then the bed starts rumbling, the framed Aces above our heads rattling against the wall, and Kirin pulls back.

"It's okay," I whisper, my skin already missing the feel of his lips. "Come back."

He kisses me again, but quickly breaks it off.

"Stevie, wait. I... I need to say something." His green eyes are glazed with desire, his breath coming out in ragged bursts, but his energy is suddenly anxious. Afraid.

I take a deep breath and dial down my cracked-out libido, reaching out for his hand and offering an encouraging squeeze. "You can tell me anything, Kirin. You know that."

Kirin squeezes me back, his body instantly relaxing. "Everything you said to me in the realm... Everything you've been saying since we first started hanging out... You *get* me, Stevie. You always have. More than anyone else in my life, you have the uncanny ability to see past the fear, past the bullshit, past the stories, straight into my heart. Despite seeing all my flaws, all my damage, you've never freaked out or bailed on me. I hurt you, and you gave me another chance. I told you the worst thing I've ever done in

222

my life—about all the people I hurt, the people I turned my back on—and still, you stuck by me." He trails his fingers down across my shoulder, making me shiver. "I can't tell you what that means to me."

I look into his eyes, his gaze vulnerable, his energy now pulsing with raw emotion, and smile. I feel his immense gratitude. His love. Even without purposefully reaching for the connection, I feel how much he truly cares about me.

But he's worried too, the anxiety still coursing through him.

"I want to be with you tonight," he continues, his voice a little shaky. "More than anything. But I can't ignore the potential for damage. The Tower energy… you know there are consequences, whether we want them to exist or not."

"Kirin, it's okay. We'll—"

"No, it isn't. *I'm* not okay—not with putting you at risk. It doesn't matter if the events of ten years ago weren't my fault or my intention—they still happened because of me. Because of an energy I can't always direct or control. I hurt people, Stevie. And no matter how much I care about you, I can't promise I won't hurt you the same way."

I nod, my heart breaking for him all over again. Even after what we went through in the realm, he's still carrying so much weight. So much blame.

"You're right, Kirin. When you told me about your past, I didn't turn my back on you. So why would I turn my back on you now? Whatever happens, tonight or *any* night, we can work through it together. I know you're scared of hurting me, but—"

"Not scared, Stevie." His grip on my shoulder tightens, his voice dropping to a whisper. "Fucking terrified."

The energy of that terror hits me hard, like ice-cold lead in my stomach.

I take his hands in mine, gently kissing his fingers until I feel his energy settle. Then, with a soft grin, I say, "Do you know what Jessa calls you?"

His brow furrows, a tiny smile quirking his lips. "Do I *want* to know what Jessa calls me?"

"Mr. Cinnamon Buns."

"Mr. Cinnamon… what? I'm not sure that's…" He clears his throat, his cheeks darkening.

"In all the years I've known her, my best friend has never given another guy a nickname on my behalf. Let alone one as cute and sexy as Mr. Cinnamon—"

"Buns, yes, I've got it." He laughs, nudging my nose with his. "So what was your point again?"

"The point, Kirin, is that I've been crushing on you forever. You once told me that the hours you spent with me every morning at Kettle Black were the best part of your day."

"They were."

"It was the same for me. Every day I opened the café, I couldn't wait for you to show up, to inspire some crazy new tea blend. Just seeing you, talking to you, it made me feel seen and connected in ways I never had before, and we didn't even know each other that well. There was just something about you."

"There was something about you too."

We watch each other for a moment, smiling like a couple of dopey kids. Finally, Kirin cracks up.

I give him a playful smack. "What on earth is so funny, Mr. Cinnamon Buns?"

"It's not funny, but... I don't know. Ridiculous? We both had such big crushes on each other, and it took you literally going to prison, me and Cass breaking you out and dragging you here, me kissing you, me *dreaming* about kissing you, all the time we spent together in the library, teaching you how to fly on a bicycle, and so many near-death experiences I've lost count before we could finally have this conversation."

I return his easy laughter. "That should tell you something. *What*, I'm not sure. But something."

He brushes my hair over my shoulder, dropping a kiss on my collarbone. "And to think, it all started with a cup of tea."

"Well, my mom always said there's no problem a perfect cup of the stuff can't fix." I smile, wondering what Mom would say now, what advice she'd have about my guys. She'd love them all, I'm certain of it, just as much as I do. And she'd wink and smile and tell me I must have a big heart to have so much room for them.

And then she'd tell me to go put the kettle on.

I smile even brighter, a new idea taking shape in my mind.

"Okay, what's that look all about." Kirin swirls his finger in front of my face. "You're plotting."

"Believe it or not, I actually have an idea." I try to get out of bed, but Kirin grabs my hand and pulls me back.

"Not that I don't love your brilliant mind, but any idea that has you leaving this bed sounds like the *worst*."

"I will only be gone a few minutes." I manage to wriggle free. "Just long enough to make tea."

"Wait, what?" Kirin laughs, his eyes shining with love and amusement.

"Tea brought us together. And like Mom said, it can fix anything."

"Even this?"

"Worth a shot."

"So tell me, Queen of Leaves," Kirin says, just like he did dozens of times at Kettle Black. "What do I need today?"

"I'm *so* glad you asked, Kirin Weber. I've got just the thing."

His smile falters, turning into a pout. "This is the part where you leave the bed, isn't it?"

"Give me ten minutes. It'll be worth it—promise."

TWENTY-FOUR

STEVIE

Exactly nine point five minutes later, I return to the bedroom with my latest concoction.

Kirin watches me expectantly, his eyes full of happiness and anticipation, his energy matching exactly.

"It's a variation of my best-selling Red-Hot Rendezvous," I explain, handing over the mug. "Chocolate Pu-erh tea blended with cinnamon, ginger, orange peel, a pinch of chipotle powder, and two rose petals. But tonight, I also added crushed witch's cauldron."

"*Stevie.*" Kirin stares at me, barely suppressing a laugh. "Did you seriously just brew viagra tea? Because I can assure you, my potency is *not* the problem here."

As if I needed proof, he peels back the sheet covering his lower half, revealing a *very* generous bulge beneath his sweatpants.

"That looks..." *Like something I need inside me right*

fucking now. I clear my throat, forcing my eyes back up to his face. "Uncomfortable."

"A side effect of your half-naked presence in the bedroom." Kirin smirks again, but his humor fades quickly. "Stevie, I appreciate this. I do. But I'm not sure how your spicy romance tea is going to help. I'm already in a state of... well. In a state. This tea—while I'm sure it's delicious —isn't going to control my Tower energy. If anything, the potency magick will make things worse."

"It's not the physical potency we need to harness— clearly you've got that covered. It's the mental potency." I sit next to him in bed, careful not to spill his tea. "Kirin, you've got all this excess mental energy swirling around your head about what it means to be with me. You're so worried about your Tower energy causing chaos that your brain is creating scenarios where one little orgasm brings the whole dorm down on our heads."

"It might."

"Okay, but what if instead of causing a six-point-five on the Richter scale, we harness that energy, channel it away from your thoughts and our external environment, and channel it instead into *us*. Into enjoying each other's company."

Kirin sips the tea, his eyes closing in pleasure, but I can tell he's still on the fence.

"You're the Tower," I continue, "and yes, that comes with a lot of intense energy, often destructive, but always illuminating. And I'm the Star. In our Arcana line, the Star appears after the collapse, so to speak—the light that shines through after the fall. I represent the healing that can take place after a tragedy, sure. But the Star can also be a beacon. Light, darkness… We exist in relation to each other. Joining together like this…" I brush my fingers along his jaw, offering a sincere smile. "It's you and me, Kirin. We belong together. Our gifts, our magick, our hearts… I know this is right. I can feel it."

He hesitates only a moment, then downs the rest of the tea and abandons the cup on the nightstand.

"Does this mean you're willing to try?" I ask, damn near giddy at the sudden change in his mood.

In response, he strips out of his sweatpants and climbs on top of me, smothering me with his delicious weight, his green eyes bright and happy once again.

"You are my favorite kind of genius," he whispers.

And then he's kissing me, deep and deliberate, the taste of chocolate and cinnamon fresh on his tongue.

Gone is the frantic fumbling in the library, the scared, gasping kisses beneath the Towers of Breath and Blade. Right here, right now, everything is perfect.

Kirin kisses his way down my chest, down my belly, tugging at my underwear with his teeth, but I can't wait another moment. I need him inside me, filling me, giving and taking all the things we've denied ourselves for far too long.

I arch my hips as he slides my underwear down my legs, and then he's coming back to me, kissing another hot path up to my mouth.

"I think your romance tea is working," he breathes, stealing another kiss.

"Was there any doubt?" I part my thighs, and with no more hesitation, no more fear, he plunges inside and fills me completely, so perfect and amazing I almost cry from the pure joy of it.

He cups my face, his eyes filling with tenderness and love, with passion, with amazement.

"You take my breath away," he whispers, sliding in deeper, never breaking our gaze. "From the first day I laid eyes on you in Kettle Black, and every day since."

I smile and pull him down for another kiss, winding my fingers into his hair, gingerly feeling my way into his slow, delicious rhythm as he brings me to the very edge of bliss. It's not long before our careful, deliberate movements give way to wild abandon, my hips arching up to meet his every thrust, his mouth hot and demanding on my neck.

My body tightens around him, and Kirin moans against my skin, sliding a hand down between us and seeking my clit.

I try to hold back, to prolong the intensity of this moment, but I'm no longer in control of my body. The softest brush of his finger has me trembling, and then he increases the pressure, drawing slow, intense circles as he fucks me harder, deeper, the last of his own control evaporating, everything inside me coiling tight and then...

"Kirin, I can't wait! I'm... *Kirin!*" I come undone in a rush, stars flickering before my eyes as the orgasm slams through me, bringing Kirin right along with it. The bed slams into the wall, the framed Aces rattling overhead, and Kirin comes with a deep sigh, burying his face against my neck as he rides out wave after wave after wave.

And then he collapses on top of me, trembling and spent, smothering me in the best possible way.

* * *

"Did the room survive?" he asks, slowly rolling over onto his back.

I look around and take stock—wall art hanging askew, blankets in a heap on the floor, half the mattress exposed and tilting off the bed. The empty tea mug is tipped on its side, rocking back and forth on the nightstand. I have no idea where his sweats or my underwear ended up.

"The room may have picked up a few battle scars." I snuggle against his chest, reveling in the strong, solid protection of his arms. "But not because of your Tower-ness."

"Are you sure?"

I nod, barely holding back my smile. "To borrow a phrase from our recent past, it's all just my regular ol' human expression of big-O excitement."

Kirin lets out a pent-up breath, his hold on me tightening. "Guess I'd better keep an eye on you, little wrecking ball."

"Eyes, hands, mouth… I'll take whatever's available, really." I lean over and kiss him, enjoying the lingering taste of chocolate and cinnamon. "Do you need more tea?"

"I don't need the tea anymore," he says with a smile. "But I do need to tell you something."

His eyes turn serious and intense, his energy prickling with fresh nerves.

I hold my breath, biting my bottom lip as my own nerves start firing. What if he didn't like it? What if it really *was* too much for him, and he's just holding it all back to protect my feelings? What if the tea pushed his mind into overdrive, and now he's grappling with—

"I'm *ridiculously* in love with you, Stevie," he says, tracing his thumb across my lips. "And I realized something tonight."

I prop my head up on my elbow, my smile chasing away the last of the nerves. "What's that?"

"As long as I get to hear you make that sound again, I don't care if we bring down every damn wall on campus."

I laugh, hooking my leg over his hips, my core already aching for more.

Kirin's eyes turn serious again.

"I was a fool to run away from you," he says, pulling me up to straddle him. His hands are big and strong on my thighs, holding me in place. "I'll spend the rest of my life making amends for that, if you'll let me."

"Hmm." I tap my lips, pretending to consider the offer. Between my thighs, his cock stiffens, and I let out a breathy moan, sliding along the hard, hot length.

Kirin grabs my backside and arches his hips, guiding himself inside me once again.

"Can I call you Mr. Cinnamon Buns?" I breathe.

Goddess, he feels amazing…

Kirin closes his eyes and shakes his head, but there's no mistaking the smile on his lips.

Before he can deny me a single demand, I lean forward and kiss him.

"Either way," I whisper, "I'm ridiculously in love with you too."

TWENTY-FIVE

CASS

Despite what my esteemed colleagues may believe, I don't —as a general rule—enjoy torture. Especially on an otherwise pleasant Sunday morning.

I find it monstrous and in most cases wholly unnecessary, not to mention messy.

But when it comes to protecting the Brotherhood? Protecting Stevie?

Let's just say my moral compass is getting a little more off-track each day.

Using the portal at Time Out of Mind and the SUV Anna so generously included with the house in Red Sands Canyon, Professor Maddox and I managed to get our prisoners relocated last night without issue. They're nice and comfortable in the basement, stretched out on two cots under a set of blinding white fluorescents, magickally restrained and required to follow my commands by the Professor's clever binding spell.

Unfortunately, that spell expires just before midnight on Harvest Eve, giving us a small window of opportunity to extract the intel we need.

I roll up my sleeves and pull up a chair next to Casey, hoping that she'll crack first. Kirin believes she's being forced into this, and I'm inclined to agree. Which means the real Casey might be fighting her way out, just as I'm fighting my way in.

"Good morning," I say brightly, angling my body so she can see the small table set up next to me, replete with a fine selection of medical instruments, magickal tools, potions, and Tarot decks. "Are you ready to have some fun today?"

"Fuck you," she snarls.

"Miss Appleton! Is that any way to talk to a man with a knife like this?" I select the largest weapon from the bunch, a dagger made from polished black onyx.

Standing across from me on the other side of the cot, Professor Maddox folds her arms over her chest and raises an eyebrow, a silent warning to not push this too far.

With an exaggerated sigh, I trade the knife for a large syringe filled with sparkling red-orange liquid, trying not to let the professor's presence irk me. I had intended on taking care of this unpleasantness on my own, but after helping me with the transport last night, she demanded we partner up.

And when it comes to the witch with absolute power over the binding spell, I'm in no position to deny *any* demands.

Casey glares up at me, her eyes fiery with rage. Under

my command, she can't move from the neck down, but that doesn't stop her from shooting daggers at me.

"Enough with this charade, Professor Devane," she snaps. "You can't hurt us without hurting the women whose bodies we're borrowing."

"I'm aware," I say calmly, turning the syringe to catch the light. "That really is a nice, rich color, Professor Maddox. Compliments to Professor Broome."

Casey laughs. "You don't have it in you to—"

I jam the needle into her neck and press the plunger, delivering the truth serum I hope will unlock the mystery.

Professor Maddox sighs. "A little harsh, Dr. Devane. Don't you think?"

"Everyone's a critic, Professor." Then, turning my attention back to our guest, I say, "Now Miss Appleton. I know we're all eager to get back home, so the faster you cooperate, the sooner we can all be on our way."

She's already struggling against the burn of the serum— a sure sign it's working its magick. "I would... rather... die."

"Somehow I doubt that."

"Go to... hell... you..."

She doesn't finish her insult. Instead, her face contorts, and she presses her lips together, almost as if she's trying to prevent herself from speaking. When she finally opens her mouth again, her next words explode in a brief but breathless rush, her gaze changing from angry to terrified in an instant.

"Devane!" she cries out. "Help me! It's—"

Her mouth clamps shut again, and I glance up at Professor Maddox.

"It's Casey," she says, and I nod, both of us letting out a relieved breath. Our theory was right. Casey Appleton isn't a party to this. She's fighting it.

"Casey, I know you're in there," I say, the breakthrough bolstering me. "I need you to keep fighting. Not just for yourself, but for your brother. Kirin needs you, now more than ever."

She nods emphatically, but whoever's got control still won't let her speak. And while I can command her lips to move, I can't command what's happening in her mind or which words make it to the surface.

I can only hope the truth serum does its job.

"Who is controlling you?" I ask.

She opens her mouth again, fighting the possession. "Dark—"

It's all she can manage, but the D-word is enough to lend credence to my other theory.

The Dark Arcana are very likely behind this, which is both good news and bad. Good, because if they're possessing non-Arcana witches like Casey and Janelle, it stands to reason they haven't yet invaded the bodies of their Light Arcana counterparts, which would be much more difficult for us to fight.

Of course, we're assuming that Lala's beliefs about how the Dark Arcana rise to power are accurate, and that Casey and Janelle are not, in fact, Arcana witches. I'm only slightly more confident about the latter.

The bad news—rather, the worse news—is that if we can't figure out how to expel them, Casey and Janelle could be possessed indefinitely.

As much as Professor Maddox doesn't want to hear it, it means we'd have to kill them.

Fortunately for my colleague, we don't have to cross that bridge just yet.

I slide my chair over to the other cot to check on Janelle. She gives me the same death stare, the same idle threats.

And she gets the same needle in the neck.

I can't lie. *That* one felt good. Even Professor Maddox doesn't flinch.

We wait for the serum to work its way into her bloodstream, but unlike Casey, Janelle remains mute, her face smooth and untroubled, even as she continues to give me the evil eye.

"The serum has no effect on her," I say.

Professor Maddox nods. We both know what that means —there's a good chance Janelle has been playing along with her hitchhiker from the start, willingly offering herself as a vessel. To what ends? That remains to be seen, but no one in her right mind would agree to something so dangerous unless she had something incredibly important to gain.

Or to lose.

I turn back to Casey for another go, alternating between reminders of Kirin and the APOA career she loves, and threats against the monster who's taken up residence inside her. But after an hour of interrogation and two more doses of serum, it's clear we've hit a brick wall.

Time to call in the big guns.

I grab an athame from the table and slice across each woman's palm, squeezing their blood into a single glass bowl. I then slice and squeeze my own palm, swirling our blood together.

Professor Maddox paces behind us, her body tense, but she keeps her mouth shut.

"Since you're both having trouble remembering your true identities," I say, setting the bowl of mixed blood on the table and retrieving a deck of Tarot cards, "we're going to try a new spell."

I drop the Moon card into the bowl, watching as it slowly dissolves, turning the blood completely clear.

"Cheers, ladies." I pick up the bowl and hold it to Janelle's lips, forcing her to drink half the liquid inside. She tries to resist me, but drinking is a command she must obey.

Casey is next, and I force her to finish the contents. Then I close my eyes, pushing my magick into their minds as I chant my spell.

> *Magick of Moon, break this illusion*
> *By blood and by will, dispel this confusion*
> *Reveal to us what darkness has hidden*
> *Reveal to us usurpers unbidden*

For a moment nothing happens, and I worry the spell wasn't strong enough. But just as I'm reaching for the bowl to make another batch, a primal scream erupts from Janelle, damn near shattering the windows. Casey follows, her head thrashing, her eyes rolling back. Janelle is foaming at the mouth like a rabid dog.

"Dr. Devane, stop this at once!" Professor Maddox reaches out to steady Casey's head, but I grab her wrist.

"Just wait," I snap. "Ten seconds."

She stills, and together we sit through the torturous screams, silently counting down...

And there it is.

Beneath the stark white lamplight, images flicker over their faces as if they're being projected from an old film reel.

Superimposed over Casey's face is a familiar one the professor and I know well.

And one I would like to murder in the most horrific way possible.

"Professor Phaines," I grind out, barely holding back the tsunami of my rage.

I stare into his film-reel eyes for so long, it takes me a minute to realize Professor Maddox has also called his name.

And that she's standing over Janelle.

"Both of them?" I shout. "He's taken over both of them?"

The rage bubbles over, and I grab Casey's shirt collar, hauling her close.

"Dr. Devane!" Professor Maddox shouts, but her voice is weak and watery compared to the one screaming in my head.

Kill him. Do it now. Kill him!

"Give me *one* reason why I shouldn't tear off his head!" I shout.

"It's not his head," she says. "Just his soul."

The image before me flickers again, revealing Casey, her eyes wide with fear.

I take a deep breath and close my eyes, forcing myself to calm down.

"Let her go, Cass," Professor Maddox says. "Just let her go."

I nod and do as she asks, laying Casey back on the cot and heading up to the kitchen for some water.

Professor Maddox gives me a few minutes to cool off, then joins me at the kitchen table.

"Can you force him out?" I ask.

"Possibly," she says. "If we can find some of his old possessions, we can probably figure out a spell. But doing so means we risk cutting him loose."

"What do you mean?"

"Right now, his physical body is probably holed up somewhere safe. As long as he's possessing Casey and Janelle, he's unlikely to leave that location, which means we can try to track him down."

"I don't understand. What's stopping him from taking off, especially now that he knows we're on to him?"

"He's essentially in power-saver mode," she explains. "Possessing even one body is energy intensive, but two? One of whom is actively fighting it? All of his focus and energy is on maintaining those links, and he's not likely to give them up easily. Binding spell or not, those women are the only reason he's still got access to the Academy. He's playing the long game here, Dr. Devane."

I nod, trying to figure out what this means for us. The last thing I want is Phaines running loose again, getting access to Stevie or any of the other students. But we can't leave Casey and Janelle in a state of possession either— especially once the binding spell breaks and Phaines is free to take control of their bodies once again.

"There's more," she says. "As far as we know, Phaines is still alive, which means he's got a physical body to maintain as well. A possession like this requires a semi-conscious state—there's no way he's managing on his own. He needs regular magickal and IV infusions, and that means someone is helping him."

"Another witch or mage," I say.

"As much as I hate to say this…" She lowers her eyes, her brow creasing. "It's likely an inside job."

I let out a bitter laugh. "And here I thought *Phaines* was our inside job."

"I suppose we were foolish to hope he was working alone."

"So what does this mean? Everyone's a suspect again?"

"Not everyone." She reaches across the table, calming me with a soft smile and reassuring pat on my hand. "Starla Milan has changed you for the better. Don't let this setback close you off again."

I open my mouth to deny it, but then, what would I deny first? The fact that I feel my walls going up again, so soon after inviting the professors, Isla, and Nat in? Or the fact that Stevie has changed me at all, let alone for the better?

"She's changed us all, Cass. Just like her mother did before her."

Memories of Stevie flicker through my mind—the first day I met her in the prison, her toughness, her stubbornness, the taste of the tea she brought me.

The taste of our near kiss in my classroom, and all the long nights I've spent replaying that moment in my mind.

Changed me?

That is a gross understatement.

Starla Milan has given me a reason to hope again. And for that, I'm falling in love with her.

Heat rises up my neck, and I clear my throat, averting my gaze and pulling out of Professor Maddox's grasp.

"Our only recourse is to find out where Professor Phaines is hiding," I say, getting us back on track. "We need to go back downstairs and try another spell. Get him to reveal—"

"You need a break."

"I'm fine."

"You're exhausted, and you're not at your best." She rises from the table and heads to the door that leads to the basement. "Go home and get some sleep. I'll take care of this."

I want to argue with her, but she's right. I haven't slept more than a handful of stolen naps in three days, and I'm getting sloppy. My reaction to seeing Phaines's face is all the proof we need of that.

Reluctantly, I nod, and she opens the basement door.

"Professor Maddox, if we don't figure this out by Harvest Eve…"

"We will, Cass. I promise."

She turns to head downstairs, but a shriek from the basement stops her cold.

"You're too late, Cassius Devane!" It's Janelle, her voice twisted and distorted as Phaines breaks through the veneer. "The clock has been set, the hours always passing. Very soon, the light shall embrace the dark, and you shall embrace your death."

TWENTY-SIX

STEVIE

The morning after our epic night of dunch and big-o dessert, Kirin and I finally drag ourselves out of bed and into the shower. As much as we'd love to hit the pause button on the rest of the world and linger in bliss, that's just not an option.

Besides, I've got plans to hang out with Ani today, and Kirin's eager to hit the library to start documenting some of our findings and comparing it with the existing lore.

Unfortunately, Baz is still a no-show. He sent a few texts this morning, assuring us he's okay, but says he needs a little more rest before he's ready for prime time. I sent him back some hearts and smileys and told him not to worry, but secretly, Kirin and I agreed to give him one more day—then we're storming down his door.

"You sure I can't entice you to tag along?" Kirin asks now, all dressed and ready to go, his face lit up with the promise of spending hours in the stacks.

I stretch up on my toes for a kiss, letting out a soft sigh of contentment. "As much as I love nerding out with you at the library, Ani is coming over later, and I need to put my bedroom back in order."

"Wait. You need to straighten your bedroom for *Ani*?" Kirin raises an eyebrow, his green eyes sparkling. "So you guys are..."

"*What*? No, why would you—*no*. I just... I mean... The place looks like a bomb went off, and I need to clean it up before company arrives. Ani and I..." A strangled laugh bubbles up from my throat. "Kirin, you *know* Ani's just..."

Kirin nudges my nose with his. "Just what? A friend you like to kiss on occasion? In my office, no less?" His tone is light and teasing, not a single shred of jealousy to be found.

"To be fair," I say, "those were extenuating circum-stances. We'd just figured out that the Arcana objects were hidden in the dream realm. I wanted to kiss *everyone* that night. I was excited."

"So was Ani. You should've seen the look on his face when you planted one on him."

I can't help but smile. There's no way around this—I do have feelings for Ani. They snuck up on me, and truth be told, I haven't been able to stop thinking about that kiss in Kirin's office, either.

"Okay, okay," I finally admit. "It's possible I might have something... feelings... for Ani."

"Hmm. Is it possible you have 'something feelings' for all of us?"

I bite back another smile and lower my eyes, heat rising in my cheeks. "More than possible, yes."

Kirin doesn't say anything right away, and for a minute I worry I've pushed it too far. Yes, he knows I have a relationship with Baz—we've been together since before Kirin and I worked things out. But maybe hearing that I'm into Ani, and possibly Doc too… Maybe that's just a little bit more than he's prepared for right now.

"Please say something," I whisper, finally glancing up at him.

But instead of the confusion or jealousy I expect, I find only amusement. Light. Love.

"I've been wondering when you might get around to admitting it," he says, brushing a curl behind my ear.

I lift a shoulder. "Maybe I was still figuring out how to admit it to myself."

"I'm glad you did. But just do me one favor." Kirin brushes his lips across mine in a whisper-soft kiss. "Put the Gingersnap out of his misery and tell him how you feel?"

"Kirin, I…" I blink up at him, fresh emotions roiling through me. Hope. Fear. Excitement. Love. All of it. Things have been so intense between Kirin and me the last couple of days… I really wasn't prepared for this to come up right now. "Are you serious?"

"As far as I'm concerned, the sooner we're all on the same page about this, the sooner we can stop tiptoeing around it and just… just move forward."

"And you're… okay with that?" I ask tentatively.

"Moving forward with a woman who loves more than one man?"

"Is that what *you* want?"

"It's… complicated. The situation with Baz is a little unstable right now. I don't know how Ani and Doc feel about me—not totally. And I have no idea whether they'd even want a relationship with me at all, let alone a relationship like this."

"That isn't what I asked you, Stevie."

A long sigh escapes my lips. Kirin's right. He's asking me what I want. How I feel. And as much as I've been living with the swirl of crazy, complicated emotions about my Arcana brothers, I've never quite put it all into words.

I've never claimed my desire.

"Yes, Kirin," I say now, a rush of rightness and empowerment washing over me. "I *do* want it. What I feel for you, for them… it goes far deeper than anything I've ever felt before. Beyond the Arcana bond, beyond friendship, beyond all of it. And that's what I want—the beyond. A life with you guys that goes beyond our Arcana obligations, beyond the Academy walls, beyond the battles we've yet to face. Dreaming about what comes next gives me more hope than I can even put into words." I look up into his eyes again, tears glazing mine. "And if any of you feel even a *fraction* of that… I think we owe it to ourselves to see what's possible."

Kirin traces his thumb across my cheek, his smile soft and warm. "Anything is possible, Stevie. You should know that by now, Queen of Leaves."

"Maybe. But love isn't tea magick, Kirin. It's not a spell I can cast or something I can master by reading a few lore books. Everything I'm feeling… it's just that. *My* feelings. You have a right to yours as well, even if you think I'm totally selfish and crazy. Even if you're jealous or worried or you just don't see yourself in this kind of relationship. You need to be completely honest with yourself about that, even if it means walking away from this. From us."

Kirin's smile fades, the look in his eyes turning contemplative. I hold my breath, trying not to hope, trying not to fear, trying not to do anything but keep an open mind and heart about whatever he decides.

But it's so hard. And I realize it's not fair, but all I really want him to do is scoop me up in his arms, tell me he'll love me no matter what, and kiss me senseless.

"Okay, listen," he finally says, and I let out my breath, hoping he can't feel the tremble in my limbs. "Maybe I *was* jealous of Baz. Seeing you with him, the connection you guys had, the… the intimacy. It was hard, and it sucked, but looking back, I don't think it was actually jealousy. I was pissed at myself for pushing you away. For hurting you. Then we got through that, and I started to see you had real feelings for him. For Ani and Doc as well—something has *always* been simmering there, even if it wasn't as obvious as you and Baz. And at first, okay—maybe I never thought I'd be good with something like this. But now…"

He slides his hands into my hair, tipping my face up toward his.

"We're a family, Stevie. All of us. In ways we didn't even

realize until you came into our lives. I can't speak for everyone, but for me? After everything we've been through together, something about this just feels right."

A smile breaks across my face, and all the hope and excitement I tried to hold back instantly floods my heart. "Are you sure?"

Kirin laughs. "I love you, my Queen of Leaves. Every complicated, amazing, multi-faceted thing about you. The fact that your heart is big enough for more than one man? It's just another piece of your puzzle, another part of what makes you so special to me. So yes, I'm okay with it. *More* than okay with it."

He lowers his mouth to mine, claiming me with a deep, sensual kiss I feel all the way down to my toes.

"Talk to Ani," he says, pulling back to offer one last heart-stopping smile before heading out the door.

"I will, Kirin. I promise."

And I mean it too. But the minute I'm alone in my suite again, nervous butterflies dance around my stomach, and my heart feels like it's going to beat right out of my chest. There's just something about Ani that makes me feel like a schoolgirl with her first crush, and the idea of telling him how I feel has me bouncing off the walls.

I've still got an hour and a half before he's due to arrive, so I put the frantic energy to work, cleaning the suite from top to bottom. By the time I'm done, my place is spotless and I'm calm and centered, not a single errant butterfly to be found.

Until my door chimes.

TWENTY-SEVEN

STEVIE

My stomach is suddenly as fizzy as a glass of champagne, and when I open the door and see Ani's brilliant smile, I erupt in happy, crazy laughter, pulling him in for a hug.

"Wow," he says, returning my embrace with just one arm. The other is tucked suspiciously behind his back. "You're either *really* happy to see me, or *really* drunk."

"Or really happy at the prospect of getting drunk with you?" I pull back, nodding behind his back. "Did you bring me wine? Vodka? Moonshine?"

"Not exactly." He steps inside, keeping his arm behind his back. "But this will definitely make your day better."

"What could be better than day drinking with my favorite gingersnap?"

"Day drinking with your favorite gingersnap while playing with this?" He ends the suspense, finally handing over a gift wrapped in shiny pink paper and silver ribbon, about the size of a shoebox.

"What is it?" I ask.

"Guess."

"Ani!" My cheeks hurt from smiling so big. I'm practically bouncing on my toes with excitement. "At least give me a hint."

"Okay, I'll give you *five* hints. But only because you're so cute right now. Seriously, Stevie. You're wearing a T-shirt covered in broomsticks. I'm overwhelmed with the cuteness."

"Five hints?" I roll my eyes. "This has nothing to do with my cuteness and everything to do with you setting me up for a joke."

"Hint number one," he says, flashing me an adorable wink that calls those butterflies back into swift action. "It's the perfect gift for the sexy, independent woman in your life."

"Oh, I know! A life-sized cutout of Dean Winchester?"

"*What*? No! Goddess, you're impossible. Okay, hint number two: batteries *are* required."

My smile fades. The butterflies do a few backflips. My thighs clench, and it's a real effort to keep my mind out of the gutter. "Robot servant? Modeled after Dean Winchester?"

Ani wrinkles his nose and shakes his head. "Three, it's waterproof. And before you say it, no, it's not Dean Winchester in a pair of Speedos."

"Um…" *Good goddess, this man is going to kill me.*

"Four," he plows on, "it's big enough to let you get a

good grip, yet small enough to fit in your purse for fun on the go."

A nervous laugh escapes. "Ani, you are such a weirdo. What is even *happening* right now?"

"Oh, I'll tell you what's happening, Stevie Boo Boo." He leads me to the couch, where we both sit side-by-side, and squeezes my knee, the heat of his touch sending a little zing right to my core. "Are you ready for the final hint? Because it's the best one. Seriously, I stayed up all night perfecting it."

"Okay, this had better be the most epic present ever, because after a lead-up like this, you are setting the bar *really* high."

"Five." Ani wriggles his eyebrows, his grin as bright as the sun. "Use it alone or with a friend, but you'll never be able to use it without thinking of me."

"Wow, you *have* been planning this joke a long time."

"Just open it."

"Are you sure?"

"Yes. You're going to love it. I promise."

I slide off the ribbon and tear open the paper, revealing a nondescript white box.

"It's the gift that keeps on giving," he says.

"How many times, exactly?"

"That depends on your personal settings, Stevie. But I will say this—it's getting a lot of *buzz*..."

I open the box and find something about the size of a cucumber inside, rolled up in a few layers of pink tissue paper.

I wrap my hand around it and pull it out of the box, those butterflies now conspiring with my lady parts to paint a *very* naughty picture.

"Um… Ani?" My jaw drops. The size, the weight, the hints… There's no doubt in my mind what this is. I just can't believe Ani would actually buy me something so… so intimate.

So fucking hot.

Heat rises to my cheeks, but Ani's obviously going all in on this prank, so I'm not about to back down either. He probably thinks I'm going to freak out and refuse to open it, then force me to admit he's the best prankster ever.

But this little gingersnap has never been more wrong in his life.

"Ani, you're the best. It takes a real man to do something like this, and I can't wait to try it out with you."

Ani doesn't respond, but the wild anticipation in his eyes is impossible to miss.

Here goes nothing…

Taking a deep breath, I close my eyes and tear open the paper, ready to rock this epic joke to its inevitable conclusion, even if it means I totally mortify myself in the process.

The paper falls away.

I open my eyes.

And there, gripped firmly in my hand and ready to set this moment ablaze, is…

Not a vibrator.

It's…

"A microphone?" I ask.

"Not just *any* microphone." Ani taps a few buttons on his phone screen, and suddenly the mic lights up, flashing with neon pink and purple lights. He taps another button, and the opening instrumentals of Stevie Nicks' *Edge of Seventeen* blare out from the built-in speaker.

"Oh. My. Goddess." I'm on my feet in an instant, laughter and excitement bubbling out of me. "You win, Ani. You totally win. That was the best joke ever, and this present is fucking amazing!"

"It's got an app with all the best karaoke tracks. And you can change up the lights too." A few more taps, and the flashing lights switch to red and blue, just in time for the first verse of the song.

Ani hops off the couch and jumps onto the coffee table, air guitar at the ready, and I raise the mic to my lips and belt it out. Verse for verse, we both keep up, dancing around the living room, jumping from the couch to the table to the floor, shaking our asses, totally rocking it out.

Our performance is fucking epic, and by the time the song ends, we're both panting, laughing so hard we're crying.

When we finally catch our breath again, I pull him in for another hug.

"Thank you, Ani. You were totally right—I love it. And I love that you picked that song."

"You never got to sing it for us," he says, a little shyness creeping into the humor. "And I really wanted to hear your performance."

"Well, Hot Shots kind of exploded." I head into the kitchen and grab us a couple of waters.

"Hot Shots may be toast," he says, "but that doesn't mean our dreams of karaoke superstardom have to come to an end."

"Clearly not." I grab the mic again, giving it a closer look. "Is this thing seriously waterproof?"

"How else would you jam in the bathtub?"

I lift a brow. Offer him a flirty little smirk. "Should we test it?"

Ani nearly chokes on his water. "Now? Are you serious?"

"Bathtub karaoke..." I pause for about half a second, then remember what Kirin said about being honest with Ani about my feelings. If this doesn't do the trick, I don't know what will.

I grab his hand and nod. "Why not?"

Ani's laughter stalls out, his cheeks turning pink. "Um... I'm not... really? You're sure you want to do this?"

"Are you scared? You look scared." I press a hand to his chest and give him a somber look. "I promise I won't drop the mic in the tub and fry any delicate parts."

"The mic's, or mine?"

Smiling mischievously, I head into the master bathroom, calling out over my shoulder, "No delicate parts will be fried in the making of this epic and wet memory."

I fill the tub and strip down to my underwear, deciding not to *totally* freak him out just yet. So far, all we've shared is a kiss and a few flirtations, and although I can sense he truly cares for me, I don't want to push him into anything he's not a hundred percent into.

A few minutes later, he joins me in the bathroom with a couple of beers, and I turn off the tap and smile.

"Water's perfect," I say, anticipation coiling inside. I have no idea where this is going to lead, but whatever happens, I know it's right. Ani is my friend before anything else, and I trust him completely. "You ready?"

His eyes trail down to my toes, and he swallows hard, blowing out a nervous breath. His energy hits me all at once—a flicker of nervousness, followed swiftly by a wave of intense, powerful desire.

Without another word, he strips down to his boxers, and we climb in the tub with our beers and our new toy.

By the time the water cools, we've worked our way through Stevie Nicks' entire catalog, including the Fleetwood Mac stuff, a good deal of Beyonce's, and an amazingly cheesy mix of eighties rock ballads I'll never be able to get out of my head.

In other words, the perfect way to spend an afternoon.

Singing. Laughing. Drinking. Half-naked in the bathtub with a ginger hottie whose infectious smile chases away the rain.

* * *

"What do you feel like doing now?" he asks. We're lying

face to face on my bed after the bathtub concert, comfy and warm in some of Baz's T-shirts and sweats we found in my closet. "Witch and Wizard Monopoly? X-Rated Scrabble? Tarot Arcana Charades?"

I shoot him a dubious glare. "You're making that up, as usual."

"Don't mock it until you've tried it."

When I don't immediately respond, he nudges my foot with his, and as I gaze into his caramel eyes, a burst of warmth fills my chest. It feels like I've known him forever. Like it's always been this way, the two of us spending lazy Sundays together, hanging out and making each other laugh.

"Come on, Stevie," he says softly. "Anything you want. Seriously. Just name it. Unless it involves me leaving, in which case, bury it. No one needs that kind of negativity in their lives."

"I don't want you to leave."

"I'm so glad we had this little chat." Ani reaches over and tugs on one of my curls. "So what *do* you want?"

A single thought comes to mind, but when I open my mouth, my throat tightens, nerves getting in the way. I lower my gaze and take a deep breath, trying to think of what to say. Scrabble might be fun. Even the charades thing.

But... no. If there's one thing I've learned about Ani, it's that he doesn't do anything halfway. He was willing to strip down to almost nothing and spend two hours in the bathtub with me, singing dumb songs until our skin pruned.

The least I can do is shore up my courage, rip off the Band-Aid, and tell him the truth.

"Honestly, Ani?" I reach for his hands and look directly into his eyes, my lips curving into a soft smile. "As much as I love *all* your ideas, especially the X-Rated Scrabble one, I kind of want to lie here and make out with you."

TWENTY-EIGHT

ANSEL

"Is that weird?" Stevie tucks her wild hair behind her ears and offers a shy smile, her cheeks darkening. "If it's weird, I totally get it if you don't want to. I just thought... Maybe?"

My heart is thundering, basically cutting off my ability to speak.

Is this really happening?

"Ani?" she asks softly.

By some miracle, I finally manage a brief reply.

"No."

Her face falls. "No, you don't want to?"

"No, it's not weird." I reach for her face, tracing a finger across her soft lips. "Not weird at all."

She laughs, a nervous rush that infects me to my core. If I thought I was falling for her before, now I'm so far gone I might as well move to Mars, because no one is going to be able to bring me back from this trip.

"Good. Because I just thought... I mean... I know a lot

has happened since then, but the other night in Kirin's office, something just came over me, and I totally wanted to kiss you. And maybe I was misreading, but I thought maybe you wanted to kiss me too, so I just kind of… went for it."

"I *definitely* wanted you to kiss me."

"But then we got taken hostage."

I laugh. "*Total* buzzkill."

"It was, right? But now I can't stop thinking about it."

"The hostage situation?"

"Kissing you!" She laughs and covers her face. "Goddess, I'm being a freakshow. I know. It's a gift. It's—"

"Adorable." I peel her hands away and hold them close, staring into her pretty blue eyes, my heart still bouncing around inside me. "Starla Milan, if you're a freakshow, sign me up for the double feature."

"Um, did you really just say that?"

"What? It was funny!"

"It was *corny*. Like, White Lion-level corny."

"And yet, you're practically throwing yourself at me. So maybe it's time to accept the fact that corny is your kryptonite."

"You're right." She lets out a soft sigh, her breath tickling my lips. "Maybe it is."

"Really?"

"Really." Still smiling, she leans in and brushes her lips against mine, a sweet, short kiss that leaves me aching for so much more.

Normally, I'd back off, wait for her to make the next move.

But that was old Ani. Sweet, good-natured, hope-for-the-best Ani.

After that kiss in Kirin's office the other night, after everything that happened at Breath and Blade, after nearly burning the whole place to the ground for her, after watching her fight her way back from the dream realm, I'm never waiting around for someone else to make a move again.

I reach up and cup her face, bringing her in for another kiss, savoring the softness, the taste, the warmth of her breath as she sighs my name, over and over.

Of course I want more. When it comes to Stevie, I'll *always* want more. I could overdose on this woman and happily sign up for another round.

But her kisses are so soft, so delicious, so perfect, I think I'll just live in the moment a little while longer.

"What are you thinking?" she whispers, pulling back to smile up at me again, her eyes sparkling.

"Just that I really like kissing you."

"I really like kissing you too."

So we spend the next couple of hours doing just that.

* * *

Long after the sun sets, we're spooning in Stevie's bed, staring out the window at the moon, when I catch sight of two small bottles on her bedside table.

"What are these?" I pick up one of them for a closer look, turning it back and forth. Inside the bottle, silvery-white liquid sparkles in the moonlight.

"That one's a dream potion," she says. "I made it when I thought I *wanted* to get in touch with the Dark Arcana. The other one is the opposite—it's for a dreamless sleep."

"How does it work?" I turn the bottle again, mesmerized by the way the light plays off the contents.

"Who cares?" She takes it from my hand and shuts it away in the drawer. "According to Doc, we still have about five days before we have to think about going back to that awful realm. Until then, I'm good with pretending it doesn't exist."

"Sounds like a good plan." I force a laugh, but inside, my mind is already churning. Five silent minutes later, and the idea has fully wrapped around my brain, anchoring itself with deep roots that refuse to let go.

All I can do now is water them. Tend them. Help them grow.

Two nights ago, I watched my best friends and the woman I love risk their lives descending into the dream realm. I watched them fight for each other, fight for all of us, fight to find a way to bring back the Arcana objects and save magick. Baz was the one who brought back the sword and pentacle, but they all share in that victory. They couldn't have done it without one another.

Right now, Cass is risking his life and compromising everything he stands for in order to interrogate our prisoners, even if it means he'll never be able to face himself in the mirror after this.

My brothers are warriors, and this is a war.

But me? Other than setting the world on fire, what am I actually doing? Telling jokes. Bringing Stevie a karaoke mic. Living my own selfish dreams by holding her in my arms, kissing her again and again.

Is that enough?

Kirin's words from the other night echo.

Ani's got the best shot at connecting with the wand...

I glance at the nightstand drawer again, envisioning the seductive little bottle inside.

A dream potion... I made it when I thought I wanted to get in touch with the Dark Arcana...

"Can you stay tonight?" Stevie asks now, pulling my arm across her chest and snuggling closer. Her sweet scent invades my senses, reminding me once again that I'd do anything to keep her safe.

Anything.

"Get some rest," I whisper, kissing the back of her neck. "I'm not going anywhere."

Stevie lets out a happy sigh, drifting away in my arms.

The moment her breathing turns long and even, I reach over and slide open the drawer, closing my fingers around the vial.

TWENTY-NINE

STEVIE

The campus burns behind me, angry black smoke blotting out the sky. Up ahead, the Cauldron of Flame and Fury glows at dawn's desperate touch, the sun fighting to break through the dark haze.

I've got one thought, one mission.

I must find Ani.

I can feel his presence all around me, but I know he shouldn't be here now, smack in the middle of my battles with darkness. There was no ritual, no dream-sharing spell like the one we did at Breath and Blade. Some otherworldly force must've yanked him into my living nightmares.

I need to get him out of here.

Choking on acrid smoke, I hike the entire rim of the Cauldron, but there's no sign of him.

I close my eyes, reach out for his energy.

Ani, where the hell are you...

There. A flicker of recognition... a warmth and eagerness that can only belong to him. I open my eyes, realizing at once where he must be.

Gingerly I make my way, scrambling down the steep, rocky trail until I finally reach the bottom of the bowl and the crevices Ani and I last explored on the material realm.

I find him with his hands braced against the canyon wall, staring into the same crevice where the Princess of Wands led us last time.

The same crevice where we sensed the Wand of Flame and Fury.

"Ani," I call, as softly as I can manage through my rush of relief.

He startles, then turns, his eyes going wide. "Stevie? What are you doing here? You shouldn't be here."

"I was about to give you the same speech."

"But... how did you get here?"

"We're dreaming, Ani. Somehow you slipped into the realm with me."

Ani curses under his breath, then steps away from the wall and pulls me in for a hug, holding on so tightly he nearly crushes my ribs.

When he pulls back, his caramel eyes are full of concern, and his energy spikes with a new emotion: guilt.

"Ani? What's going on?"

"I just thought... I wanted to see if I could find the wand myself." He flashes a disarming grin. "Save you guys a trip."

His otherwise heart-melting smile is nowhere near enough to eradicate the anger surging inside me.

"We can't stay here," I snap.

"I won't be long," he says. "I just need—"

"Ani!" I gasp and shove him against the rock wall, hoping like hell we weren't spotted. My heart is slamming into my chest, my mouth going dry.

Because there, gazing down at us from the rim, is Dark Judgment. He's pacing back and forth, the tip of his staff glowing red.

"Ani, listen to me," I say firmly. "We can talk about all this later, but right now, we need to leave. We need to wake up."

"But we're so close."

"He's here," I whisper. "Judgment."

Ani's face pales, the first indication that he understands even a modicum of the danger we're in.

I have no idea how to wake us up from this, so I try the only thing I can think of.

I close my eyes and chant, calling with desperate urgency on the combined power of my elemental Princesses.

"Stevie, no!" Ani grabs my shoulders, imploring me to stop, begging me to let him undertake this quest, but it's too late. I can already feel their magick bolstering me.

"Don't do this!" Ani cries. "Stevie, please!"

I open my eyes and take Ani's face between my palms, magick singing from my fingertips.

"Ani," I whisper. "Wake up."

* * *

We jolt up in bed, both of us gasping for air. It takes a moment for my body and mind to sync up, and the moment they do, I turn to check on Ani.

He's staring at me, his gaze holding a mix of disbelief and hurt.

"I *wanted* to be there, Stevie," he says. "We were so close. I could feel the wand's energy, just like that day at the Cauldron."

"You could've died," I say, fighting to keep the sting of betrayal from my tone. "You could've been lost in the realm like Baz was, only this time no one would've even known to come looking for you! What the hell were you thinking?"

"That my best friends are in trouble? That your life is in danger? That there's nothing I won't do to protect you?"

"We all feel that way about each other." My anger softens, and I reach up and run a hand through his red hair. "But you didn't have to do this alone. We were supposed to make a plan. We were supposed to go together."

"I couldn't ask you to do that. Not after what happened to Baz. I won't risk that happening to you. Or to him, for that matter."

Anger's winning out again, and I glare at him, torn between kissing him and strangling him. "So you risk yourself instead? That's your grand plan?"

"Stevie, you don't understand." He climbs out of the bed and heads toward the window, crossing his arms over his chest and staring out at the moon. When he speaks again, his voice is soft, his energy full of sadness and regret.

"When I was a kid, my parents got divorced because of me."

"What do you mean?" I ask.

Keeping his back turned, he gives me a quick sketch about his mother's affair and the manifestation of his magick that revealed the truth: the man who raised him couldn't possibly be his father. "The truth destroyed my family. And after that, for the rest of my life, I grew up thinking I was the problem. Whatever went wrong, *I* was the problem. Well you know what, Stevie?" He finally turns to face me, his eyes blazing. "For once, I have a chance to be the solution."

I rise from the bed and join him at the window, taking his hands in mine.

"Ani, I can understand how you'd feel that way as a kid, but now… You have to know it wasn't your fault."

"I do. Logically." He offers a faint smile, full of heartache for what could have been. "But it still hurts. That kind of ache… It doesn't just go away."

Looking into his golden caramel eyes, I can't imagine a family that wouldn't love him. One that wouldn't know how blessed they'd be to have him in their lives.

"I can't speak for your parents," I say. "But I can tell you this." I stretch up on my toes and give him a soft kiss. "You're my rock, Ani. I don't know what I'd do if I lost you."

He sighs and pulls me against his chest, pressing a kiss to the top of my head.

"Promise me I'll never lose you," I whisper, knowing how ridiculous it sounds. Knowing I need to say it anyway.

Ani cups my face, lowering his mouth to capture me in a deep, lingering kiss, gently leading me back to the bed. We climb in together and hold each other, falling right back into another sensuous kiss. Behind my eyes, images of the sun shine bright, warming my skin with the touch of summer—the effect of our combined Arcana magick.

With every breath, every touch, every gentle summer breeze, I know how much he cares about me.

And I know he'd do anything for me—anything I ever asked—except for the one thing I most need.

He won't say the words.

He won't promise me I'll never lose him.

THIRTY

ANSEL

It's wrong. I know it's wrong. Dangerous too—there's no doubt about that. But I was so, so close to getting the wand. How can I walk away now?

Certain she's asleep again, I take another dose of the potion and fall back into the realm. It's easier the second time, and within minutes I find myself right back at the bottom of the Cauldron, searching the rocky walls for the crevice that will lead me to—

"I've been waiting for you, Ansel."

I turn on my heel, nearly faltering when I see him. The sight of him—up close, impossibly powerful—brings tears to my eyes.

Awe. Fear. Joy. All of it swirls inside me, making my blood sing.

Standing before me is a druid dressed in a white tunic and green cape, his hood drawn low. There's an ancient horn hanging from a rope around his waist, and in his hand, he holds a staff so tall and powerful, it's almost as if it's growing right out of the earth itself.

I know at once it's what I've come for—the Wand of Flame and Fury.

Just like I know, despite his presently clean appearance, this is Dark Judgment, the evil druid who feasts on babies and torments witches and mages until they can hardly tell the difference between reality and fear-induced hallucinations.

Everything in me is screaming at me to run, to fight, to do *something* other than just stand here.

But suddenly my lips are moving, forming words I don't even remember thinking.

"I've been... waiting for you too," I say. As soon as the words leave my mouth, I know they're true. I mean them. From the bottom of my very soul, I mean them.

The druid smiles, his sharp teeth flashing like metal in sunlight. Logically I know that nothing about this moment is right, but I can't force myself to walk away.

It *feels* right.

"You've come for this, I presume?" He tips the staff forward, the tip glowing red, captivating me.

I try to keep a neutral expression, but it's too late. My desire is too raw, too primal. My hands itch to grasp it, to feel its potency, to fuse its magick with my own.

He knows how badly I want it.

"The Sun Arcana is often associated with twins," he

says. "As such, *you* are a twin, Ansel. Not with a sibling, no. But deep within your own soul. Light and darkness, flame and shadow, truth and deception—always two parts of the whole." He raises the staff, and the smoke choking the sky finally clears, revealing a sunrise so bright I have to shield my eyes. "All sides exist for us, at all times. But our true power lies neither in the light nor the dark, but in the spaces between—the spaces where potential energy gathers, preparing to leap from one side to the other in an endless, eternal dance…"

He's rambling, but I'm not paying attention to the words. I'm watching the staff, my heart beating in sync with the red flame pulsing at its tip.

I don't even realize he's stopped talking until the darkness descends, smoke once again blotting out the sun.

I blink up at the sky, only to realize it's not the smoke causing the darkness at all.

The sun has set. Night has fallen. I've been standing here for hours, completely entranced.

Judgment seems to understand that I've come to this realization, and he nods sagely, reaching out to touch my shoulder.

I flinch instinctively, but his touch isn't frightening or painful. It's warm. Welcoming.

It feels like a promise of good things to come.

Baffled, I look up to meet his gaze.

He looks back at me with kind eyes, his smile that of a normal man once again.

I was wrong to fear him. Wrong to want to run away.

"You may visit me in this realm as often as you like," he says. "When you awaken again in your realm, you will not remember this conversation. You'll remember only your desire, your thirst for power." At his words, the flame on the staff glows brighter. "Your thirst will bring you back to me night after night. But for now, you must return home."

"But... But I can't," I say, emotion choking off my words. The idea of leaving without the staff fills me with a cold dread so all-consuming, I fear it will end me. "The Wand of Flame and Fury... It's my birthright. I... I need it."

The druid smiles again. For a second, I think I see another flash of metal, but I blink, and then it's gone.

He's just a man, I remind myself. *A druid priest. He cares about me. He wants to help me...*

"I will consider your needs, Ansel," he finally says, and I let out a breath of relief. "But in return, I shall ask the same of you."

"I understand."

Without hesitation, he hands me the staff.

I wrap my fingers around it and smile, my chest expanding with love, with joy. The wood is smooth and warm, the feel of it perfect in my hand. It *belongs* in my hand. I've never been so sure about anything in my life.

I'm struck mute by the rush of power coursing through my blood. The heat. The fire. There is *nothing* I won't do to claim this. Nothing.

But as soon as the heat and magick rise inside me, they vanish, along with the staff.

my way with you," I whisper. "A very *punishing* sort
[o]ay, for a very *naughty* boy."

[H]e doesn't say anything about that, but judging from
[a] new bulge growing in his pants, I think we're on the
[sam]e page.

[S]liding my fingers into his hair, I pull him down for
[ano]ther kiss, and he presses against me, giving me a
[pre]view of just how *much* he missed me. I moan softly,
[de]epening our kiss, my hands twining into his hair...

A not-so-subtle throat-clearing reminds me we have an
[au]dience, and I pull back with a shy smile, heat rising in my
[ch]eeks.

"Guess my punishment will have to wait," he whispers.

"Probably for the best, considering Ani's still asleep in
[m]y bedroom."

Baz's eyebrows shoot up, but before he can say another
[w]ord, Kirin says, "We brought pastries."

"Muffins," Doc adds, holding up a big paper bag. He
[t]ries for a casual smile, but he can't hide the heat blazing in
[h]is eyes. He must've been the one who cleared his throat,
interrupting my kiss with Baz.

I smile back, holding his gaze just a beat longer than
necessary.

"We didn't know what you wanted," Kirin says, "so we
just got one of everything."

"Perfect. One of everything is *exactly* what I wanted."

The guys grab a few plates and napkins and settle into
the living room while I finish up the tea.

It's Monday, the first school day after our epic weekend

The druid is holding it once again, leaving me cold and
wanting.

"Come." He turns his back and heads toward the trail
that leads out of the Cauldron, gesturing for me to follow.
"You and I have much to discuss."

THIRTY-ONE

STEVIE

I've just put the kettle on when my d⟨
announcing the arrival of three of my four m⟨
men.

Kirin, Doc, and—most surprising of all—Ba⟨
spent the last two nights hiding out and dodging
we weren't sure he'd make it for our group me⟨
morning. But suddenly… Here he is.

"Hey," I say softly as he straggles in behind th⟨
his hair as rumpled as his clothes. He looks a little ⟨
the wear, but his eyes shine with familiar misch⟨
when he scoops me into his arms and spins me arou⟨
tight hug, I know he's finally back.

"Goddess, I missed you," I whisper.

"I missed you too." He sets me on my feet, leaning
a quick kiss. "More than you know."

His kiss lingers, heat sparking between us.

"I have half a mind to drag you to the bedroom

The druid is holding it once again, leaving me cold and wanting.

"Come." He turns his back and heads toward the trail that leads out of the Cauldron, gesturing for me to follow. "You and I have much to discuss."

THIRTY-ONE

STEVIE

I've just put the kettle on when my door chimes, announcing the arrival of three of my four most favorite men.

Kirin, Doc, and—most surprising of all—Baz. After he spent the last two nights hiding out and dodging our calls, we weren't sure he'd make it for our group meeting this morning. But suddenly... Here he is.

"Hey," I say softly as he straggles in behind the others, his hair as rumpled as his clothes. He looks a little worse for the wear, but his eyes shine with familiar mischief, and when he scoops me into his arms and spins me around in a tight hug, I know he's finally back.

"Goddess, I missed you," I whisper.

"I missed you too." He sets me on my feet, leaning in for a quick kiss. "More than you know."

His kiss lingers, heat sparking between us.

"I have half a mind to drag you to the bedroom and

have my way with you," I whisper. "A very *punishing* sort of way, for a very *naughty* boy."

He doesn't say anything about that, but judging from the new bulge growing in his pants, I think we're on the same page.

Sliding my fingers into his hair, I pull him down for another kiss, and he presses against me, giving me a preview of just how *much* he missed me. I moan softly, deepening our kiss, my hands twining into his hair...

A not-so-subtle throat-clearing reminds me we have an audience, and I pull back with a shy smile, heat rising in my cheeks.

"Guess my punishment will have to wait," he whispers.

"Probably for the best, considering Ani's still asleep in my bedroom."

Baz's eyebrows shoot up, but before he can say another word, Kirin says, "We brought pastries."

"Muffins," Doc adds, holding up a big paper bag. He tries for a casual smile, but he can't hide the heat blazing in his eyes. He must've been the one who cleared his throat, interrupting my kiss with Baz.

I smile back, holding his gaze just a beat longer than necessary.

"We didn't know what you wanted," Kirin says, "so we just got one of everything."

"Perfect. One of everything is *exactly* what I wanted."

The guys grab a few plates and napkins and settle into the living room while I finish up the tea.

It's Monday, the first school day after our epic weekend

adventures, but all classes have been canceled until further notice. None of us was surprised at the announcement; Trello's blaming the explosion and flood at Hot Shots on a gas leak, and says the quote-unquote *team* needs time to investigate.

She also says APOA is running a bit short-staffed this week, with Casey Appleton called away suddenly on urgent matters overseas. In a shocking coincidence, our new librarian, Janelle Kirkpatrick, was called away by a family emergency.

Lots of exciting comings and goings at the Arcana Academy of Bullshit.

"Ah, the Sun finally rises." Baz laughs as Ani emerges from my bedroom, sheet marks creasing his face, his T-shirt on inside out and backward. "Rough night, Gingersnap?"

Ani smiles, then looks at me and winks. I return his easy grin, but something about his energy feels off this morning.

He joins me at the kitchen counter, helping himself to a mug of tea and leaning in to kiss my cheek. Behind us, Baz and Kirin whistle like the man-children they are, and Doc lets out a soft chuckle.

But all I've got is a huge sigh of relief.

That kiss just made everything right in the world again.

"You okay?" I ask him softly, squeezing his hand.

"Better now." He sips his tea, then lowers the mug to grin at me. "I kind of like waking up to you."

"I kind of like that you kind of like waking up to me."

Another throat-clearing, and I lower my eyes, biting back a smile.

The guys continue their gentle teasing, but I know it's just that. There's no jealousy in their energy, no rivalry. Just brotherhood and friendship. Just family.

Ani and I bring the others their tea, and I take a seat on the couch between Kirin and Baz, reaching for a chocolate coconut muffin.

We spend a few more minutes enjoying our breakfast and one another's company, but there's only so long we can put off the inevitable.

After polishing off my second muffin, I finally lean back on the couch and say it.

"Okay, Doc. I really appreciate that you didn't sully my orgasmic chocolate muffin experience with bad news, but we all know why we're here." I take a sip of tea, knowing it's probably my last chance for a little pleasure before Doc drops a bomb. "What's happening with Casey and Janelle?"

The energy in the room shifts, apprehension and concern filling my suite like poison gas. It's the first time we've all been together since that night at the Towers of Breath and Blade, and nothing about this situation has gotten easier. Doc has spent the last two days interrogating possessed prisoners who threatened to kill us and steal the Arcana objects; I can't imagine his news will be particularly uplifting today.

"There is no easy way to say this," he begins, setting his mug on the coffee table between us. "I'm just going to put it out there. Professor Maddox and I have made a breakthrough with our guests, and we've got good news and bad. The good news is—there's only a single entity possessing both Janelle and Casey, which means we can narrow our focus."

"If that's the good news," Baz says, "I'm almost afraid to ask for the bad."

"As you should be." Doc lets out a long breath and meets my gaze, and I know before he even says the words what's coming next.

"That single entity," he confirms, "is Professor Phaines."

A sharp pain pierces my chest, the memories of my torture at that man's cruel hands never far from my mind.

"Great." Baz is on his feet in a heartbeat, a surge of anger rushing through his energy. "So when can we go dismember him?"

"I'll get the chainsaw," Kirin says, squeezing my knee.

Ani raises his hand. "Flamethrower. Just say the word."

"I'd love nothing more than to do just that," Doc says, still holding my gaze. "And we *will* usher that monster to his darkest end—I promise."

"But?" I ask.

"But we have to find him first."

THIRTY-TWO

STEVIE

As far as we know, APOA's search for Professor Phaines hasn't let up since his initial escape. With no immediate ideas about where *else* to look for our elusive Dark Hierophant, Doc wraps up the meeting on a happier note, giving us a preview of tomorrow night's Harvest Eve menu. By the time he gets to the desserts, the pain in my chest is all but forgotten, my memories of Phaines fading back into the darkest corners of my mind where they belong.

With all the talk of sweets and delectables, it's not long before we're all in relatively good spirits again, looking forward to the feast tomorrow night. To forgetting our problems and celebrating the good things, even for a little while.

"Feeling better?" Doc asks, following me to the kitchen to clear away the dishes.

"Talking about French pastries never fails to perk me up."

"Good." He smiles, his eyes sparkling. "Mission accomplished, then."

"Definitely."

He stands with me at the sink a moment longer, fingers wrapped tight around a stack of plates, scrutinizing my face as if he's got a *lot* more to say on the matter. Despite his smile, uncertainty throbs through his energy like a drumbeat.

"Doc—" I begin, just as he says, "Stevie, are you—"

"Sorry." I laugh, taking the stack of plates from his hands and setting them into the sink. "You go ahead."

"No, it's just... I just wanted to know if you were sleeping okay. Since you got back, I mean."

I nod, but we both know that's not the full truth. I'm just not sure how to answer his question. Yes, I've been sleeping some, thanks in part to Kirin and Ani taking turns in my bed, keeping me safe and secure in their arms. But I'm supremely worried about Baz, and the whole dream realm thing with Ani last night left a bad taste in my mouth too. I'm also not thrilled about the fact that we've left Doc and Professor Maddox with the dirty work of interrogation. And Isla and Nat have been calling to ask how they can help, but I keep putting them off—I don't want to put their lives at risk any more than we already have. Besides, what could they possibly do? At the moment, it just feels like we're all playing an epic waiting game.

I open my mouth to try to put some of this into words, but decide against it. We've had enough anxiety-inducing news for the day—no need to add to it with my rambling worries and what-ifs.

"I'm good, Doc, all things considered." I reach for his arm and give it a squeeze. "I'll just be a whole lot better when all of this is over."

He cups my cheek, his touch warm and tender, and I lean into it and close my eyes.

"Me too, Stevie," he whispers. "Me too."

With the muffins and tea decimated and the kitchen restored to neutral, Doc and Ani finally say their goodbyes. Doc needs to get back to Janelle and Casey, and Ani said something about an overdue lab assignment on gem and crystal identification. But Baz and Kirin, still lounging on the couch, make no move to leave.

After what happened in the realm—and now that Baz is on the mend—it seems the three of us have adopted an unspoken agreement to stick together.

I'm *more* than good with that.

"No plans today, boys?" I tease.

"Oh, we've got *tons* of plans," Baz says. "But Cass wants us to keep an eye on you, so here we are."

"Is that so?" I laugh. "You don't have to throw Doc under the bus just to find an excuse to stay with me. But if it helps your fragile male egos, I'll play the damsel-in-distress card... Just for today, though. After that, it's back to all-badass, all-the-time mode."

Kirin beams at me. "Aww, you're the sweetest."

"I know, right? I settle onto the couch between them

again. Kirin puts an arm around me, and I lean back against his chest. Baz takes my feet into his lap.

Damsel or badass, it doesn't matter to me. In that moment, there's nowhere else I'd rather be.

We spend the rest of the day together, just hanging out and watching Netflix, eating snacks, ignoring the mountains of self-study assignments our professors are piling on in light of class closures.

At one point Kirin decides to hop in the shower, giving me some alone time with Baz.

Kirin's not even out of the room yet when Baz pulls me into his lap, assaulting me with hot, devastating kisses.

For a few blissful minutes, I lose myself in his touch, letting the power of his mouth chase away all my worries. But no matter how delicious his kisses, they can't keep the anxiety at bay for long.

"Baz," I say, finally pulling back, "we need to talk about what happened the other night. Are you okay? Really?"

His eyes lock on mine, full of sadness and shame, and for a minute I think he might just let loose. Not just about how he's been feeling the last couple of days, but about what happened in the realm. About his demons.

But then he just brushes the curls away from my face and says, "I'm okay. I really was exhausted. I didn't mean to make you guys worry."

"I thought I lost you," I whisper, my throat suddenly tight. I can barely get the words out.

"I'm not that easy to take down, Little Bird. You should probably know that about me."

I force a smile, but it doesn't last. Baz may think he's fooling us—maybe he's even fooling himself—but I can feel his energy. The truth is... Our little trip to the dream realm left a dark stain on all of our hearts. But whatever he's been through, it's obvious Baz is carrying the heaviest weight, whether he's ready to admit it or not.

"That night," I say, "in the realm..." I close my eyes, trying to gather my thoughts. My strength. There's so much I want to ask him, so much I want to say, but suddenly I'm terrified to utter a single word about it. "Baz, I—"

"Thank you," he says softly—so softly I'm not even sure he really said it. But when I open my eyes and look at him, he smiles and cups my face, his energy flooding with pure gratitude.

"Why are you thanking me?" I ask.

"You and Kirin fought for me when I was damn near ready to give up on myself. And when I completely lost my shit in that house, you didn't freak out. You didn't turn tail and run. You just... you just waited for me to work through it. So thank you, Starla Milan. Thank you for just... for being you."

I wait for him to continue, to explain what happened in the house, to give me even the tiniest glimpse into the past that still haunts him.

But Baz says nothing. Once again, the door on that subject has apparently closed.

I'm starting to realize I have to be okay with that, though. To just be here and wait for him and let him work through it, just like we did in the realm.

But he also needs to know he's not alone. He needs to know how I feel.

"I'll always fight for you," I say, tracing a thumb over his eyebrow. "And no, not just because I signed my name in a book."

"No?" He smiles and slides his hands up my thighs, his tone light and teasing once again. "Then *why*, Little Bird?"

"Because I love you, Baz Redgrave. It's as simple and as complicated as that."

He pulls me in for another kiss, picking me up off the couch and carrying me into the bedroom just as Kirin steps out of the bathroom. He's wearing nothing but a towel, his muscles hard and slick, his hair curling in damp waves.

A soft whimper escapes my lips.

Baz laughs, tightening his hold on me. "So, are we drawing straws tonight, Weber?"

Kirin takes one look at me and Baz, then at the bed, then back to me and Baz. "No straws. I'll... I'll take the guest room. Give you guys a chance to catch up. Or whatever."

"Oh no you *don't*," I say, wriggling until Baz finally sets me down.

"So *I'm* taking the guest room?" Baz asks, his disappointment washing over me in waves.

"I have a better idea." I look from one to the other, my heart rate kicking up, my mind churning with possibilities, everything in me hoping like hell they're on board with this. "Why don't you *both* stay with me tonight?"

"As in... All together?" Kirin asks. "In the same bed? At the same time?"

"I've just decided I don't want to be more than six inches away from either of you," I say.

"That might be a problem," Baz teases, "considering I've got at least *nine* inches of—"

"And Kirin's got ten," I say brightly, flashing a big grin. "But who wants to do math in the bedroom? Am I right?"

Without another word, I quickly strip out of my clothes and climb into the bed, my body trembling with anticipation. Nerves. Giddiness.

The two of them just stand there, gaping.

"Honestly," I huff. "It's like the two of you have never seen a naked woman before."

"Did she really just do that?" Baz finally asks Kirin.

"You mean strip naked and get into bed? After inviting us both to join her? Yes, I believe she did."

Without further ado, Kirin drops his towel and beelines for the bed. Not one to be left behind, Baz tears his clothes off so fast he practically shreds them.

Warmth rushes over me as my men surround me, the three of us shifting around under the blankets to find the best position. I know this isn't the first time we've been naked together—this is exactly how we got into the dream realm the other night. But tonight, everything about this moment—and everything that comes after it—is *our* choice. No threats, no do-or-die missions, and best of all—no audience.

The brotherhood oath has never meant more to me than it does right now. But this thing between us... It's so much more than loyalty and protectiveness, so much more than friendship, so much more than the Arcana bond. I'm in *love* with them. And I want to be with them tonight—*really* be with them.

Together.

In the same bed.

At the same time.

Truths and lies have this in common—both are easier in the dark. So with no more than the moonlight illuminating the space around me, I take a deep breath, shore up my courage, and...

"Guys?" I whisper. "Are you still awake?"

"Yes," comes the unanimous reply. Their breathing is rough and shallow, and I know that if I pressed my hands to their chests, I'd feel the same frantic drumming.

"I need to tell you something."

The silence is so heavy, I swear I can *hear* those wild hearts beating.

"The Arcana bond may have brought us together," I say. "But the feelings I have for you are... something else. I'm... I'm in love with you. Both of you. And I want to be with you tonight. Like... the three of us..." I trail off, not entirely sure how to put my desires into words.

"You know how I feel about you," Kirin whispers into my hair, nuzzling my neck.

Baz slides a hand up my stomach, tickling the spot below my breasts. "Me too, baby."

"But this is different," I say. "It just... I know we've talked about this, but it still doesn't seem fair of me to want more than one man."

"I already told you," Kirin says, "if your heart has room for more, I wouldn't dream of denying you that."

"None of us would," Baz says, fingers trailing down to brush between my thighs, then back up, tracing slow circles on my stomach.

"I'm an excellent sharer." Kirin kisses my ear, my jaw, my neck. "At least, I'll learn to be."

I laugh, suddenly remembering something Ani said on our first hike together.

"What's so funny?" Kirin asks.

"Ani."

"Slow your roll, hotcakes." Baz's fingers go still. "So I was right all along? You've got a thing for the Gingersnap too?"

"I... yes." What's the point in denying it?

"Insatiable," Kirin whispers.

"Not to mention a total buzzkill," Baz teases. "Ani? We can't compete with that. That man is the best one of the lot."

"Maybe so," Kirin says, his lips buzzing along my jaw again. "But he's not here now, is he?"

Baz lets out a soft sigh, his breath tickling my bare shoulder as he shifts to get closer.

"No," he says, pressing a kiss to the other side of my neck. "He's not."

"He said I should... I should admit my feelings," I say, struggling to hold onto the words as Kirin and Baz send my heart into overdrive, their kisses getting more intense. "That maybe we could... find a way to... to share."

"Honestly, I don't see how we have a choice," Baz says.

"It's right there in our oath."

Kirin laughs, reciting the very line I know Baz is thinking of. "Among brothers in blood, all things are shared…"

I let out a nervous laugh, goosebumps erupting over my skin. "Well, if it's in the oath, who are we to deny it?"

"Exactly." Kirin flutters light kisses along my shoulder, his fingers slowly trailing down between my thighs, teasing me as Baz slides his hand up to cup my breast. He rolls my nipple between his fingers, then follows with his mouth, sucking hard, then releasing, blowing a cool breath across my flesh.

A rush of heat floods my core, and I let out a soft sigh, my hips already writhing, my back arching for more.

I've never been with two men at the same time. Before meeting Kirin and Baz, I'd barely been with *one* man; my last pre-Baz, pre-Academy encounter was a rock climber from Colorado passing through Tres Búhos—nothing more than a quick roll in the sack that ended before I was even sure it began.

But now… *Goddess*, the feelings are so intense, the images coming to my mind unbidden as my mages work their own brand of magick on my body—Cernunnos and his forbidden meadow, the flashes of lightning and thunder I've come to associate with Kirin. My Devil and my Tower, each of them so different, yet coming together tonight so perfectly, their eager, seductive touch fulfilling my wildest desires. Healing my heart. Showing me how much they love me, falling in love with me just as I have fallen in love with them, over and over again, a little more with every kiss.

I don't know where to feel. Where to focus. I'm surrounded by them, by their hands, by their mouths, by their hard, smooth cocks pressing urgently against my outer thighs. I can't get enough.

In a tangle of limbs and heat and soft moans of pleasure, the three of us find our way down this new, enticing path. I roll onto my hip and thread my fingers into Baz's hair, pulling him back up to kiss my mouth as his fingers slide down to my clit, stroking and teasing with a featherlight touch. Behind me, Kirin bites the back of my neck, gripping my thigh, urging my legs to part for him. The head of his cock teases my entrance, and I arch back, begging him to take me.

Baz sucks the tip of my tongue into his mouth, and slowly, agonizingly, Kirin slides into me from behind, moaning in my ear as Baz increases the pressure on my clit. Kissing his way back to my breasts, Baz grazes my nipple with his teeth, then bites gently, flicking it with his tongue, making me cry out in pleasure and pain, all of it conspiring to shatter me.

Kirin's cock thickens inside me as his slow thrusts become more erratic, deeper, less retrained. Baz returns to claim my mouth in a searing kiss, and I reach down for his cock, stroking him hard and fast, knowing none of us will be able to last much longer. The moment is just too intense, too hot, my mages and I caught up together in a wild, uninhibited frenzy of pure euphoria.

My heart is racing as fast as my breath, my skin slick with sweat, my ears filling with the sounds of their deep moans as we drive each other to the absolute brink, and oh my *Goddess* I have never felt so alive, so electric.

Kirin tightens his grip on my hip, his pace quickening, his whole body slamming into me as I tremble from the delicious force of his thrusts, from Baz's fingers on my clit, from their hot, wet mouths on my bare flesh.

"Stevie, I'm right there," Kirin groans, and I arch back against his thrusts, tightening my body around him, urging him right over the edge.

That's all it takes.

Kirin cries out in ecstasy, shuddering hard against my backside, setting off a chain reaction inside me. I come in a white-hot rush, moaning into Baz's mouth as I squeeze his cock, stroking him until he tumbles right over the cliff with us.

The room is spinning, my whole body vibrating, my skin tingling with the best kind of magick. When our heartbeats finally return to normal and I manage to catch my breath, I roll onto my back and take their hands in mine, holding them against my chest. Maybe it's wishful thinking, considering everything we've already been through together. Everything we still have to face. But when I whisper into the darkness that I love them, and I feel the fierce, overpowering energy of their love returned to me, I know in my heart that this is what forever truly feels like.

And I never want to let it go.

THIRTY-THREE

BAZ

The chill comes hard and fast, crashing through me like a New England winter. Despite the heat of Stevie's skin, of her breath on my bare shoulder, I'm damn near shivering.

But the worst part isn't the cold. It's what follows.

The emptiness. The nothingness. It comes for me, just like the ghosts of my past in the dream realm, all my secret shames. The self-pity, the revulsion. The utter blackness.

It's been happening ever since we got back from that fucked-up place, and each time it's getting worse.

I can't let her see me like this. Can't let *either* of them see me like this.

Sitting up in bed, I look over my shoulder and take in the sight of her hair spilled across the pillowcase, her dark mouth parted, her cheeks pink, Kirin's big hand spanning her stomach, and I know I should feel something. It's not like I don't remember holding her, kissing her.

Tasting her.

Telling myself that falling for this woman is crazy.

Knowing that it's too late for that; I've already fallen for her. Headfirst, no holds barred.

But looking at her now, I don't feel any of that. There's my brain, reminding me. And then there's my heart, cold and empty.

All I want to do is get the fuck out of here, leave her and Kirin to whatever comes next.

Get out. Now. Leave. Unwanted. Unworthy. Dirty. Broken.

Somewhere in the dark recesses of my fucked-up head, something is screaming at me to stay. To wake up, to stop being such a dick. To feel what I remember and remember what I feel—get my brain and heart on the same fucking page.

But no matter how hard I strain to hear them, I can't make sense of the words. Can't obey the commands.

The walls are closing in.

I need air.

I need out.

"Baz? You okay?" Stevie's eyes flutter open, her sweet face coming to life in the moonlight, her midnight smile cracking through the ice around my heart.

I reach for her, but another jolt of ice slams into my gut, a new voice hissing at the back of my skull.

I will come for you, boy. One night, I will come. And when you hear my clarion call, you will beg me to set you aflame...

There's a druid, and a wand... fire... searing my flesh...

I shake my head, blink the images away. The bedroom comes back into view. Rumpled sheets. Another man in the bed. I'm pretty sure he's my best friend, but I can't remember his name.

There's a tug inside, some nagging feeling that I'm forgetting something, or…

What am I even doing here?

Ah, yes. Leaving. *That's* what I'm forgetting.

Ignoring the woman's confused and disappointed gaze, I climb out of the bed and sweep my shirt and pants from the floor. I'm dressed in thirty seconds flat. Can't find my shoes, but fuck it, I don't need them.

"I'm just gonna take off," I announce. Not that it matters. I don't give a shit what anyone thinks.

Only what *he* thinks.

The druid.

"You're leaving?" the woman asks.

Was she always this annoying? Add it to the list of shit I just can't remember.

"You'll miss all the fun, brother," the dude says, rolling on top of the woman and patting the empty space next to her, undoubtedly still warm from my body.

Something inside me tells me I should probably feel something about *that* too; I'm pretty sure the two of us just spent half the night giving her intense pleasure, sharing her, making her scream our names.

Hell, I must've screamed hers a time or two. But fuck if I remember it now.

Once again, I don't feel a damn thing. Not about that, and not about anything else.

I'm a wasteland inside. Barren. Cold.

I glance at her bedroom door, the outer door visible just beyond it, and all I can think is...

Freedom. Now.

And I'm on my way without a backward glance, wondering why the fuck I lingered so long in the first place.

THIRTY-FOUR

STEVIE

Among brothers in blood, all things are shared...

It should've been the best night of our lives. The first of many more to come. Safe in their arms last night, their mouths hot on my bare skin, I imagined our first shared "morning after" would play out *very* differently.

But instead of enjoying another three-way in the shower or introducing Baz to the concept of naked dunch or living out *any* of the dozens of delicious dreams I'd envisioned for this day, I'm spending my so-called "morning after" sequestered in the archives, alternately paging through Mom's old notebooks and pulling Tarot cards.

Seeking. Forever seeking.

But when it comes to Baz and whatever's going on in his head right now, the answers I'm getting from the universe are always the same:

Six of Cups reversed, the children on the card speaking to me of the past, the reversal suggesting Baz's difficult adolescence—his abandonment, his struggles growing up with the Kirkpatricks.

Three of Swords reversed, the wise tree scarred by three blades permanently balanced on a heart of stone. I feel the deep, endless ache of old wounds refusing to heal, forcing us to relive their pain again and again.

Judgment reversed. That motherfucker is self-explanatory, and it's all I can do not to tear the card to shreds.

Whatever Baz saw in the realm—whatever Judgment pushed to the forefront of his mind—it's clear that Baz has not escaped. Not from the Dark Arcana. Not from his own dark past.

And Kirin and I are powerless to help him. It feels like we're in the house in the dream realm again, the two of us standing by while Baz falls apart, our hearts breaking, knowing there's not a damn thing we can do to ease his pain.

I shove the cards back into the pile, shuffle again. A card jumps out, landing on the table in front of me.

The Hierophant.

My stomach tightens. Another reminder of our enemies. Of all the things we haven't been able to change, no matter how hard we try.

I slide the card back into the deck and shuffle again, turning over three new cards. Six of Cups reversed. Three of Swords reversed. Judgment reversed.

I pick up the deck to reassemble it and try again, the bottom card winking up at me.

The Hierophant.

Goosebumps erupt along my arms and scalp, making me shiver. Thanks to the epic glamour Kirin and Doc pulled off after Phaines's attack, the archives lab feels like a peaceful summer retreat—one of the only reasons I've been able to come back and work without freaking out. I still love this place—truly. And I love that Kirin and Doc cared enough to try to make it better for me.

But at the end of the day, the archives will *always* be the place where Professor Phaines first showed his true colors —where he beat me, spelled me into paralysis, and kidnapped me for his twisted sacrifice to the Dark Magician. So the fact that his namesake card keeps showing up here uninvited? Yeah. Can't say I love it.

I close my eyes and take a deep breath, trying to convince myself it's not some kind of terrible omen...

"I thought I'd find you here," Kirin says. His voice startles the hell out of me—I didn't even hear him come through the security system.

I look up at him and try to smile, but we both know it isn't working. The anguish and frustration must be written all over my face.

Kirin takes one look at the cards and notebooks spread out before me and gestures toward the adjacent chair. "Do you mind?"

"Of course not." Despite my sour mood, I can't help but be glad he's here.

"Stevie..." He reaches for my face, knuckles brushing softly down my cheek. "What happened last night... You have to know Baz isn't himself."

"Have you heard from him?" I ask.

"He hasn't returned my calls or texts. I tried knocking on his door, but that only got a few curses and something thrown at the wall, which I guess was better than getting something thrown at my head."

"At least we know he's alive in there." I try to laugh, but just like my smile, it falls short.

"It isn't Baz," Kirin says, his hands warm and reassuring on my shoulders. "You *know* Baz. We both do. And the man who walked out on us last night isn't him."

I let out a deep sigh. I want to agree, but I can't.

"You're wrong, Kirin. It *is* Baz—right now, the only version we've got. Something may be broken inside of him, but he's still *him*. He's still *ours*. And unless we figure out how to put him back together again, it's the only version of him we'll ever know."

"We *will* figure it out." He swipes my tears with his thumbs. "You can't think like that."

"How could I not? I felt his energy last night, Kirin. I don't know how it happened, but in that moment, right before he left? Something just... just turned off, like a switch flipping. He meant everything he said last night, everything he did."

Kirin shakes his head, still not buying it. "If you sensed his energy when he left, then surely you sensed it *before* he left too. Those moments when we were all together... When we all... You felt it, Stevie. I know you did." Kirin's eyes darken with desire, memories of last night's shared moments playing out in his mind, just like they're playing out in mine.

Shared moments we should be reminiscing about with Baz. *Recreating* with Baz.

"He cares for us both," Kirin continues. "And he's *crazy* in love with you, just like I am. That's the real Baz. And we're not giving up on that."

"No, of course not." I close my eyes and take a deep breath.

Kirin's right—I *did* feel those things last night. More than that. And I know it was real.

But something happened in the moments that followed —something that turned his heart to stone, just like in the Three of Swords card.

"It's like he's shut down," I say.

"Protecting himself, more likely." Kirin picks up one of my notebooks, flipping through some of my notes about the realm. "You said the realm forced you to face your worst fears, right?"

A shiver rattles down my spine as the images come back to my mind—the rush of water, my father's bloated body. Luke, hauling me to safety only to turn on me, then burn alive.

My mouth fills with the taste of salt and bile, my stomach threatening to revolt.

"I wouldn't say I faced it," I say, swallowing hard. "*Survived* it, maybe. But facing something implies dealing with it, and I think we're all a long way from earning *that* particular merit badge."

"Maybe so," Kirin says, "but the point is... Whatever Baz went through, it's just hitting him a lot harder than we thought. It's not surprising that he's running hot and cold, getting close and then retreating. Putting up those walls. He's terrified, Stevie. Not just of what he experienced in his past, but what that might mean for his future. His relationships. All of it."

I look into Kirin's eyes, marveling at the confidence I find there, at the certainty that this will absolutely work out. "How can you be so calm about this?"

He grabs my hand, then nods at the mess on the table. "Because we've got you on our side. And I know better than anyone... You won't stop digging until you find something to fix this. In the meantime, all we can do is just be there for Baz in whatever way he'll let us, and keep the faith."

His optimism gives me a much-needed boost, and I finally return his smile—probably the first real smile I've shared today.

Feeling at least fifty percent better than I did when I got here, I stand up and reassemble the stacks of notebooks and Tarot cards.

"So, are you about ready to head out?" Kirin asks, helping me clear the table. "We should probably get going, or we'll be late, and everyone will ask where we were, and we'll have to tell them we got distracted making out in the library *again*..."

Kirin's talking, but his words are a jumble in my mind.

Right now, all I can see—all I can focus on—is the card that just dropped out of the deck.

I snatch it up before Kirin spots it, shoving the Hierophant into the middle of the deck.

"Don't tell me you forgot," Kirin says, eyebrows raised in question.

"Forgot what?"

"Cass's place? Harvest Eve dinner?"

Shit. I *totally* forgot.

"I didn't forget, I just… I lost track of time." I grab my bag, stow the Tarot cards, and follow him toward the exit. "I just need to stop home first, change into my holiday outfit, and get my mulling spices."

"And get naked. I think you forgot that part."

"Kirin! Didn't you say something about being late?"

"Hey, if I have to traipse all the way back to Iron and Bone for a wardrobe change and some mulling spices, we're going to take full advantage of the few minutes of alone time we can get."

THIRTY-FIVE

STEVIE

"Where were you guys?" Ani asks as we step into Doc's apartment, slightly off-kilter and slightly more than fashionably late.

"Mulling spices!" Kirin and I blurt out.

"So *that's* what we're calling it now?" Ani shakes his head and laughs, then grabs me to steal a long, sweet kiss.

The warm scents of fresh bread and cinnamon fill the apartment, reminding me of past Harvest Eves, and I relax into Ani's embrace, letting the festive mood take over. And even though my heart hurts to know Jessa's not here with me, and Baz is shutting us out, I'm still so happy to be celebrating today—so happy we're here to celebrate at *all*, given the brewing storm with the Dark Arcana and everything unfolding outside Academy walls.

So many witches and mages don't have the privilege of celebrating tonight, or they're being forced to do so from behind bars. That sobering realization was almost enough to make me stay home, but in the end, I just wanted to be with my family. Celebrating with them tonight, reflecting on what we're grateful for... It's the best way I know to honor this holiday. To honor our magick.

As Ani twirls me around and whistles his approval for my Harvest Eve dress—a strapless, wine-colored little number that flares out above the knee, paired with a sheer black scarf and black lace-up boots—I let out a laugh, the burdens of the day drifting away on the pumpkin-pie-scented air.

"So, did you finish your assignment?" I ask Ani as we head into the kitchen to start the mulled wine. Despite his upbeat mood, he looks a little tired, dark circles shadowing his eyes. I figure he probably pulled an all-nighter or something, but then he just cocks his head, his brow knitting in confusion.

"Gems and crystals?" I remind him, pouring a few bottles of red wine into the pot.

"Oh, right! Yes! Yes, I did finish. Took a lot longer than expected, but I think I have a handle on it now."

I narrow my eyes, sensing a spike of tension in his energy, but the sound of the front door opening saves Ani from further grilling.

"Happy Harvest Eve, heathens," comes the boisterous greeting.

I don't need to turn around from the stove to know it's Baz. His voice sends shivers up and down my spine, kicking my heart into overdrive.

I focus on the wine, refusing to budge. Refusing to even acknowledge his presence. Because if I turn around and look into those red-brown eyes and see so much as one tiny *shred* of the cold, lifeless man who walked out on us last night, I won't survive it. Not tonight. Not again.

But suddenly the air shifts behind me, and two strong, warm hands slide over my bare shoulders, thumbs pressing into the muscles, kneading lightly. My breath hitches, and Baz leans in close, brushing a feathery kiss along the shell of my ear.

"I'm so, so sorry," he says, his voice low. "I honestly don't know what the fuck is going on with me lately, and yeah, we probably need to talk about it. But all that aside…" He nuzzles the sensitive skin behind my ear—a favorite spot for both of us—and I already feel my resolve crumbling. "I just need you to know how much I love you, Stevie. Don't *ever* doubt that. Because if you doubt that for even *one* second, I swear—"

I cut him off, turning around and stretching up on my toes to kiss him. He melts against my mouth, his arms sliding around my waist, pulling me close.

When I finally break for air, I take a chance and look up into his eyes.

And there, gazing back at me, is Baz Redgrave. The *real* Baz Redgrave. Haunted, confused, and completely exhausted… But whole. Happy.

At least for the moment.

It's a small victory, and for now I take it, sneaking in one more kiss and giving him a wide smile in return.

I want to believe last night was the last of it—the last time he'll go cold, the last time he'll walk out on us like he doesn't even know our names. But the truth is, I'm not sure how long this present happiness is going to last, and I'm pretty sure Baz is struggling with the same worries. Kirin too, judging from the glare he's shooting Baz right now, wordlessly watching us from the other side of the kitchen.

After a long, uncomfortable silence bordering on tense, the two of them finally embrace, wishing each other a Happy Harvest Eve. But Kirin's energy is vacillating between angry and guarded, and a wave of Baz's guilt hits me right in the chest.

Goddess, please *let us get through tonight without incident...*

Turning back to the stove, I sprinkle in my homemade blend of spices and set the wine to simmer, then head off in search of Doc.

"Where's our illustrious host?" I ask Ani.

"Still in his room."

"Don't tell me he's sulking because you guys wouldn't let him cook this year."

"He said he'd be out soon," Ani says with a shrug. "But that was earlier. He's been in there over an hour."

"An *hour*? I better go check on him." I head down the hallway, trying to keep my concerns at bay. The guys don't seem worried, but why would Doc be hiding out from his own Harvest Eve party? Did something happen yesterday with Janelle and Casey? He checked in last night with a text

—it didn't sound like anything was wrong, but maybe I missed something. Did they locate Phaines?

My stomach twists at the thought. It might explain why the stupid Hierophant card was stalking me all day, but... no. Doc wouldn't sit on news like that.

"Doc?" I strum my fingers on the closed bedroom door, not wanting to startle him. "It's me. Are you in there?"

"Stevie? I'm... Sure, come on in."

I step inside, closing the door behind me.

The room is small and stuffy, with a few basic pieces of generic bedroom furniture, some hotel-style wall art, and little else. Not surprising, considering this is just a temporary home for Doc—something Headmistress Trello and her APOA buddies encouraged after limiting faculty travel in the wake of the attacks on campus.

I glance quickly at the queen-sized bed, then look away, my cheeks hot. Generic or not, being in such close proximity to the place where Doc lays his head at night is already inspiring a few fantasies he'd certainly call *highly inappropriate.*

He's half-standing, half sitting on the edge of a computer desk, head hung low, but he smiles when he sees me, his otherwise melancholy energy pulsing with desire.

"Stevie," he says softly. "You look beautiful."

"Thank you." I lean forward and kiss him on the cheek, lingering just a moment to enjoy his clean, masculine scent. He's dressed in dark gray trousers and a crisp white button-down, the top few buttons undone, and it's taking every bit of my restraint not to run my fingers over that exposed stretch of smooth, warm skin.

Lingering one final moment, I reach behind him for the bottle I know he's got stashed there and remove the cap, helping myself to a healthy swig.

Doc raises an eyebrow. "I didn't know you were a fan of whiskey."

"Not my favorite," I admit as the liquid burns my throat. "But it's Harvest Eve, and I'm determined to show my appreciation for *everything*."

Doc cracks a smile, there and gone again.

It's quiet, the smallness of the room making it feel like we're in our own private little world.

"I miss you," I admit softly, passing back the bottle. "I feel like we haven't... connected much since the other night at Breath and Blade."

"No, I suppose we haven't." Doc takes a swig, but he doesn't say anything else, just looks down at the bottle and frowns, as if he thought it might have all the answers and has just figured out the simple truth of it: whiskey doesn't know shit.

"Doc, I wanted to thank you," I say, desperate to erase the sadness from his eyes. "For doing this tonight. I... it's been a long time since I've had anything even *close* to a family celebration."

His energy pulses at the word *family*, and I can't help but wonder about his. He's never mentioned much about his origins, about his home, about his life before he became the illustrious Dr. Devane, and the more time I spend with him, the more I want to know about him.

But just as I sense his energy, I also sense that now is not the time for prying questions.

More than anything, I think he really just wants to be left alone.

Swallowing my disappointment, I squeeze his arm.

"Listen, if something is upsetting you tonight, we can wrap it up out there. I know there's a lot going on... Maybe you got in over your head with this dinner party. We're a lot to handle—I get it."

I grin, but my gentle teasing is met only with more silence. More sadness. I'm just about to abandon my policy of not prying when Doc finally opens his hand, revealing a small photograph. It's old and weathered, as if it's been carried around in a pocket and looked at a thousand times.

Judging from the reverent way Doc's holding it, I'm sure it *has* been.

"Is that *you*?" I ask, pointing at a chubby little boy on the left with a head of dark hair. He looks to be about seven or eight, and he's got his arm around another little boy—a blonde with big dimples, maybe a year or two younger than the dark-haired boy. They seem inseparable, like two peas in a pod.

"It is," Doc says. "Me and my brother."

"Really?" I turn and hop up on the desk, sitting next to him and leaning in for a better look at the photo. "You have a brother?"

He nods, but I can tell by the heaviness in his eyes and the wave of sadness in his energy that something is very, very wrong.

"Xavier," he finally says, his voice breaking at the end. "That was his name. He died when I was... well, I suppose it's been about twenty years now. This is the only picture I have left of him."

I hold in a gasp of shock and say nothing, knowing first-hand there aren't any words to make this right.

"*Goddess*, sometimes it feels like yesterday," he says. "Other times, it's like it never happened at all—like it was someone else's life. A story from a past I never knew but only read about in a book."

"I know," I whisper.

"Holidays are... not the easiest for me," he admits. "Especially this one. Harvest Eve was his favorite. Every year I think it will get better, that the pain won't be so fresh. But it's always there, just... right there." He massages his chest, struggling to find his words. "We had so many traditions..."

I rest my head on his shoulder and take his hand in mine. He flinches, but just before I pull away, he turns his hand over and laces our fingers together, resting his cheek against the top of my head.

For now, it seems the rules of propriety are on pause again, granting us a moment of humanity instead. A surge of affection rushes through me, and I fight back tears, not wanting to make him more upset than he already is.

Words may be useless and clunky right now, but there's something I want to say anyway.

"Doc, sometimes it's okay to… I don't know. To make new traditions, to celebrate… It doesn't mean that we're forgetting the ones we've lost. I mean, how could we? Loving someone… It changes us on a soul-deep level. And in that way, we always carry them with us."

Doc lifts his head and turns to cup my face, and I look up at him with a soft smile. "I'm sorry. I don't know how to find the words for this," I whisper, finally losing the battle and letting a tear escape. "I wish I could take away your pain."

Doc closes his eyes, touching his forehead to mine. "I wouldn't allow it, Stevie. Not in a million years."

He holds me like that—his hands on my face, our lips close—for several heartbeats, both of us just breathing, just existing in this moment.

That we've both suffered the death of loved ones is something that bonds us, just as our Arcana magick bonds us. But there's more between us—so much more. And for the first time since this whole thing started, since I felt those very first sparks between us, I think Doc is finally starting to allow for that possibility too.

"The fact that you're here is enough," he says.

"You too, Doc."

"Starla," he whispers, sliding his thumb across my lips, making me shiver with intense pleasure. I feel the tug-of-war raging inside him, tearing his heart in two. He *wants* this. He feels the intensity of our connection just as strongly as I do.

But something in his heart won't let him give in to his feelings. Won't let him take the leap.

"When I was in the dream realm," I say softly, our faces still close, "one of the things that gave me strength was you. Just knowing that you were watching over us, waiting for us on the other side, never giving up hope that we'd return."

He opens his eyes and pulls back, his brow furrowing. "Why would I give up hope? You promised you'd come back to me, and you never break your promises."

The first sparks of humor alight in his eyes.

"I promised myself something too," I say. "That I'd... I'd do something when I returned, and I haven't done that yet."

"What's that?"

I lower my eyes, my lips still tingling from the touch of his thumb. When I finally speak again, my words are no more than the faintest whisper. "I promised myself I'd kiss you."

His sharp intake of breath draws my attention back to his mouth, his full lips parting in surprise and desire. It washes over me in a rush, unleashing all those highly inappropriate fantasies all over again.

But Doc goes completely still.

"Unless you don't want me to," I say, offering him an out.

His lips curve into an apologetic smile, and sadness

washes through him once again. "Believe me, Stevie. There's *nothing* I want more."

"Yet you're still fighting it."

"Because it's dangerous." He rises from the desk, pacing his tiny bedroom. "This attraction between us—"

"Is not just attraction. We've already established that. On more than one occasion, I think."

"Regardless, this... this connection... It's dangerous."

Okay, now I'm just getting annoyed.

"Just because you're scared of something doesn't mean it's dangerous," I point out.

"Just because you're reckless doesn't mean it *isn't*."

"*Reckless*?" I hop off the desk and stand before him, frustration competing with annoyance now. Jabbing a finger at his chest, I say, "Look, Dr. Control Freak, I am *not* reckless. Not when it comes to stuff like this. So maybe the most obvious explanation is the right one here."

"What explanation?"

"You've got *issues*!"

"You have *no* idea," he says, his eyes blazing, his jaw tense.

The air between us is crackling with possibility, with heat, every second conspiring to push us together no matter how much we bicker. Doc and I could go a hundred rounds, hurl a hundred insults, and we'd be right back where we started, every single time.

What are we even doing?

It's Harvest Eve. We should be celebrating, not fighting.

And he's obviously in pain. I never should've pushed him like this.

I let out a sigh, then let it all go. I don't want to fight with him. Not tonight. Not ever again.

"I'm sorry," I whisper, lowering my eyes. "I shouldn't have said that. You're—"

In a flash he's got me pinned against the wall, one hand wrapped around my throat, the other gripping my hip, his mouth hovering no more than a hair's breadth from my lips.

Sliding his thumb down my throat, he presses closer to me, his cock stiffening against my belly.

"I'm *consumed* with you, Starla Milan," he says, voice low and sexy as his gaze sweeps down my face. "My dreams, my waking thoughts... You've *thoroughly* invaded me. No matter how hard I try to fight it, to pretend this thing between us is just a minor infatuation..." He closes his eyes, the barest brush of his lips against mine a painful tease of everything he's holding back. "Yours is a pull I can't resist."

A deep and endless ache blooms in my core, and I swallow hard, afraid to move, afraid to blink, afraid that even a single breath will shatter this moment between us...

A swift knock on the door does it for me.

"Dr. Devane?" a soft voice asks. "Stevie? It's Isla. Nat's here too."

"We brought bacon-wrapped brie!" Nat says excitedly, which—let's be honest—who can blame her? "Are you guys coming?"

322

"Apparently not tonight," I mutter.

Doc closes his eyes and curses under his breath.

"Be right out," he calls. His hand is still wrapped around my throat, his eyes blazing with a desire not even Isla's ill-timed interruption can cool. "Stevie and I were just discussing some... mental magick... theories."

"Big ones," I add, glancing down at the situation below his belt, which is only getting worse. "Just give us five minutes!"

Doc arches an eyebrow, and I arch one back, both of us likely wondering the same thing.

How much can we get away with in five minutes...

But in the end, I finally shake my head, pulling out of his enticing grip.

"You're... leaving?" he asks, dropping his hands. "Right now?"

I force out a laugh, doing my best to put some icewater on this situation before we burn the place down. "I mean, you gave me quite a thrill there, Doc. *Woo!* Five stars, would *definitely* recommend. But..."

"But...?"

"Didn't you hear?" I look at him like he's the most clueless man on earth. "There's *bacon.*"

He opens his mouth to argue, but then shuts it, finally letting loose a smile. "Fair point, Miss Milan. Fair point."

"Are you coming?"

"Apparently not tonight," he parrots back.

His eyes blaze again, and a wave of new heat washes through me. Now *I'm* the one with the internal tug-of-war.

Do I laugh at his attempt at humor, or do I hike up my dress, push him onto the bed, and ride him into the sunset, confirming *exactly* how much we can get away with in five minutes?

Choices, choices...

"Let me rephrase that," I finally say, forcing myself to be at least ten percent more sensible. I pop my hands on my hips and focus on a spot just above his shoulder, because if I look into those eyes again, or anywhere near his sexy mouth, I'm going to do something likely to get us both in trouble. "Will you be joining me and the rest of the guests in the dining room for dinner? Which, I might add, is happening in *your* home, at *your* request?"

"Yes... Remind me again why I invited so many people?"

"Because you love Harvest Eve, and you love us." I smile, the words tumbling out before my brain has time to catch up. When it does, I'm nearly choking to suck them back in. "I mean, you love... people. Guests. In your home. Because Harvest Eve is a time for celebrating the bonds between friends and good food and happy memories *aaaand* I'll just be right out... there... somewhere else."

I reach for the doorknob, hoping like hell my friends aren't listening from the other side.

"You go on ahead," he says, adjusting his pants. "I'll be out in... just a moment."

"Perfect. I'll save you a seat."

"As long as it's not next to Baz." He points at me in

warning. "That man has no qualms about stealing food from other people's plates. He's barbaric, Stevie."

"Your seat will be next to *me*, Doc. *That's* going to be our new tradition. First of many." Then, with a smile and a wink to dissipate the intensity, I add, "As long as the food is good, I mean. If not, I'm spending next Harvest Eve at Smash, eating my weight in mashed potatoes and liquid cheese, and you're on your own."

Doc grins. "I would expect nothing less, Miss Milan."

THIRTY-SIX

STEVIE

After making our separate exits from Doc's bedroom, likely fooling absolutely *no* one, we fill our glasses with wine and gather with the others around the dining room table.

The spread is magnificent, covering the table with so many different meats, vegetables, and rich, creamy sauces I'm getting overwhelmed just trying to decide where to start. And the bread? Oh, those French people *really* know what they're doing there.

But before we can eat ourselves into a proper food coma, Doc insists on making a toast, gesturing for us all to raise our glasses.

Turning first to me and the guys, he says, "You came to me as students, and quickly became friends and brothers. In our time together, I've come to know you as my family in the deepest sense of the word." He glances at me, his eyes sparkling. "And because of you, Stevie, our family continues to expand, to strengthen." He nods at Isla and

Nat, both of them beaming, and I swear I'm ready to throw caution to the wind and kiss him, right here in front of everyone, propriety be damned.

He has no idea how much all of this means to me, and I smile, my eyes blurring with tears. Happy ones, this time.

"To family," he says, savoring the moment.

"To family," we repeat, tipping our glasses back.

After the toast, I squeeze his hand and smile, whispering another heartfelt *thank you.* The world may be falling down around us, but seriously. Tonight couldn't be any more perfect.

Then the doorbell chimes.

We all look around expectantly, wondering who it could be. With Professors Maddox and Broome spending the night with Casey and Janelle, the list of possibilities is basically zero.

But Doc winks at me, his eyes twinkling with new mischief, and a fizzy feeling erupts in my stomach, making me light-headed in the best possible way.

"Speaking of our ever-expanding family," he says cryptically. "Stevie, would you mind getting that?"

"I... guess not." I head over to the door, ready to welcome our newest guest with a big fat Happy-Harvest-Eve grin.

But as soon as I open the door and see that sleek black bob and fashionable red lips, I lose all sense of decorum, letting out a squeal instead.

I can't even speak. Seriously, I don't remember how to make words or even move my lips.

"Happy Harvest Eve," my best friend Jessa says softly.

"Jessa?" I finally manage, still not totally trusting my eyes. "But what... When... How is this possible?"

"I have an old friend in Mexico," Doc says from behind me, brushing his knuckles down my arm, "not far from where Jessa's family lives. The mage is a retired portal magick specialist, and he owed me a favor."

"You did this," I breathe, my eyes still not leaving Jessa's. "For me."

"I know how much you miss her, Stevie," he says. "And this holiday is about honoring and remembering those we love."

"You did this for me," I repeat, still trying to catch up. I feel like everything is happening in slow motion, except for the fact that my heart is slamming into my ribs.

"It's only for a couple of hours," he says, keeping his voice low. "I wish she could stay longer, but it's too dangerous—I'm talking about *real* danger, Stevie. If anyone outside our circle found out she was here, she'd become an instant target. She's the easiest way to get to you, and she's got no magick to defend herself."

I nod, my brain finally clicking back into gear. Doc doesn't have to explain—I agree with him completely. My heart breaks to know I'll have to say goodbye so soon, but spending even one *minute* with Jessa on Harvest Eve is more than I ever could've hoped for.

And it's one more thing to be grateful for on the holiday meant for just that.

Brushing away my tears, I beam at the woman standing inexplicably in Doc's doorway—my best friend.

"I'll just have to hug her extra tight, then," I say.

Jessa squeals, and I squeal again, and she launches herself into my arms, holding me for what feels like an eternity while everyone around us cheers.

As predicted, Isla and Nat fall instantly in love with her, something that started on our very first Witch-'N-Bitch Happy Hour chat and has only intensified with the in-person visit.

I introduce her to all the guys, eager for her to welcome them into her heart like I have. She already knew Kirin from his many visits to Kettle Black, but it doesn't take long for her to get comfortable with the others, and by the time we finish the first course, she's basically inherited four new big brothers.

Jessa and I hold hands under the table all through dinner and dessert, eating pie off each other's plates and falling into our old conversations and jokes like no time has passed. I tell her about my classes, and she tells me about her new place in Mexico, and even though I know the clock is ticking, I try to stay in the moment, memorizing every detail of this night filled with friendship, food, laughter, and—most importantly—love.

It's the best night I've had in a very long time.

We've just finished our second helping of chocolate torte

when the doorbell chimes again, and Doc squeezes my shoulder and nods.

Tears fill my eyes. It's time to say our goodbyes.

"But who's at the door?" I ask.

"An old friend offered to escort Jessa home tonight," he says. "Actually, she'd like to speak with you first. She'll be waiting outside."

While Jessa says her goodbyes to the others, I head outside in search of Doc's second mystery guest of the evening, wondering just how many more surprises my heart can take tonight.

Thankfully, it's got room for one more. Because there, standing in the shadow of a huge saguaro cactus, is a kind, beautiful woman I didn't think I'd ever see again—not in this realm, anyway.

"Lala!" I reach for her hands and squeeze, returning her big, youthful smile. She's wearing her glamour tonight, her skin flawless, her brown eyes full of their usual depth and wisdom.

Her outfit is a little less mystical than it was on our last encounter; she's traded in the star-spangled skirt-and-cape ensemble for a much more sensible pair of stretchy jeans and a mustard yellow off-the-shoulder sweater.

I want to tell her how super-cute she looks tonight, but I'm not sure that's a thing you say to the High Priestess, so instead I say, "Happy Harvest Eve."

"And to you as well, Starla," she replies.

"I'm glad you're here. I never got a chance to thank you

for your help in the realm. I don't know what I would've done without your guidance."

"There's no need for thanks." Lala flashes that mysterious smile of hers. "I promised your mother I would do what I could to protect you, so that is what I've done. What I will always do."

My heart warms at the mention of my mother, and I recall something Doc said to me the first time I met Lala.

"Doc once told me you were a friend to my parents," I say. "That you stood by them when things went south at the Academy."

"Yes." Her smile turns sad, her eyes misting with tears. "It was a difficult time for all of us. Your mother... It was so very hard for her to communicate all that she'd learned through her divinations. She knew her days were numbered at the Academy, just as she knew you would ultimately find your way back here, no matter how desperately she and your father tried to protect you from it."

"But that's the funny part, isn't it?" I ask. "In the end, the Academy wasn't even something I needed protection from. I'm *glad* I enrolled. For the first time in my life, I feel like I belong." I glance back toward Doc's front door, the murmurs of happy conversation and laughter drifting on the air. "I'm accepted here."

Lala reaches up and touches my cheek. "You were always accepted. Loved. You belonged to a family that was willing to die to protect you."

"I know that," I say softly. "And I loved my parents more than anything. But as much as they protected me, they also stifled me. They kept me from learning my magick. They tried to convince me it was a curse."

"It wasn't your magick they feared, Starla. Nor the Academy nor the brotherhood." She lowers her head, a single tear splashing into the dirt at her feet. "Your mother was trying to save your life, though she'd seen your death a thousand times over. She hoped that by altering your course, she might also alter its final outcome. Alas, that was not to be."

Her earlier words come back to haunt me, hanging in the air between us like something rotten.

Thus her ache shall find no ease, so shall the daughter of The World surrender to the emptiness, to the void within and without. By her own hand, of her own volition, The Star shall fall. Henceforth she shall take her eternal breath in utter darkness...

I open my mouth to defend against this prophecy, to deny it once again, but what's the point? We've already been down this road many times.

"It would bring her peace to know that you have your brothers now," she says. "That the Light Arcana bond remains strong, despite the rise of the Dark Magician."

At the mention of public enemy number one, her jaw tightens, her fists clenching at her side. But in her eyes, I find something else: regret.

The kind of harrowing, lifelong regret that can only come from deep personal experience.

"You knew him," I gasp, the realization hitting me hard. "You knew the Dark Magician."

It feels like an eternity before she answers, and when

333

she speaks again, her anger has softened into something more like resignation. "In a former iteration, yes. He was... Well, *he* was actually a *she* then. And she was my beloved, Starla. Not in this body or time, but in another, many centuries ago."

"I don't understand," I say, which has become a common refrain when it comes to Lala's cryptic confessions.

"For the Magician and the High Priestess," she continues, "One and Two of the Major Arcana, this bond has always been so. In one lifetime he was my brother; in another, a cherished student. In our last lifetime together, he was a she—my wife. She was a powerful Light Arcana, but she died of natural causes. When she was reborn, it was again as a man, and though I could sense the event of his incarnation, his soul remained hidden from me."

"Hidden from you? But how were you able to connect with him... I mean her... Um, *them*... all these lifetimes?"

"The Magician and I are forever bound, much as you are now bound to your brothers." At this, she frowns, her eyes filling with fresh tears. "And while part of the woman I once loved still remains, it is a very small part now—one the Magician's dark soul no longer even recognizes in itself."

"Wait. You two are still in touch?"

"In a manner of speaking, yes. We are still connected. We do not communicate the way you and I are communicating now, but a bond such as ours does not sever completely. You are only just beginning to experience such a bond, but in time, you will rediscover the lost memories of your previous lifetimes, and you will understand. You will know just how deep your connection to your Arcana brothers runs, like roots running to the very core of the earth."

An image of the guys comes to mind again, and my heart races. Is that the kind of connection we share? When one of us dies, will the rest of us feel when that person is reborn? Will our connection change too, like it did for the High Priestess and her Magician? Lovers one lifetime, siblings the next, parents and children another, neighbors, colleagues... It's almost impossible to fathom.

"The Magician has turned inward," she says, "consumed by a thirst for power and revenge. He will not rise from this darkness. He is bent on your destruction, Starla—yours more than any other—and he will not rest unless he succeeds. Until your mother's prophecy is fulfilled."

Again, the words echo, chilling me to the marrow.

By her own hand, of her own volition, The Star shall fall. Henceforth she shall take her eternal breath in utter darkness...

"But why me?" I ask. "I understand he's got a hard-on for magick and world domination, but why is he targeting me specifically? Don't we all pose a threat to his master plan? Besides, I should be the *last* witch he's worried about —I'm still a total newbie!"

"*You* are the Star. Despite your lack of experience, he knows you represent his greatest threat." A smile touches her lips. "Hope."

I sigh, wishing I could return the smile. "I'm sorry, Lala.

I appreciate your kindness. I just don't feel very hopeful at the moment."

Thoughts of Baz swim through my mind, my fear of losing him closer than ever, despite his earlier assurances.

Tucking a curl behind my ear, Lala offers another warm smile. She knows exactly who I'm thinking about—she always knows.

"Baz will find his way back to you, child," she says. "As will all your brothers, any time one is lost. As long as your light shines bright, they will always know the way home. Even in death."

A shiver runs down my spine, but I can't think about death right now. My death, their deaths… No. There's no room for that. Not tonight.

"I just wish I knew what to do for him," I say. "He's so lost. *I'm* so lost. I feel useless, Lala."

"In all things, you must trust yourself to know what is right." She holds my gaze a moment longer, then pats my cheek. A breeze ruffles my hair, and Lala goes quiet and still once again.

I know instinctively our conversation has come to a close.

The door opens behind us, light spilling out onto the path as Jessa makes her way out.

Wordlessly, Lala bows, turning and walking a few paces away to give me a minute alone with my best friend.

"Oh, Jessa." I pull her into my arms, wishing I didn't have to let her go. Our time together went by entirely too fast. "There's so much I want to tell you, so many things I wish I could show you. And, *Goddess*! Isla and Nat are dying for a real girls' night with you—live and uncut."

She pulls back, her cheeks stained with tears. But she's smiling, just like me. "And you *will* show me all those things and more. Including a full tour of the campus. And a detailed flowchart explaining how it is you're in love with four guys, and none of them have killed each other yet."

I crack up. "Yes, that does require a flowchart. Probably a few Post-it notes too. And some very juicy details I've yet to share."

"Starla Eve Milan!" She smacks my arm, cracking up. "I can't believe you're holding out on me!"

"It's a cliffhanger," I tell her. "Leaves you wanting more. That's how I know you'll come back."

"Of *course* I'll come back, bitch. Who else is gonna rock that karaoke mic with you?"

"Ani told you about that, did he?"

"He sure did. Epic present, by the way."

"Epic and waterproof. Did he tell you about the bathtub sessions?"

Jessa's eyes bulge out of her head. "The *what* now?"

"Cliffhanger," I sing-song. "See how that works? But Goddess, what about *you*? I still have so many questions about Mexico! I want to know about your family and your friends and how you spend your days... How is it that you just got here, and now you're leaving again?"

Sadness slips in around the edges again, and we both tear up.

"Don't worry," she says softly. "We'll have plenty of time to catch up soon."

I nod, letting out a resigned sigh. "Doc's right. It's not safe right now. But hey, I'm not complaining. Seeing you tonight… It was the best surprise ever."

She pulls me in for a hug, and I hold her tight, drawing strength from her love, from her loyalty, from all the amazing, ass-kicking things about the absolute best friend I've ever had.

All too soon, Lala's back. It's time to let Jessa go.

I give her one more tight squeeze, and then we leave it at that, neither of us acknowledging the painfully obviously truth:

That when we say it's not safe right now, "right now" is totally relative. Because unless we can defeat the Dark Arcana, there's a very good chance it will *never* be safe—not for any of us.

I head back toward the door, in desperate need of a group hug and a pep talk. But just as I pull it open, someone else storms out, nearly barreling into me in his rush to escape.

"Baz? Wait!" I call after him, but he doesn't acknowledge me or even stop to see if I'm okay after he practically ran me over. It's like I'm not even here.

I don't bother chasing after him. I know he's already long gone.

Back inside, I sit on the couch, trying not to lose it. My

best friend can't visit me for more than a few hours because we've got dangerous magickal psychopaths on the loose. Students are being attacked on campus. Just last weekend, we were taken hostage by witches possessed by the very mage who tried to kill me. One of the men I love is losing the battle against his inner darkness, and none of us knows how to save him.

And I'm pretty sure the wine is gone too.

Kirin sits next to me, sliding an arm around my shoulders while the others pace the living room, none of us quite sure what to do next.

"He was fine," Nat says, clearly worried. "He said goodbye to Jessa like normal, then he came into the kitchen to help me pack up some of the leftovers. When Isla asked if she should put on the kettle for tea, his face went totally blank. He looked at her like she was crazy. Like he didn't even know who she was, or what *tea* was for that matter."

"That's when he left," Isla says. "Didn't say another word—just stormed out the door."

"That sounds about right," I say with a heavy sigh. "Goddess, I really hoped this was behind us."

"How long has it been going on?" Doc asks.

"Since we got back from the realm." Kirin fills everyone in on the details, thankfully leaving out the part about our epic night together. "At first we thought he was just exhausted after the ordeal—that's what he kept saying."

"Sounds like it's a lot more complicated than that," Doc says, frustration and worry darkening his energy. "Do we have any idea what we're dealing with here? Dark magick? PTSD? Something else?"

"I've been researching the lore," Kirin says, "but so far I haven't found anything on the side-effects of traveling in the dream realm. I've put in a request for more books from the APOA's library system, and there's another collection online that may shed some light as well. We need to figure out what this is—not just to help Baz, but to ensure our next trip to the realm doesn't have the same outcome."

"No one is going back there until we know exactly what we're dealing with," Doc says. "And exactly what to do about it."

Kirin nods. "We'll fix this. I promise."

"I hope so." Ani shoots me an anxious look. "I really, really hope so."

But Star Arcana or not, I'm done relying on hope as a strategy.

I'm done relying on books too. Done asking the Tarot. Done consulting the lore.

Because when it comes to cracking the code of Baz's dark past, there's only one person who can help us.

"No more books, no more research." I take a deep breath and pull out my phone, trying to heed Lala's advice about trusting myself to know what's right. "It's time for the nuclear option."

THIRTY-SEVEN

STEVIE

I'm no expert, but I'm pretty sure the Goddess invented Harvest Eve for overindulgent dinners and copious amounts of mulled wine. Or reading an entire romance novel, cover to cover, totally uninterrupted. Or doing deep, coconut-oil conditioning treatments.

Or literally *anything* other than this.

But tonight I'm on a mission to save the man I love, which sounds a lot more epic than it is. Because right now, saving the man I love means—

"*Really*, Twink?" Carly's gaze flicks over my hair as I head to her table at Jumpin' Jack's Java, her nose wrinkling in disgust. "Would it kill you to put in some highlights?"

"Probably not." I toss my curls over my shoulder and smile. "But Baz is always going on about how much he *loves* my hair, so I'm not changing a thing."

Carly grimaces.

Goddess, she really brings out the bitch in me. It's a

wonder I can maintain any composure in her presence at all.

Still, she did agree to meet me tonight, despite the short notice and my complete vagueness on the phone. All I said was that it was about Baz, it was super important, and could we please go somewhere to talk?

I still can't believe how quickly our perfect Harvest Eve celebration unraveled. I left Doc's in a hurry, too anxious to meet up with Carly to even say goodbye. Baz is still MIA, not returning anyone's texts. And now I'm worried about Ani too.

He offered to keep me company on the walk to the café tonight, but he was strangely quiet the whole time. Just before we parted ways, he asked if he could wait for me back at my place—said he had to talk to me about something kind of important. When I pressed for details, he shook his head and frowned.

"Later," he promised. "In private." That and a quick kiss on the forehead was all I got from him before he walked away.

I wouldn't be surprised if it's related to his little white lie about the crystal homework. Something is definitely going on with him... I just hope he's not still upset about our dream realm argument. I really thought we were on the same page about that—especially now, given everything Baz is dealing with after his own post-realm return.

After grabbing my honey vanilla cinnamon latte from the counter, I settle into the chair across from Carly, trying to figure out where to start this conversation. I'm about to ask her if she's heard from Baz tonight when she blurts out, "Hierophant!"

"What? *Where*?" My heart jumps up into my throat so fast I nearly choke on my latte. I whip my head around, scanning the tiny café.

After a minute, realization dawns. She isn't talking about Professor Phaines.

She has no idea what the H-word means to me.

I force out a laugh, hoping to convince her it was just a bad joke.

"Are you always such a psycho?" She rolls her eyes, stirring another sugar packet into her cappuccino. "When you sat down, the card popped into my head. That's all."

"What does it mean?"

"That's up to you to decipher. As a *clairvoyant witch*, I'm just the messenger." She says *clairvoyant witch* like someone might say *lord of the manner* or *billionaire heiress*. "So remind me… *Why* did I leave my Vampire Diaries rewatch marathon for this little date?"

She continues to stir her drink, spoon clanking angrily against the mug, and a twinge of sadness works its way into my heart. She was spending Harvest Eve alone watching Netflix… and her mother is currently our prisoner, magickally restrained in a basement in Red Sands Canyon.

She has no other family here. And her friends… well, they've never seemed like real friends to me. Not from the outside, at least.

But now is not the time to get sentimental about Carly Kirkpatrick.

"Like I said on the phone, it's Baz," I say, trying to keep my voice steady. Just saying his name out loud nearly breaks me. "He's just... Something's wrong with him, Carly."

She practically snorts. "*Obviously.* I mean, look at the company he's keeping."

I close my eyes and sip the latte, forcing my inner bitch back into her cage before trying again.

"What I mean is... He's gotten really distant lately, and now he's having these extreme mood swings. Sometimes he won't even answer his door—not even for his best friends. And sometimes he just gets this look on his face... It's like he's fallen so deep inside himself, he doesn't even remember who we are. That's the best way I can describe it."

Genuine worry flashes through her energy, but she shrugs like it's no surprise.

"Listen, Twink. You're on your own with this one. He's not returning my calls, either—that's just what he does." She digs into her shoulder bag and pulls out a shoebox, sliding it across the table. "The only reason I agreed to meet was so I could give you this."

"What is it?"

"What does it look like?"

"Um." I lift the lid, peering inside. "A faded gray T-shirt that probably used to be black, a few glamor shots of someone's Barbie dolls, and an old cell phone with a Pokemon sticker on the back?"

"It's a *breakup* box," she explains, enunciating every word like I'm a toddler who just can't grasp the concept. "So the next time you see that man, you tell him we're over. And I mean it this time, so he better not come crawling back to me when he gets tired of you. And don't *you* come crawling back to me either, saying I didn't warn you. Baz is *not* the boyfriend type."

I replace the lid on the *breakup box* and grab my latte, taking a deep, energizing gulp. Then I look at her and let loose.

"Listen, Carly. It's clear you need to get laid and possibly find a good therapist, maybe even a super hot, totally unethical therapist so you can kill both birds with the same stone, who am I to judge? But do you *honestly* think I'd call you out here on Harvest Eve for *relationship* advice? With *Baz*? For fuck's sake, Carly, I'm here because this is fucking *serious*, and you're the only person I could think of who might possibly—and that's a small possibility, by the looks of things—be able to help him. So you're either in, or you can tell me to fuck off, but your little mean-girl mind games are *not* on the menu tonight. Clear?"

She opens her mouth to respond, but then thinks better of it, taking a sip of her drink instead.

I take that as an invitation to continue.

"I know Baz lived with you guys for awhile, and I know a little about his parents and brother. Beyond that, the details aren't important at the moment. What *is* important is that he's recently come face to face with some of those old ghosts, and he's not handling it well. It's... it's changing him. Messing with him, somehow."

Carly's energy spikes with real fear, and for the first time, I look into her eyes and see her genuine love and concern for Baz—a look that goes far beyond her infatuation with him and her frustration that he chose me.

She *really* cares about him. As a friend, as a pseudo-brother, as an old crush, I don't know. But one thing is certain: her feelings are real. And whatever they are, however complicated and messy things might get between us, for once Carly and I are on the same team.

Team save fucking Baz.

"What do you mean he's come face to face with old ghosts?" she asks.

I take another sip of my latte, trying to figure out how much to reveal.

"Basically... I think he's... having nightmares," I finally say, deciding it's as close to the truth as I can get right now without putting everyone else at risk. "Really vivid ones, even during the day. He seems to be reliving things from his family situation and childhood that he never fully dealt with."

Again, her energy spikes—alarm mixed with revulsion. But for once, her revulsion isn't directed toward me.

"And you think I can help fix... whatever this is?" she asks.

"You basically grew up together. There are things you

must know about him... Things you guys share that I can't even *begin* to guess at."

"No, you couldn't," Carly says, but there's no animosity or pride in her tone. Instead, sadness weights her shoulders, and a darkness seeps into her energy, so cold it makes me shiver.

"I'm not asking you to share the details," I say. "I was just hoping you could talk to him, maybe offer a shoulder. See if you can help him open up about it."

Carly nods, lowering her gaze to the cappuccino. She traces her finger around the rim, lost in thought, lost in her own private pain.

After a few beats, she finally looks up at me and says, "Do you know where my mother is?"

"Janelle? Um... why do you ask?"

Deflect! Deflect! Deflect!

"Baz isn't the only one not returning texts and calls. I haven't heard from my mother since Friday, which would normally be fine by me. But she's been up my ass like a hemorrhoid ever since she took the librarian job—I swear the woman can't go an hour without nagging me. Now it's just radio silence." Carly shakes her head, her brow furrowing. "Not only that, but Trello messaged me last night saying she had to send my mother overseas on urgent library business, which would've been weird enough, because what the hell could be so urgent about the library? But then she sent out that memo yesterday saying Mom was called away by a family emergency. But my dad is our only family, and if something happened to him, they would've told me."

The mention of Anna Trello momentarily shifts my attention from Janelle.

"Yeah, that whole memo was bullshit," I say. "That stuff about the gas leak? Trello said the explosion caused the water main break, which caused the flood. But when we saw you that night on our way to Hot Shots, you told us the bar was already closed because of the leak. That was *before* the explosion."

Carly points at me, her eyes lighting up. "Exactly. She's *so* shady. Which is why I'm a little worried about what's really going on with my mother. What if she and Trello had an altercation? What if something happened and Trello's covering it up? What if—"

I hold up my hand to stop her, her sudden neurosis feeding into my guilt.

I can't keep hiding this from her. She deserves to know *something*, even if it's only part of the story—namely, that her mother was working with Phaines, and is now being detained for questioning.

I close my eyes and attempt to gather my thoughts, no idea where to start. Yes, I was on the "go team, we need all the help we can get" kick with Doc, but this feels different. I *trust* Isla and Nat. Our professors too. Even Casey, when she's not being hijacked by an ancient dark mage.

But Carly? What reason has she given me to trust her?

I'm here tonight because I believe that for all her faults and fuckups, she really does care about Baz. But I'm not naive enough to believe that her loyalties extend to me. And if I tell her about Janelle threatening us, I'll have to tell her what Janelle and Phaines wanted in the first place, and that means filling her in on the artifacts, the legends, and the prophecies too. But *that* opens up the can of worms about—

"It wasn't fair," she says suddenly.

"What?" I meet her eyes again, surprised to find a flicker of warmth there.

"How I treated you," she says. "How I'm *still* treating you."

Her observation takes me completely off guard, and it takes me a few beats to respond.

"I... I could've been a little less antagonistic too," I finally manage.

"Maybe," she says. "But petty games aside, you've been pretty decent toward me. Even that first night, over at Smash? You invited me to sit with you guys and you didn't even know me. I was being a total bitch to your friends, and you still tried to be kind. That meant a lot to me, even if I didn't show it. It still means a lot, Stevie."

"Wait." I smile. "You just called me by my name. Does this mean I'm back on the invite list for the exclusive coven?"

"Don't flatter yourself." Carly rolls her eyes, but she's laughing now too. "Honestly, there was never a coven. That's just some mean-girl bullshit I let Blue talk me into."

"Really? Why?"

Carly shrugs. "I don't even know anymore. Sometimes

you just get so caught up in other people's ideas of who you *should* be, you start forgetting who you really *are*. And by the time you remember, it's too late to go back."

"It's never too late to remember who you are."

"I…" Something shifts in her eyes, and Carly shakes her head, as if she just woke up from a nap. Forcing a laugh, she says, "Thanks for the After School Special, Twink, but I think I'm good."

"If you say so." I smirk at her over the rim of my mug. Carly can crow all she wants. The truth is, I saw something human in her tonight, and I'm not going to forget it.

"Anyway," I continue, setting down my mug, "regardless of how you feel about me, I know you love Baz. I believe you'd do anything to protect him. So I'm asking you—"

"No."

My gaze shoots back up to hers. "*No*?"

"You don't have to ask me anything. I'm there. Whatever you need." Carly smiles, humanity overriding her superbitch factory settings once again. "I mean, I'm not saying I'm ready to pick out BFF charms at Time Out of Mind, but in addition to helping you with Baz, if you ever want, like, advice on how *not* to dress like someone's emo prostitute grandma, I'm definitely your girl."

I don't even know what an emo prostitute grandma is, so I just thank her and smile, then take a deep breath, shoring myself up for what I'm about to say next.

"I'm not sure if you've got any plans this weekend, but I'm having Isla and Nat over on Friday. My best friend Jessa joins us on video chat too. We call it the Friday Night Witch-'N-Bitch Happy Hour."

"Sounds… charming."

"It is! You should totally join us."

Carly offers a noncommittal shrug, but her energy pulses with longing.

"You could even bring your friends," I offer, cringing inside as I imagine what Isla and Nat are going to say about this. Still, in the effort of solidarity… "I bet Blue and Emory would appreciate the opportunity to get to know me a little better, especially now that you and I are getting along so famously."

"Blue and Emory hate you."

"Just think about it, okay?" I sigh and take my latte mug to the bus bin, knowing I've done all I can to reach out to her tonight. We've got Baz in common, but if she's going to come around to the idea of building an actual friendship with me, it'll have to be on her own terms.

"What the *hell*?" she blurts out.

I turn back to find out what I did wrong this time, but Carly's not looking at me. She's peering out the window, watching someone on the path outside.

"Hello, Sketchy McSketcherton," she mutters into the glass. "Where are *you* sneaking off to tonight?"

I head back over to the table and lean in close to get a look at her target. "Is that… Trello?"

"Sure is. And the minute I saw her, I got this intense vision of a room. I really feel like she's heading there."

"A bedroom?"

"No, like..." She closes her eyes and presses her fingers to her temples—*super* dramatic, but hey, whatever works. "It's dark and dusty, with no windows. Lots of file boxes and rolls of paper stacked on shelves. I'm getting a flash of... bottles? Canning jars? Something like that. Oh, wait... there's some kind of cot... No, it's a hospital bed."

"Any people?" I ask. "A patient? Anything else about the room, the walls, the shelves, anything at all?"

"No. But I keep seeing the number five."

"Could be an address."

"Wait, no—it's a keypad. I'm seeing a code—five, seven, nine, nine, six, two, four. Write that down. Hurry!"

I grab my phone and tap the code into my notes app.

She opens her eyes, then reaches for my phone to check the code. "We need a list of all the local hospitals and hospices. Maybe we should check out newspapers and commercial printers too? There was a *lot* of paper in there."

I crack up. "Carly, not that I don't respect your craft as a *clairvoyant witch*, but you know there's a much easier way, right?"

Carly blinks up at me, equally annoyed and confused.

"Get your things, Frenemy." I grab my phone out of her hands and flash her a wicked grin. "Time to go find out what that crazy, two-faced bitch is up to."

THIRTY-EIGHT

STEVIE

Once we're out of the coffee shop, it's not hard to figure out where Trello's heading. In this section of the campus, there's only one place that makes sense, given Carly's visions and the direction of Trello's path.

The library.

Despite Janelle's absence and the cancellation of classes, the Academy decided to keep it open after a bunch of graduate students pitched a fit about losing precious hours of research time.

It doesn't explain why Trello would be heading there now, on Harvest Eve of all nights, but that's what we're about to find out. I'm tired of her secrecy, her demands, her stupid out-of-an-abundance-of-caution emails. I'm tired of the fact that she brought me to the Academy, enrolled me, insisted I use my super special spirit-blessed magick to decipher Mom's prophecies for the good of all witch-kind, and then cold-shouldered me every day since.

Whatever happens tonight, I'm getting some fucking answers.

"There's storage in the basement," I explain as we head inside. "That might be what you saw in your vision."

Even on a holiday, the library is no ghost town, with several dozen graduate students situated at various tables or roaming the stacks. It's better for us this way; if we get busted at any point on our misadventure, we can easily claim we got lost looking for some obscure manuscript.

Wouldn't be the first time.

There's no sign of Trello yet, but I can sense her energy. She's definitely here, and definitely close.

I've never been down to the basement, but Kirin pointed it out once—a heavy metal door at the end of a long corridor behind the elevators on the main floor. He told me they dump a lot of old scrolls and unbound manuscripts down there—mostly donations or purchases from private auctions. It's a treasure trove of knowledge and lore, but with no assigned staff to catalog the stuff, it usually ends up in the basement graveyard, forgotten.

I lead Carly there now, scanning for Trello as we pass by the stacks. Just before we reach the elevators, I spot her at one of the tables, consulting with a student over a stack of manuscripts.

"Let's go," I whisper, quickening the pace.

We head down the corridor, passing supply closets and custodial offices until we finally reach the big metal door. I'm just about to open it when Carly points up at the ceiling.

"Look. The cameras are busted."

I follow her line of sight, and sure enough, two white security cameras that were probably aimed at the door are now bent at odd angles, wires protruding from both. I have no idea how long they've been that way, but it's obvious their current condition is not an accident.

"We need to keep moving," I say, opening the door and heading to the staircase. When the door closes behind us, we both take out our phone flashlights, slowly making our way down the concrete steps to the basement level.

The room is a lot like Carly described in her vision—a dark, gray-walled chamber about the size of a lecture hall, with high wooden and metal bookcases jam-packed with scrolls, file boxes, books, even paper grocery bags full of stuff. But other than the shelves and a couple of abandoned metal desks, there's nothing of note down here. No jars or bottles—not unless they're shoved in a box somewhere. No keypad. And certainly no hospital bed.

"Keep looking," Carly says. "I know this is the place. I can feel it."

"Yes, it *is* the place. The place where they store old manuscripts, just like you saw in your vision." I sigh, realizing what a waste of time this was. She's already agreed to help out with Baz—that's all I really wanted from her tonight. This whole Trello thing was pointless. She's here working with students, overseeing the library in Janelle's absence. That's what professors and headmistresses do, isn't it?

A wave of exhaustion rolls over me. Suddenly, all I want

to do is go home to Ani, make some tea, sing some karaoke, and fall asleep in his arms.

"Stevie, there's more," Carly says. "There *has* to be more. I don't get visions of random places just for the hell of it. They come with, like, mojo."

"Define *mojo*."

"Okay. I saw Trello outside the café, right? And then all of sudden this icy cold feeling washed through me, and the images started popping up. Then I got the tugging feeling in my chest, which is my sign for, 'Bitch, some shit's about to go down, so pay attention!' It's the same thing that happened the night I had that vision of you with Professor Phaines."

My stomach lurches, but I nod. She saved my life that night—thanks to her vision, she was able to alert Baz, and the guys were able to find me before I bled to death in the Forest of Iron and Bone.

"Okay," I say, resigned. "Let's keep looking then."

We each take a side and walk the perimeter, shining our lights along the walls, searching for something—anything else. I come up empty, but Carly's gasp from across the room suggests she just hit pay dirt.

"Stevie! Here!"

I find her behind one of the old desks, standing in front of a wide, chest-high door that looks like a bank safe. It's almost the exact color of the wall and nearly impossible to see unless you're really looking for it.

And there, on the lower right side, is a keypad.

My adrenaline spikes, and I pull up my notes app, reading off the code she saw in her vision.

She punches in the numbers, and the indicator light turns green and beeps, the locking mechanism releasing. She pulls open the door and peers inside, a rush of cold air leaking out around her.

"Ew," she whispers. "This place reeks. And what is that sound?"

I cock my ear, picking up on the sounds of a dripping pipe and some kind of scuttling, scratching noise that could either be roaches, scorpions, snakes, giant rats, or some or all of the above.

In other words…

"Okay, well, thanks again for meeting me tonight, Carly. I should probably get back home. Ani and I have plans, so..."

Carly glares at me. "Are you serious right now? We made it all this way, and you're bailing in the home stretch?"

"Dark, danky-ass basement chambers are where people go to die."

"Where did you hear that?"

"Hello? Every horror movie *ever*?"

"Stay here if you want to, but I *know* this is the place from my vision. I need to see what's down there—preferably before Trello finds out we're snooping."

Before I can stop her, Carly's heading into the murder-chamber, leaving me no choice but to follow. Because that's the other thing every horror movie fan worth her blood-curdling scream knows: as soon as you split up, you die.

There's another keypad on the inside, and after testing it to confirm it uses the same code to exit, we close the vault door behind us. We head down another staircase, this one narrow and claustrophobic, the whole chamber obviously built before fire codes were a thing.

"Holy shit," Carly whispers. "This is it. This is *exactly* it."

Coming up behind her at the bottom of the stairs, I shine my phone light around, taking in the horror movie set we've just stepped into.

This room is smaller than the main storage room above, the walls unpainted, the floor no more than hard-packed dirt. Bookcases and storage shelves fill almost every available space, each one jammed with so many jars and bottles, we could give Professor Broome's potions classroom a run for the money. But unlike the stuff on Broome's supply shelves, the bottles we're looking at now aren't just ingredients. They're active potions, glowing and swirling in their glass containers, some casting a faint magickal hum.

Carly reaches for one of the glass bottles and brings it in for a closer look. The liquid is milky white, almost iridescent. When she swirls the bottle, the contents illuminate, casting her skin in a pale glow.

"It's essence," she says.

"Holy shit," I breathe. Essence can only come from one source.

Other mages and witches.

"Look." I head behind the shelves, spotting a massive bulletin board that spans the entire back wall, divided up with masking tape into tiny squares. Tacked inside each square is a tiny ziplock bag about the size of a Saltine cracker. Each holds a lock of hair.

Whenever I touch one of the baggies, one of the bottles on the shelf glows brighter.

"The hair is the connection to the source of the magick." Carly says.

"Carly, remember the students who got attacked on campus? Casey Appleton told us they'd been found with chunks of their hair missing."

"Well, now we know why they lost their magick," she says, barely suppressing a shudder. "It's here. Someone is siphoning it."

"But who the fuck would do something like this?"

"It has to be Trello," she says.

"But why would Trello steal power from her own students? For one thing, she has her own magick. And for another, this isn't a very sustainable practice. When word gets out that students are losing their magick, who's going to enroll here?"

"Let's just keep looking," she says. "I want to find that hospital bed."

I hold up my phone and snap a few pictures, then follow Carly out from behind the shelves.

Leaving the terrifying collection of hair and bottles behind, we continue exploring the room, each section containing more of the same—magick spells, essences, grimoires. I pick up one of the spellbooks, but before I can take a look, Carly's calling me over to her side of the room, panic edging into her voice.

"What is it?" I ask as I approach.

Her face is sheet-white, her eyes wide. Whatever it is, it's got her so freaked out, she can't even speak.

My heart stalls out, certain we've been busted. I'm almost afraid to look, so sure Anna Trello will be standing there with an ax, ready to steal our hair and our essences and chop us into tiny magickal bits...

"Stevie..." Raising a trembling hand, Carly points into the darkness behind me. Slowly, I turn around, preparing for the worst.

But it's not Trello with an ax. It's not *anyone* with an ax.

It's something much more horrific than that.

There's another small chamber branching off of this one, the ceiling low, the walls rough and slanted, as though it was dug hastily out of the earth with no real thought or care.

And there, right in the middle of the makeshift room, is a hospital bed. An old man lies in it, unmoving but for the rhythmic rise and fall of his chest, his body hooked up to dozens of IVs. Not just regular saline IVs, but magickal ones, each bag a different color, some swirling like the potions on the wall, some bubbling.

"Professor Phaines," I whisper, my magick immediately picking up on his energy. Right now, he's just a sickly old man in a stained T-shirt and a pair of sweats, but I *know* it's the ferocious, treacherous monster who nearly killed me. The same monster who's possessing Casey and Janelle. The very reason the Hierophant card kept jumping out of my Tarot deck, and why Carly saw it tonight when I first sat down at the café.

He was right here under the library. Literally under our fucking noses.

For how long? Since the first night he supposedly fled campus after trying to kill me? Or did he come back at a later time?

Did Janelle *help* him?

Kill him. Wrap your hands around his throat and press your thumbs into his fucking windpipe until his head turns the color of a rotten eggplant...

The voice inside my head is loud and convincing, but I can't kill him. As far as I know, the binding spell is still in effect on Janelle and Casey for at least a few more hours. I have no idea what would happen to them if Phaines died while still possessing their bodies. But if there's even a *chance* that Kirin's sister could die, I can't risk it.

I snap a quick, shaky picture, then turn around and grab Carly's arm, steering her back toward the staircase. "We need to leave. Right now. We need to call Dr. Devane and—"

The chamber door beeps, then clicks open. High heels clack on the concrete stairs, and my heart drops into my stomach.

There's no doubt in my mind it's Trello. Whether she has an ax is irrelevant. She's involved in this—the hair, the essences, Phaines. That's reason enough to fear for our lives.

"Hide," I whisper, and Carly and I scuttle behind a bookshelf, crouching down and praying to the goddesses Trello can't see us.

She reaches the chamber and crosses the dim room as if she's done it a thousand times before, heels clacking with purpose as she beelines straight for the antechamber with the hospital bed.

In her hand, I spot large two syringes filled with glowing red liquid.

My heart is hammering so loudly I can barely think straight, but I manage to hear Trello's words as she reaches Professor Phaines—short and to-the-point, as usual.

"You've drawn far too much attention, Professor Phaines. I'm afraid our agreement must come to its end. We've reached the end of the road."

There's a rustling sound, and then a strangled moan escapes his mouth, fading quickly into a gasp, and then… nothing.

We can't see what she's doing from our current vantage point, but it doesn't take much imagination to figure it out.

Minutes later, she's on her way out, crossing the room and heading back up the stairs as if this were no more than an annoying errand.

The chamber door beeps, opens, then closes again, locking behind her.

Certain we're alone again, Carly and I creep out from our hiding place and check on Phaines.

He's dead.

* * *

"Stevie? Where are you?" Doc barks into the phone. "I just got a call from Professor Maddox. Phaines's connection to Casey and Janelle has been severed. The witches are alive, still bound to my command. But we have no idea what happened to—"

"Phaines is dead." I tell him the short version, still trying to catch my breath as Carly and I jog back to the café, desperate to get away from the library.

"Kirin and I are on our way. Stay there."

True to his word, Doc and Kirin rush into the café no less than ten minutes later. With no concern for propriety, Doc swoops me into his arms, holding me against his chest, pressing his lips into my hair.

"Are you all right?" he asks, his breath hot on my skin, his heart jack-hammering.

I manage a nod, then turn to hug Kirin.

"Where's Ani?" Doc says, his voice tinged with alarm as he scans the café.

"He's at my place," I say. "I was supposed to meet him after my date with Carly."

Doc glances at Carly, noticing her for the first time.

"Dr. Devane? What's going on?" she asks, her voice trembling.

"There's no time to explain," he says, already ushering us back toward the exit. "Let's go. Stevie, we need to get Ani, pack your things, and get you off-campus tonight."

"What about Trello?" I ask.

"I'll deal with her later. Right now, my bigger concern is Phaines. With him dead..."

Doc trails off, but he doesn't have to explain. With Phaines dead, the Hierophant energy could be anywhere, waiting to incarnate again. Light, dark, no one knows for sure. But given what Lala said about the Dark Magician— about him not rising again from this darkness, not resting until my mother's prophecy comes to pass and I'm destroyed— something tells me the Hierophant won't be returning to us as an ally, either.

"Where's Baz?" I ask.

"We're still trying to reach him," Kirin says. "He'll meet us later. I know he will."

"What about me?" Carly asks, wrapping her arms around herself. "Should I just... go home?"

Doc hesitates, glancing my way as if I have the answer.

And for once, when it comes to Carly Kirkpatrick, I do.

I put my arm around her and nod at Doc, the circle of trust getting a little larger by the hour.

"Looks like you're coming with us," he says.

* * *

The four of us race into my suite, nearly tumbling through the door in our rush to get to Ani.

But the place is dark and silent, not a single light turned on, not a single candle flickering.

"Ani?" I call out.

"Let's go, Ani," Doc calls, flipping on the lights. "We need to get to Red Sands Canyon. We'll explain on the way."

Ani's not in the living area or the kitchen, but he's definitely here. I can sense his presence, though his energy is beyond weak.

Worry shoots through me, but I try to keep it in check. There's an explanation. There *has* to be.

"He must've fallen asleep," I say, heading to the bedroom.

It's dark and silent in there too, and for a moment I wonder if he decided to go home after all. But then I spot a dark shape slumped over on the chair in the corner.

I should be relieved, but something about it doesn't feel right.

"Ani?" I call softly, flipping on the light. "What are you—"

A scream cuts me off, and it takes me a beat to realize the sound of terror is coming from my own mouth.

Ani, my sweet, big-hearted, laugh-a-minute ginger, is unconscious in the chair, blood leaking from his nose and mouth, his breathing shallow. His eyes are half-closed, his legs twitching.

"Goddess, what happened?" Doc rushes past me and drops to his knees before Ani, checking his pulse. "He's alive, but barely."

"Ani…" I whisper, tears spilling into my mouth, my legs refusing to move, even as I reach out for him.

Doc takes Ani's face between his hands, peering into his half-closed eyes. "No. No. No no no. Don't do this to me. Not you. Come back, Ani. Come back."

Doc's voice breaks, his composure cracking, sending a fresh bolt of terror into my heart.

"He's holding something," Kirin says, reaching for Ani's clenched hand. "What the *hell*?"

He pries open Ani's fingers and removes a small vial, holding it up to the light. Silvery-white film coats the glass, but it's otherwise empty.

Dread fills my insides like wet cement. The knot in my throat is so massive, I'm not sure I'll ever be able to breathe again.

A strangled gasp finally escapes my lips, and I stare at the vial as if it's a bomb about to go off.

In so many ways, it is.

Kirin hands it over. "Do you recognize it?"

I nod, squeezing the vial so hard it bursts in my hand.

"What is it?" Doc demands. "What's happening?"

I close my eyes, the room spinning, my heart breaking into a thousand pieces.

"He's… he's in the dream realm," I whisper. "Ani's trapped in the dream realm."

THIRTY-NINE

ANSEL

Yes, I know all the signs. Of course I do.

My mother was an addict. After my not-father finally bailed, the rest of her life exploded spectacularly, and she used booze and sex and nicotine to patch up all the holes. It was never enough, though. Even when she burned through most of our money and all of our dignity, there was always one more bottle to buy, one more hookup to find, one more night of debauchery to endure like a downpayment on some future happiness that never, ever materialized.

According to her, she was blameless in her misery. It was all because of me, naturally. The cursed, red-headed, magickal freak.

I haven't seen my mother in years. I'm sure nothing has changed, though. If she were here, she'd look at me now, eyes full of scorn as she ashed her cigarette into the sink.

Well honestly, Ansel. What did you expect?

That's what she'd say.

And I'd tell her to go fuck herself, because no matter what the evidence says now, I'm *not* like her. I'll *never* be like her. What I'm doing here, the risks I'm taking, the secrets and lies... They're all part of a bigger plan. An important plan.

Stevie will understand one day. All of them will.

So for now I bear the guilt, endure the burn of it like my own private albatross.

How could I not? No great victory comes without sacrifice. In the end, it will all be worth it.

"You have returned to me," my dark druid says, beaming with pride. No longer at the Cauldron, we now meet in the mist beyond the holly and mistletoe, at the mouth of the cave carved with spirals—the place he calls home. A small child plays at his feet, naked and unafraid.

I kneel before them both and bow my head.

"Your loyalty is admirable, Ansel," he says.

"Thank you, sir," I reply.

Suddenly, it doesn't feel shameful. In fact, the more time I spend here, the less I can remember about my life before.

Why was I so worried that my friends wouldn't understand? That Stevie would try to talk me out of this?

This partnership we're forging is a good thing. My brothers simply need to come to that understanding on their own.

They misjudged the druid, as did I. An honest mistake.

I will help them see it.

"I know you will not disappoint me," he says.

I smile so wide, my cheeks hurt. The idea of disappointing him is so ludicrous, it's almost offensive.

Gesturing for me to rise, he comes to stand before me, finally giving me what I most desire.

I grip the Wand of Flame and Fury in my hand, feeling its immense power twine with my own magick. My entire body trembles to contain it, but I've never been so certain, so resolute before.

I raise the wand to the skies, and a blinding, red-orange flame sparks to life at the tip. A surge of dark magick races down through my hand, my arm, straight into my heart.

On the bare skin of my chest, the mark of Judgment glows bright.

"Ansel McCauley," the dark druid begins. "Are you prepared to do what needs to be done, no matter what the cost?"

I meet his eyes. Blood runs down his chin, staining his robes. The child is gone, but I am not afraid. Not anymore.

I kneel before him once again. Blood pools at his feet, soaking through my pants. I welcome the warmth of it. The rich, coppery tang. Hunger burns inside me, but I know he will take care of me. He will *always* take care of me.

"I am ready," I say, making my sacred vow. "By the power of Flame and Fury, by the magick of the Sun, I am yours to command."

* * *

In the battle against the Dark Arcana, can Stevie and her

fiercely loyal mages save the world of magick without losing their own souls? Find out what happens next in **Tarot Academy 4: Spells of Blood and Sorrow!**

* * *

If you loved reading this story as much as I loved writing it, please help a girl out and **leave a review on Amazon!** Even a quick sentence or two about your favorite part can help other readers discover the book, and that makes me super happy!

If you really, *really* loved it, come hang out at our Facebook group, Sarah Piper's Sassy Witches. I'd love to see you there.

XOXO
Sarah

MORE BOOKS FROM SARAH PIPER!

Paranormal romance fans, do you know I've got another sexy series ready to heat up your bookshelf? The Witch's Rebels is a complete supernatural reverse harem series featuring five smoldering-hot guys and the kickass witch they'd kill to protect. Read on for a taste of book one, Shadow Kissed!

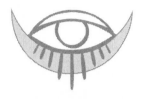

SHADOW KISSED EXCERPT

Survival instinct was a powerful thing.

What horrors could we endure, could we accept, could we embrace in the name of staying alive?

Hunger. Brutality. Desperation.

Being alone.

I'd been alone for so long I'd almost forgotten what it was like to love, to trust, to look into the eyes of another person and feel a spark of something other than fear.

Then *they* came into my life.

Each one as damaged and flawed as I was, yet somehow finding a way through the cracks in my walls, slowly breaking down the bricks I'd so carefully built around my heart.

Despite their differences, they'd come together as my protectors and friends for reasons I still didn't fully understand. And after everything we'd been through, I had no doubts about who they were to me now. To each other.

Family.

I didn't know what the future held; I'd given up trying to predict it years ago. But I didn't need my Tarot cards or my mother's old crystal ball to know this:

For me, there was no future without them. Without my rebels.

"Gray?" His whisper floated to my ears.

After several heartbeats, I took a deep breath and opened my eyes.

I heard nothing, saw nothing, felt nothing but the demon imprisoned before me, pale and shattered, fading from this realm.

"Whatever you're thinking," he said, his head lolling forward, "don't."

Looking at him chained to the chair, bruises covering his face, blood pouring from the gashes in his chest, I strengthened my resolve.

His voice was faint, his body broken, his essence dimming. But the fire in his eyes blazed as bright as it had the day we'd met.

"Whatever horrible things you've heard about me, Cupcake, they're all true..."

"Please," he whispered, almost begging now. "I'm not worth..."

His words trailed off into a cough, blood spraying his lips.

I shook my head. He was wrong. He was *more* than worth it. Between the two of us, maybe only one would make it out of this room alive. If that were true, it had to be him; I couldn't live in a world where he didn't exist. Where any of them didn't exist.

This was my fate. My purpose. My gift.

There was no going back.

I held up my hands, indigo flames licking across my palms, surging bright in the darkness.

The demon shuddered as I reached for him, and I closed my eyes, sealing away the memory of his ocean-blue gaze, knowing it could very well be the last time I saw it.

* * *

2 Weeks Earlier...

Don't act like prey, and you won't become it. Don't act like prey...

Whispering my usual mantra, I locked up the van and pushed my rusty hand truck down St. Vincent Avenue, scanning the shadows for trouble.

It'd rained earlier, and mist still clung to the streets, rising into the dark autumn night like smoke. It made everything that much harder to see.

Fortunately it was my last delivery of the night, and I'd brought along my favorite traveling companions—a sharp stake in my waistband and a big-ass hunting knife in my boot. Still, danger had a way of sneaking up on a girl in Blackmoon Bay's warehouse district, which was why most people avoided it.

If I hadn't needed the money—and a boss who paid in cash and didn't ask questions about my past—I would've avoided it, too.

Alas...

Snuggling deeper into my leather jacket, I banked left at

the next alley and rolled to a stop in front of the unmarked service entrance to Black Ruby. My hand truck wobbled under the weight of its cargo—five refrigerated cases of O-positive and three AB-negative, fresh from a medical supplier in Vancouver.

Yeah, Waldrich's Imports dealt in some weird shit, but human cops didn't bother with the warehouse district, and the Fae Council that governed supernaturals didn't get involved with the Bay's black market. The only time they cared was when a supernatural killed a human, and some-times—depending on the human—not even then.

Thumbing through my packing slips, I hoped the vampires weren't too thirsty tonight. Half their order had gotten snagged by customs across the bay in Seattle.

I also hoped someone other than Darius Beaumont would sign for this. I could hold my own with most vamps, but Black Ruby's owner definitely struck me as the shoot-the-messenger type.

No matter how sexy he is…

Wrapping one hand discretely around my stake, I reached up to hit the buzzer, but a faint cry from the far end of the alley stopped me.

"Don't! Please!"

"Settle down, sweetheart," a man said, the menace in his voice a sick contrast to the terrified tremble in hers.

My heart rate spiked.

Abandoning my delivery, I scooted along the building's brick exterior, edging closer to the struggle. I spotted the girl first—she couldn't have been more than fifteen, sixteen at most, with lanky brown hair and the pale, haunted features of a blood slave.

But it wasn't a vampire that'd lured her out for a snack.

The greasy dude who'd cornered her was a hundred percent human—just another pervert in dirty jeans and a sweat-stained henley who clearly thought runaway kids were an easy mark.

"It'll all be over soon," he told her.

Yeah, sooner than you think...

Anger coiled in my belly, fizzing the edges of my vision. I couldn't decide who deserved more of my ire—the asshole threatening her now, or the parents who'd abandoned her in the first place.

Far as I was concerned, they were the same breed of evil.

"Well now. Must be my lucky night." The man barked out a wheezing laugh, and too late, I realized I'd been spotted. "Two for the price of one. Come on over here, Blondie. Don't be shy."

Shit. I'd hesitated too long, let my emotions get the best of me when I should've been working that knife out of my boot.

Fear leaked into my limbs, and for a brief instant, I felt my brain and body duking it out. *Fight or flight, fight or flight...*

No. I couldn't leave her. Not like that.

"Let her go," I said, brandishing my stake.

He yanked the kid against his chest, one meaty hand fisting her blue unicorn hoodie, the other curling around her throat. Fresh urine soaked her jeans.

"Drop your little stick and come over here," the man said, "or I'll break her neck."

My mind raced for an alternative, but there was no time. I couldn't risk going for the knife. Couldn't sneak up on him. And around here, screaming for help could attract a worse kind of attention.

Plan B it is.

"All right, big guy. You win." I dropped the stake and smiled, sidling toward him with all the confidence I could muster, which wasn't much, considering how hard I was shaking. "What are you doing with a scrawny little kid, anyway?"

He looked at the kid, then back at me, his lecherous gaze burning my skin. The stench of cigarettes and cheap booze lingered on his breath, like old fish and sour milk.

"I've got everything you need right here," I purred, choking back bile as I unzipped my jacket. "Unless you're not man enough to handle it?"

His gaze roamed my curves, eyes dark with lust.

"You're about to find out," he warned. "Ain't ya?"

He shoved the kid away, and in one swift move, he grabbed me and spun me around, pinning me face-first against the bricks.

He was a hell of a lot faster than I'd given him credit for.

"So you're an all talk, no action kind of bitch?" He wrenched my arms behind me, the intense pain making my eyes water. His sour breath was hot on the back of my neck, his hold impossibly strong, my knife impossibly out of reach. "That ends now."

A few blocks off, an ambulance screamed into the night, but it wasn't coming for us. The kid and I were on our own.

"Mmm. You got some ass on you, girl." He shoved a hand into the back pocket of my jeans and grabbed a handful of my flesh. "I like that in a woman."

Of course you do.

After all these years making illegal, late-night deliveries to the seediest supernatural haunts in town, this wasn't my first rodeo. The one-liners, the threats, the grabby hands... Human or monster, guys like this never managed to deviate from the standard dickhole playbook.

But this was the first guy who'd actually pinned me to a wall.

At least he'd ditched the kid. I tried to get her attention now, to urge her to take off, but she'd tucked herself behind a Dumpster, paralyzed with fear.

The man pressed his greasy lips to my ear. "No more bullshit, witch."

You don't know the half of it, asshole.

He didn't—that much was obvious. Just another dude with a tiny dick who tossed around the word "witch" like an insult.

My vision flickered again, rage boiling up inside, clawing at my insides like a caged animal searching for weak points.

It wanted out.

I took a deep breath, dialed it back down to a simmer.

God, I would've loved to light him up—spell his ass straight to oblivion. But I hadn't kept my mojo on lockdown for damn near a decade just to risk exposure for *this* prick.

So magic was out. I couldn't reach my knife. And my top-notch negotiating skills had obviously failed.

Fuck diplomacy.

I let my head slump forward in apparent defeat.

Then slammed it backward, right into his chin.

He grunted and staggered back, but before I could spin around or reach for my knife, he was on me again, fisting my hair and shoving my face against the wall.

"Nice try, little cunt. Now you eat brick."

"Don't!" the girl squeaked. "Just… just let us go."

"Aw, that's cute." He let out a satisfied moan like he'd just discovered the last piece of cake in the fridge. "You'll get your turn, baby."

Okay, she'd saved me from a serious case of brick-rash —not to mention a possible skull fracture—but now she was back on his radar. And I still couldn't get to the knife.

Time for plan B. Or was this C?

Fuck it.

"Hey. I've got some money," I said. "Let us go, and it's yours."

"Yeah?" He perked up at that. "How much we talkin'?"

"Like I said—some."

Lie. At the moment, I was loaded. Most of the $3,000 I'd already collected tonight was in the van, wrapped in a McDonald's bag and shoved under the seat. I also had $200 in a baggie inside my boot and another $800 in my bra, because I believed in diversifying my assets.

My commission depended on me getting the cash and van back to the docks without incident. I couldn't afford incidents. Rent was due tomorrow, and Sophie had already covered me last month.

But I couldn't—wouldn't—risk him hurting the kid.

"It's in my boot," I said. "Left one."

"We'll see about that, Blondie." He yanked me away from the wall and shoved me to the ground, wet pavement biting into the heels of my hands.

With a boot to my back, he pushed me flat on my stomach, then crouched down and grabbed my wrists, pinning them behind me with one of his meaty hands. With his free hand, he bent my leg back and yanked off my boot.

Bastard.

"I hope you feel good about your life choices," I grumbled.

Another wheezing laugh rattled through his chest, and he coughed. "Choice ain't got nothin' to do with it."

Whatever. I waited until he saw the baggie with the cash, let him get distracted and stupid over his small victory.

The instant he released my wrists and went for the money, I pushed up on all fours and slammed my other boot heel straight into his teeth.

The crunch of bone was pure music, but his howl of agony could've called the wolves.

I had just enough time to flip over and scamper to my feet before he rose up and charged, pile-driving me backward into the wall. The wind rushed out of my lungs on impact, but I couldn't give up. I had to keep fighting. Had to make sure he wouldn't hurt the girl.

I clawed at his face and shoved a knee into his groin, but *damn it*—I couldn't get enough leverage. His hands clamped around my throat, rage and fire in his eyes, blood pouring from his nose and mouth as he spit out broken teeth.

He cocked back an arm, but just before his fist connected, I went limp, dropping to the ground like a pile of rags.

The momentum of his swing threw him off balance, and I quickly ducked beneath his arms and darted behind him, crouching down and reaching for the sweet, solid handle of my knife.

"You can't win," he taunted as he turned to face me. Neither his injuries nor the newly acquired lisp diminished his confidence. "I'm bigger, stronger, and I ain't got no qualms about hurting little cunts like you."

Despite the tremble in my legs, I stood up straight, blade flashing in the moonlight.

"Whoa. Whoa!" Eyes wide, he raised his hands in surrender, slowly backing off. "Hand over the knife, sweetheart."

"Not happening."

"You're gonna hurt yourself, waving around a big weapon like that."

"Also not happening."

"Look. You need to calm the fuck down before—" A

coughing fit cut him short, and he leaned against the wall, one hand on his chest as he gasped for air.

I held the knife out in front of me, rock steady, finally getting my footing. Chancing a quick glance at the girl, I jerked my head toward the other end of the alley, willing her to bolt.

Her sudden, panicked gasp and a blur of movement beside me were all the warning I had before the dude slammed into me again, tackling me to the ground. My knife clattered away.

Straddling my chest, he cocked back an arm and offered a bloody, near-toothless smile. "Time to say goodnight, witch."

"Leave her alone!" No more than another flash in my peripheral vision, the kid leaped out from behind the Dumpster, flinging herself at our attacker.

She scratched and punched for all she was worth, eyes blazing and wild. I'd never seen anyone so fierce.

But he simply batted her away like she was nothing. A fly. A gnat. A piece of lint.

She hit the ground hard.

I gasped, heart hammering in my chest, shock radiating through my limbs. She *wasn't* a fly or a gnat. She was a fucking child in a unicorn hoodie, lost and scared and totally alone, and he'd thrown her down.

Just like that.

Still pinned in place, I couldn't even see where she'd landed.

But I would never forget that sound. Her head hitting

the pavement. The eerie silence that followed. Seconds later, another ambulance howled into the darkness, nowhere close enough to help.

"What did you do?" I screamed, no longer caring who or what might've heard me. "She's just a kid!"

I clawed at the man's chest, but I was pretty sure he'd already forgotten about me.

"No. No way. Fuck this bullshit." He jumped up to his feet, staggered back a few steps, then took off without another word.

Still trying to catch my breath, I crawled over next to the girl, adrenaline chasing away my pain. Blood pooled beneath her head, spreading out like a dark halo. Her breathing was shallow.

"Hey. I'm right here," I whispered. "It's okay, baby."

She was thin as a rail, her wet jeans and threadbare hoodie hanging off her shivering frame.

"Jesus, you're freezing." I shucked off my jacket and covered her body, careful not to move her. "He's gone now. He can't hurt you anymore."

I swept the matted hair from her forehead. Her skin was clammy, her eyes glassy and unfocused, but she was still conscious. Still there, blinking up at me and the dark, cloudy sky above.

"What's your name, sweet pea?" I asked.

Blink. Blink.

"Hon, can you tell me your name?"

She sucked in a breath. Fresh tears leaked from her eyes. That had to be a good sign, right?

"Um. Yeah," she whispered. "It's… Breanne?"

"Breanne?"

"Sometimes Bean."

"Bean. That's a great nickname." I tucked a lock of hair behind her ear, my fingers coming away sticky with blood. "Hang in there, Bean. I'm going for help."

"No! Don't leave me here. I—" She reached for me, arms trembling, skin white as the moon. "Grape jelly. Grape—"

Grape jelly grape, she'd said. And then her eyes went wide, and I watched the spark in her go out.

Just like that.

"Bean!" I pressed my fingers beneath her jaw, then checked her wrist, desperate to find a pulse.

But it was too late.

Here in the middle of vamp central, the sweet kid in the unicorn hoodie—the one who'd ultimately saved *my* life— was dead.

* * *

Ready for more? Dive into the sexy supernatural world of The Witch's Rebels! Order your copy of Shadow Kissed now!

ABOUT SARAH PIPER

Sarah Piper is a Kindle All-Star winning urban fantasy and paranormal romance author. Through her signature brew of dark magic, heart-pounding suspense, and steamy romance, Sarah promises a sexy, supernatural escape into a world where the magic is real, the monsters are sinfully hot, and the witches always get their magically-ever-afters.

Her works include the newly released Tarot Academy series and The Witch's Rebels, a fan-favorite reverse harem urban fantasy series readers have dubbed "super sexy," "imaginative and original," "off-the-walls good," and "delightfully wicked in the best ways," a quote Sarah hopes will appear on her tombstone.

Originally from New York, Sarah now makes her home in northern Colorado with her husband (though that changes frequently) (the location, not the husband), where she spends her days sleeping like a vampire and her nights writing books, casting spells, gazing at the moon, playing with her ever-expanding collection of Tarot cards, binge-watching Supernatural (Team Dean!), and obsessing over the best way to brew a cup of tea.

You can find her online at SarahPiperBooks.com and in

her Facebook readers group, Sarah Piper's Sassy Witches! If you're sassy, or if you need a little *more* sass in your life, or if you need more Dean Winchester gifs in your life (who doesn't?), come hang out!